Under Nushagak Bluff

Under Nushagak Bluff

a novel

Mia C. Heavener

This is a work of fiction. Names, characters, businesses, places, events and incidents are either the products of the author's imagination or used in a fictitious manner. Any resemblance to actual persons, living or dead, or actual events is purely coincidental.

Book Design by Mark E. Cull

Library of Congress Cataloging-in-Publication Data
Names: Heavener, Mia, 1978– author.
Title: Under Nushagak bluff : a novel / Mia Heavener.
Description: First edition. | [Pasadena, CA] : Boreal Books, [2019]
Identifiers: LCCN 2019024653 (print) | LCCN 2019024654 (ebook) | ISBN 9781597098090 (trade paperback) | ISBN 9781597097970 (ebook)
Subjects: LCSH: Yupik Eskimos—Alaska—Fiction. | Nushagak (Alaska)—Fiction.
Classification: LCC PS3608.E28377 U53 2019 (print) | LCC PS3608.E28377 (ebook) | DDC 813/.6—dc23
LC record available at https://lccn.loc.gov/2019024653

The National Endowment for the Arts, the Los Angeles County Arts Commission, the Ahmanson Foundation, the Dwight Stuart Youth Fund, the Max Factor Family Foundation, the Pasadena Tournament of Roses Foundation, the Pasadena Arts & Culture Commission and the City of Pasadena Cultural Affairs Division, the City of Los Angeles Department of Cultural Affairs, the Audrey & Sydney Irmas Charitable Foundation, the Kinder Morgan Foundation, the Meta & George Rosenberg Foundation, the Allergan Foundation, the Riordan Foundation, Amazon Literary Partnership, and the Mara W. Breech Foundation partially support Red Hen Press.

First Edition
Published by **Boreal Books**
www.borealbooks.org
An imprint of Red Hen Press
www.redhen.org

For my parents, Nina and Bob Heavener
and Ilona Karmel

One

The tide is still going out, so we may have a while on this sandbar. Not much we can do now but sit and wait, because there isn't a fishing boat for miles. I don't see one, do you? Well, don't blame me. You're the one who needed to get off shore, who wanted to run from the village. Now here we are—in the middle of the channel with our kicker prop run aground and our hull sucked to the silt. It's not good to have your stern anchored, but you already knew that. Let's worry about capsizing when the tide shifts. It will probably happen. I don't mean to scare you, but it will. You know how it goes when waves hit you from both angles. And all it takes is that one rogue wave. Happened to a crew out in Kvichak Bay last year. Remember?

My girl, I'm sorry. I'll start with that. One, for maybe cutting your life short. But if we get off this bar there will be a time when you'll want to know your father. And you will look for him in the eyes of strangers and cannery men to see if they match your own. And you'll ask and beg me to tell you where he is. You might even want to hit me. But I'll have to tell you, I don't know. The story that you are really searching for doesn't sleep with me. Your story is different, one that could be told by the shape of the beach we just left. It is years before me. And it begins with a storm—one of those kind that everyone remembers.

Yet, few outside the Bristol Bay region in Alaska knew about this rare summer storm that gutted the beach of Nushagak Village during the height of the red salmon season. The rising tide could have washed away the dock and all the homes along the shore, and the reports in Anchorage would have still been about the new air navigation silo that recently opened in King Salmon. The Japanese and the Russians had been seen scouting out the islands farther down the chain, and territory lawmakers were anxious to announce Alaska as the first line of defense.

But all the talk of self-defense and the war coming to the territory matters little to our story. As you know, the war came and went, but on that day it was the storm that brought Anne Girl out of her house. Very few things caused Anne Girl to panic, especially a few droplets of rain. Not even the crossways wind made her shudder. But on that day, in that storm, Anne Girl felt a change coming her way. Perhaps it was the seagulls climbing and diving that made her think of her future. I know it's hard to understand what I am getting at, but one day you will understand why I am telling you. You will want to know.

Coastal storms bring gifts. For Anne Girl, the sharp smell of salt and bloated salmon brought in from the storm would be forever linked to John Nelson's stringy, yellow hair. Before she had even met him, she felt his arrival and blamed him for all the scattered driftwood, the knotted net, and her mother's blunt tap on her shoulder, telling her that it was time to inspect their skiff.

Although downpours and floods were common in the bay, they rarely occurred in the summer when the coast was littered with double-enders and drift nets, when the fish were so thick you could walk across the bay on their dorsal fins. But when the swells curled into themselves and the sky rattled with lightning that only God could have sparked, all the fishermen in the bay, including Anne Girl and her mother, Marulia, pulled up their boats to wait it out.

Around the same time that Anne Girl and her mother were tying an anchor to their coiled net so that it wouldn't float away, John Nelson grounded his sailboat several miles down the beach. Anne Girl felt the bottom hit and clutched her stomach as the boat skidded onto the gravel, grinding her abdomen into a knot. Her mother nudged her, and said that now wasn't the time to rest. The water was rising.

Two days after, when the clouds parted and the mountains across the bay could be seen rising out of the silty green water, Anne Girl and Marulia returned to their skiff. Marulia could hardly wait until the whitecaps no longer frothed before gathering her boots and gloves. She poked Anne Girl with a bent finger that was stiff from years of sewing fur parkas. "We have to see if we still have a skiff left. The ghosts from the Aleut wars might have sailed off with it. Or maybe they drowned on the way. Better yet, huh."

Anne Girl peered out the window and saw only grayness beyond the waving grasses. Although the beating wind had paused for the moment, the rain still raced towards them like shooting pebbles. There seemed to be a lot more weather coming with the promise of more wind. Even the gulls squawking above agreed with her, but Anne Girl wasn't about to say anything. Her mother already had her gloves on and a hood wrapped around her face like a tight bonnet. She tapped her finger impatiently on the door frame as she waited for Anne Girl to get ready.

Outside, the air was damp with hints of an early winter—the fireweeds were bent low and their tips had begun to seed. Anne Girl followed her mother down the grassy path toward the beach. The grass stalks were wet, and she felt the cold rise in little bumps on her legs, numbing her skin. But Marulia walked as if she didn't notice, as if she were floating across the grasses to the beach.

Marulia's home was exactly in the middle of the village, in the lower section of the bluff, and from her bedroom window Anne Girl could hear the entire village play out its drama before her. During the summers, when the cannery was open, she could see all the movement in the new part of the village, where the houses progressively grew taller on stilts and the land flattened into a beach that projected out into the bay. Where the houses ended, the cannery began with rows of buildings that always had fresh, painted siding and clean white steps.

Even at midnight, Anne Girl could see the cannery working around the clock, taking in salmon and more salmon. And if she shifted her head slightly toward the bluff, she could see the years worn into the grassy paths and trace the village's movement up the slope as it tried to escape the annual floods. But even with her generous view, she always felt too far from either side of the village. The bluff side and the sod homes with crumbling clumps of grass and dirt reminded her of the tundra across the bay, where it was said that the salmonberries grew so thick that they could not be picked. There was the chapel, a clinic, and newly whitewashed homes that were too square and clean for her. There was an order on that side of the village that made her feel as if her *qaspeq* was a sloppy shirt rather than a loose pullover that allowed the salt of the bay to move through her.

When the grassy trail met the gravelly beach, Marulia paused in mid-stride. Her eyes fell toward the cannery and the cluster of buildings that were oddly silent on this day. Usually at the height of the summer, the noise was endless, reaching across the bay with an arm of money. As more fish were delivered, the canning machines coughed and steamed all night long, louder than the seagulls who squawked as they claimed the discarded guts, eyes, and heads. It was a never-ending chatter between the cannery and the gulls. Everyone wondered how the missionaries could stand to listen to all the noise rattling their windows. It was worse than the screeching coming from the chapel organ.

Marulia clicked her tongue at the chapel's growing steeple as if it were a large tooth feeding on the villagers. She wondered why they stayed when their congregation was a rotating tide of drunks and repentant sobers. It made her dizzy just thinking about it.

"I hear there's a new one staying with them," she said, pointing to the missionaries' home. "Got lost or something in the storm. How can anyone get lost here?"

Anne Girl made no answer, but she grinned at her mother's backside, because her senses were correct about the new man in the village. Anne Girl's abdomen hadn't stopped fluttering since the day of the storm, and all the teas on the tundra gave her no relief. Of course this had to be because he was staying with the Killweathers. Who in their right mind would want to stay with them? He probably had nowhere to go.

She had been inside the Killweather house only once. When Nora and Frederik first arrived, everyone visited them, brought them *akutaq*, stinky head, and secrets of the tundra so they could look at Nora's pale face and Frederik's glasses. Anne Girl hadn't brought anything to share, because she had only wanted to see the inside of their home. Nora, with her long skirts that danced around her body when she walked, gave the impression that her house was pink and smelled of June. Anne Girl expected flowers in vases on every windowsill and honey set neatly on the table. Yet, although the missionary's wife had honey on her table, her house wasn't nearly what Anne Girl had expected, as the main room was a small, yellow square with a narrow doorway to the kitchen. How much Anne Girl had wanted to see the kitchen, to know if it was as clean as Nora carried herself. She wanted to count how many pots and pans Nora had, to see if it explained the many boxes that followed the Killweathers upon their arrival. But Nora wasn't giving tours, and all Anne Girl could do was stare at the large cross on the wall and wonder why it didn't have two crosses like the one she had seen at the cannery store. Marulia had said that the cross was "them Russians" still praying for fish, since they took all the seals. This cross had been different. Everything about these missionaries was different. They planned to stay.

"Maybe he knows them," Anne Girl said, although she didn't think so. She felt that this new man was an accident waiting to collide, and he probably ended up at the Killweathers' because he didn't know any better. She wondered when they would finally meet, because there was no way she was going to invite herself over for tea.

Two steps behind her mother, she walked quickly along the shore, feeling the wind beat against her cheeks, until Marulia stopped suddenly. She pointed at the loose gravel, where their skiff was supposed to be anchored. And it was anchored; it was more secure than they had hoped, and Anne Girl could hear her mother's teeth grinding in long, slow circles, filing her teeth down to her nerves.

A double ender turned on its side balanced on top of their skiff; the mast dug deep into the gravel as if it had finally found its roots on the beach. A large wave had picked up the boat and placed it perfectly into the bed of their skiff. The wooden frame of their skiff stretched and bowed under the weight, and it appeared that its seams were breaking, flattening the ribs into twigs. A gray seagull with a black-tipped beak strutted along the mast while eyeing the women. Marulia clicked her tongue and tapped the wood.

"Some storm to make boats fly like this. Probably had spirits running like crazy." She waved over her head. "Funny that I don't see any other boats on this beach." Marulia sighed and looked up and down. Her hand went to her chest as if to make sure her heart still moved against its cage. It wasn't the broken shape of the skiff, Marulia knew, that caused shortness of breath. This was different, as if something were growing branches in her body, stretching itself from her chest to her gut. "*Akeka,*" she muttered under her breath.

"No, it's that man's who's staying at the Killweathers'. Didn't even know how to anchor his boat," Anne Girl said. "It's too late in the summer to repair the skiff. Everyone's fishing and no one is going to want to patch a boat." She ran her hand along the wooden seams of the boat and felt the creases beneath her fingertips eat at her skin. Her hand paused at the wooden cleat that was sheared off, exposing the brightness of the brown grain. She imagined a thin man with long legs that made catwalking up and down the rails easy. He was blond with cheeks that slightly reddened against the wind, and so his skin was smoother than the bay when the water was like glass. He was completely unlike any villager or cannery man with the tough skin, and Anne Girl couldn't decide whether she should put a hole in his boat or ask him if he wanted to join her at the next potlatch.

"He must be pitiful with this kind of boat," Marulia said. Her fingers lingered in the air, painting it. "I heard that he don't know how to fish. I heard he can't sit still during church."

"You hear a lot."

"I do," Marulia conceded and tapped her forehead. "I hear more than you think."

Anne Girl saw hours of labor wrapped in the coils of rope that were knotted around the sailboat. They definitely would need help from some of the men in town to free the boat from the skiff. It was nothing but a bloated tree. She tugged on one end of the rope, but when it didn't budge she thought of the Killweathers' visitor and decided that even if he was good-looking, she hated him.

With her hands still on her hips, Marulia stared at the boat that jammed her skiff into the bank. She ran her tongue over her bottom lip. "Makes you wonder why he couldn't see the cannery. All that wood piling is hard to miss, you know? You need to tell him to get his boat off our skiff."

Two

Despite the storm, the salmon quickly returned to the bay as they always do, and in the next high tide, Anne Girl found her net loaded to the gills. Her skiff was still trapped under the weight of the sailboat, and in order to pick out the salmon, Anne Girl had to pull the net onto the beach. She cursed the tide and John the entire time. That morning, Marulia had woken up ill and her skin was hot to touch, but she pushed Anne Girl out the door so she could make medicine teas. So Anne Girl picked alone, thankful, because she knew that today she would see John Nelson.

Although she was ready to meet him, had him traced out in her mind of how they would look standing next together or lying side by side, she didn't hear his quiet approach. The salmon had her complete attention. She bent over each one and pulled and yanked them out until silver was flying all around her, raining silver dollars. She would ask him how he came this far north. No, she would tell him that she was going to burn his boat for firewood. No, she would tell him to go home, because they already had too many fishermen in this bay.

"You have quite the load there," John said as he approached. He stopped in front of the snaking wooden corks with his hands jammed in his pockets.

"You get your boat off my skiff?" Anne Girl said without looking up. She continued picking out the salmon and throwing them around her, narrowly missing John.

John laughed nervously. "That was your skiff? I haven't yet, but I'm sure there's a way we can do it. Frederik was telling me that the cannery has some rollers we can put it on . . ."

Anne Girl stood up slowly and stretched her back. She nodded toward John, barely taking him in, and picked up the cork end of the net where a salmon was entangled and handed it to him. And then she returned to where she had crouched before and continued to pull out salmon after salmon.

John took the salmon and turned it in his hands. But when he tugged on the line, it slipped from his fingers and fell to the ground, coating itself in a layer of gravel.

Anne Girl glanced up and saw John redden as if caught in a lie. His cheeks and forehead flushed until it seemed that his blond hair would catch fire too. Watching him, she saw his story in those colors. She knew before he said anything that he had left Seattle, telling everyone that he was going to Alaska to fish the deep waters for salmon or crab or anything that lived beneath the waves. Of course he had read about Bristol Bay and how it was swimming with heads and tails and millions of dollars. Or maybe he thought, because he looked like a Norwegian, that fishing was in his blood. Her stomach sank, because she knew she was stuck with him and that it was going to be a while before she would get her skiff back.

"Don't say nothing," she said, and took the salmon by the gills. She yanked it twice and the fish dropped freely to the ground. She handed him a different section of net.

John took another salmon and mimicked her hands. He pulled hard until the web was securely lodged in the gills. He pulled again and ripped the gills clean off. He held the bloody salmon by its tail fin in front of Anne Girl and smiled.

Once again, Anne Girl stopped and stared at him, her eyes dark and peering as if she were trying to make a decision about this large white man before her. She didn't have a pretty face, and when she was thinking, her broad forehead became one horizontal crease in the middle. But no one would disagree that she was hard and sturdy. Her skin was light tan, like that of most of the residents in the village, but seemed almost gray against the color of her black hair.

"You here to fish?" she asked. Her voice carried over the crash of the waves. "'Cause you don't know nothing about fish." She took the salmon from him and showed him how to pull a salmon from a net without getting its gills further caught or ripped off. "Fish are food, uh."

"I thought about fishing, but maybe I'll work for the cannery." John nodded toward the little town on stilts and winked at her.

"You don't want to work for them," she said. "See these hands." She took off her gloves and held up her hands. The knuckles were swollen, and the fingers were scarred white where they had been repeatedly nicked and burned.

"Oh, you've worked then in a cannery, I see. Which one?"

"No, I never. I still got all my fingers, and they work too." She laughed. "You like your fingers? You shouldn't work in the cannery." She wiped her forehead, leaving a string of slime gleaming on her skin.

Anne Girl saw John's pale skin become whiter, as if the moon had risen inside of him, making his eyes lighter. He was weak-blooded too, she thought. She laughed again and pointed toward another caught salmon. "I jokes. Maybe you can fish. Here, fish with me." She picked up a flounder and traced its white underside with her finger. "You know the Killweathers, then?" she asked.

"Well, not really. We're accidental friends," John said.

As John recounted his arrival to Nushagak Village, of how he left at high tide from Dillingham and ended up on the beach, Anne Girl kicked the gravel to the rhythm of his speech, enjoying the fact that she was correct about him. Right down to the length of his legs. She almost believed that she had made him appear before her. She partially listened to his story about tea with Frederik and Nora and how their daughter, Kristen, was teething. It was too much detail for Anne Girl. His voice was getting in the way of her thinking. Her foot continued to tap, and her head nodded as a smile played out on her face.

Tap, tap, tap. And here he was.

Three

You see our prop is bent. I am pretty sure of it. Where the hell is everyone? Don't people fish around here? This isn't like the old days with the double ender sailboats where we could try to make an outrigger with the mast. We wouldn't have to worry about capsizing then.

I was talking about Marulia, huh? Yes, there are so many things I wish I could share with you about her, like how she did her hair or whether she loved hard or just enough so it was easy to say goodbye. You might want to know these things about her one day, just as I wanted to know. Yet, your Nan spoke little of her mom. Yes, there were other stories, but not the juicy ones. So Marulia's story is locked up with the village women, who prefer to talk over smoked fish and a cup of dark tea. The village women, you say? Oh yes. Wait till you meet them. They are round and skinny, loud and quiet. But it is the fat one you will like the most. But I am not there yet. You will meet her in time.

The sailboat remained latched to the skiff until it was clear to everyone that John was not leaving. His presence made Anne Girl restless, but she had always been on edge. Born on the shores of the salty waters in Nushagak, she grew up with mud in her fingernails and tundra leaves in her hair. The farthest she had traveled was to King Salmon, so that she could work in the cannery. She didn't last long in that village, though. The buildings there were stacked against each other, and Anne Girl couldn't breathe. It reminded her of flies swarming around a dead fish, and she felt like she was suffocating. She didn't even make it to the run before she returned home to help her mother put up meat for the winter.

It was difficult for Anne Girl to sit too long in one spot. She found that if her hands kept busy, then she felt better, calmer. But once they stopped, a rising anxious knot formed in her stomach that made her want to run to that place where the tundra met the blue sky. Where there was an end to the earth. She was scared of the knot and always felt its presence, even during the summers when she was too busy fishing, berry picking, and gathering wood. Some days were devoted to avoiding its tightness, and when she was still short of breath after gathering wood for the *maqi* or putting up fish, Anne Girl understood that the knot might never leave.

One afternoon, Anne Girl and her mother pulled the cutting table down the beach where the salmon that Anne Girl had picked earlier lay gleaming on the gravel floor. The seagulls flapped in irritation and scattered as they approached but landed just far enough so that when the cutting began, their meals of guts and tails would be fresh.

While Anne Girl filled a bucket with water, Marulia stood near the table sharpening her *uluaq* with a round stone. She tested the half-moon blade with her finger before lobbing off the head of the first salmon.

"You were with that *kass'aq* again fishing today? He looks clumsy." She grunted and threw the silver head in a bucket. They would have boiled heads sprinkled with wild celery tonight.

"Yeah, he's no good at fishing," Anne Girl agreed. She didn't let on that John's clumsiness made her laugh, that watching slime trickle down his forearms as he wrestled with a salmon made her want to reach out and pick off the scales that stuck to his skin. She could almost feel his arms beneath her fingertips and imagined how the coarseness of her own hands would soften against his.

"He's staying at those missionaries' place, then?" Marulia asked. "You know how long?"

Marulia didn't give Anne Girl the chance to answer, and continued with her question. She set down her *uluaq* and waved her arm to the seagulls. "Did he invite you to the church, saying 'Please join us for services and cookies. We are the only ones on the beach with cookies and Bibles in Yup'ik.'?" She chuckled to herself and remembered how when the Killweathers first arrived, they tried all kinds of ways to become part of the community. They brought cheese and offered to work with the elders. They did this so they could teach the way to heaven through the elders. Most were happy to learn, happy to sit down and eat new foods with bleached flour and sugar. But because she had lived with missionaries as a child, Marulia saw through Frederik and Nora and waited for them to scold the villagers as if they were children. Waited for them to demand an end to potlatches and ivory carvings.

"He's supposed to go fishing soon," Anne Girl said. She rinsed mud from the gills and fins, before plopping the salmon onto the table. He was supposed to leave at the next high tide, but part of Anne Girl hoped he would change his mind.

He was a storyteller. Anne Girl wanted to share that with her mom, because if anyone understood a good story it was Marulia. Yet his stories were written in a different color than the silty green of the bay, and Anne Girl found herself thinking about them long after they parted ways on the beach. Steamships, Norway, trapping, Canada—they were words, yet he made them real and separate from the endless bluff that were her days. Anne Girl couldn't explain it, especially to her mother when she was holding a knife.

The older woman huffed. Sweat had gathered around her neck and trickled down her back as she cut the meat. She wanted to warn Anne Girl that she never mixed with the fishermen and hunters who used the village as a pit stop. Most of the time they took what they wanted, but never stayed long enough to see who gave it to them. *Kass'aqs* only meant trouble when the fish came. They always smelled like booze and dirtied the village, especially after a good fishing season. Too much money in the bay made smelly, hungry men and babies. She didn't have time for that, and she didn't want Anne Girl to mix with them. But Marulia was silent for another reason. She felt this was her last summer. The pain in her gut had grown stronger, and it took all her strength to put up these strips with her daughter. Soon Anne Girl would be alone.

"I loved a *kass'aq* once. But he flew away." Marulia grunted as she scraped the darkest blood of the salmon from its spine.

Anne Girl raised her eyebrows. She had only seen a plane a few times in her life, and she doubted her mother had seen as many planes, much less known someone who flew. Flying in Bristol Bay was new, and the whole village stopped and ran to the beach when a plane was circling the bluff. Whatever man her mom was talking about could not be a pilot. "Nah, you joke. There's not even a place for planes to land here."

"*Kita.*" Marulia handed Anne Girl the bloodless fish. "You going to change my story? Now, I loved a *kass'aq* once. He was pink like this meat and licked his lips to keep the cold from biting them. He fished better than your John too. We fished together, and when the bay dried up and all we caught was flounders and jellyfish, he stretched his arms up"—Marulia motioned with her hands, raising her bloodied fingers in the air—"and left."

That's what Anne Girl loved about her mother—how she held her hands above everything and said what she thought people needed to know. But despite her mother's warnings, Anne Girl liked the fact that this blue-eyed man, who claimed to be a fisherman, didn't know the difference between a king and a silver. Or that he didn't know which flounders were good to eat and which ones were tough on the teeth. But she loved that he tried. He didn't know it yet, but she would make him fish good.

"It's time you find a man though," Marulia said. She sucked in air to catch her breath. "What are you—twenty already? Going to dry out soon, you know. What are you waiting for?"

"For a tall Norwegian, maybe like your pilot," Anne Girl answered. She flung two slabs onto the table. She felt the tension rise in her throat and debated whether to admit her feelings about John. His name was forming on her lips until she looked at her mother. Marulia's head was bent down in concentration, taking large gulps of air as she tried to split the fish. Anne Girl couldn't. Now wasn't the time.

At the end of the summer, when the last of the fishermen pulled up their nets and returned to civilization in the States, John's boat was still sideways with its bow pointing toward the peaks across the bay. Anne Girl had shrugged and said, "Hell, you might as well stay. But I better not have to ask Amos or Gil to push it off." John smiled and promised that the sailboat wouldn't be a problem ever again, that he wished he never saw the damn thing. "You going to the chapel this week? I'll be there."

The question caught Anne Girl off guard. He hadn't seemed like the type to advertise the missionaries. She was disappointed and wondered if he was going to say something about being saved. Even some villagers on the bluff tried to corner Anne Girl and her mom. They would say that the women needed to get ready for salvation and Marulia would retort that she needed to put up fish for winter, and that they better steer clear of her. And yet they always returned. It burned Marulia, who would mutter in a nasally voice, "This is right—that's wrong. Always something!" Out of respect for her mother, Anne Girl kept to herself. But it even bothered her when Nora first came around, urging her to go to chapel. She was tired of being tracked down and cornered—first the villagers, then Nora, and now John. Anne Girl swallowed and told herself that if she had to, she would suffer splinters on those hard, wooden benches if it meant she could sit next to John for an hour. No one said she had to listen. Two hours would be pushing it, though.

Four

Although her mother gave her long, tired glances, Anne Girl secretly met with John. They walked up and down the beach, creating a space for themselves between the cannery and the bluff side of the village as they searched for new paths when the tide was high. John told different types of stories, ones that filled Anne Girl's head with black and white images, like those she saw printed in the *Life* magazines at the cannery store. Her favorites were the summer covers that usually showed a girl in a fitted swimsuit with bare shoulders looking out to the ocean. It made her laugh to think of herself in such a getup, trying to pick fish. Yet, the images always fascinated her, and she pictured them when she talked to John. She saw them in his words when he described his home and family in Seattle. And the more John talked, the easier it became to fit herself into his stories as if she came from the same roots. He was Norwegian, with a grandfather as old as the canneries and straight from Norway. John didn't have to tell that story twice. Even with his soft hands, she knew that Norwegians were workers. That's what every village woman on the bluff said. The cannery was built by Norwegian and Swedish hands. You can't let a worker go, even if he doesn't know what he is doing. Even Marulia couldn't disagree with that. Yet, Anne Girl wondered why someone who traveled so far would decide to remain in her village, where the winter quiet becomes hungry and you have to yell just so you know that your voice still works.

They walked toward the cannery and onto the boardwalk where the buildings loomed from on top of wooden decking. The cannery had shut down weeks ago, and there was a new stillness in this part of the town. Although all of the windows were boarded up and the doors locked, she could feel the echoes of the cans of salmon being steamed shut. She could hear the seagulls fighting for the last bits of gills.

"You're quiet today."

Anne Girl nodded and took John's hand. Before she had left the house, she had helped her mom into bed and pulled the covers up to her chest. Marulia told her to bury her on high ground and to make sure all of her clothes were burned. She had made Anne Girl promise to marry a fisherman, someone who knew how to mend nets with one hand. Until that moment, they hadn't mentioned death before, and Anne Girl had found herself without a response. She nodded and moved to put more wood in the stove, because her mother continued to repeat that it was too cold.

"The temperature dropped in the last few days. It's going to be a cold winter," Anne Girl told John. "Did you see how fast the berries came this summer? I couldn't pick them quick enough. They were falling into my bucket. Just so you know, my *kass'aq*, when the berries ripen early, then everything shifts." Anne Girl motioned with her hands, moving them side to side.

"Yeah, that's what Frederik says. He says you haven't had a really deep freeze in a long while."

Clearing her throat, Anne Girl pulled John toward the boat house. "He always says that. He hasn't been here long enough to know. Come, I'll show you where we used to sneak into the boat house as kids."

They weaved between the alleyways, passing the bunkhouses, the mess hall, the net loft, the small clinic with a front porch painted white, to the heart of the cannery with the boat house and mechanical rooms. It was here where the rumble of the cannery generators grinded their wheels. It was here where all the fishermen stored their equipment and spent hours painting and repairing their boats before the season began.

Anne Girl walked to the side of the boat house and began tapping the sheet-metal until one panel rattled louder than the others. She pulled the tin sheet from the wall, revealing a narrow, black hole, and grinned.

"Kind of small. You fit through there?" John asked.

"Used to. Had to hold my breath to get by the metal edges or they would cut deep."

"What did you do in there?"

"Play. The cannery men always left good things to play with. Once they left tools, so I took them home." A smiled spread on her face. "Do you want to play now?"

John reached for Anne Girl's waist. "When are you going to let me meet your mother?"

Anne Girl pulled away and let go of the tin flap. She stared at him. Of all the things he could say to her now, he *had* to ask about her mother! But as he stood waiting for her answer, Anne Girl realized that she could neither lie nor tell the truth. She wanted to tell him that he would never meet her mom, that Marulia cringed every time Anne Girl mentioned his name, and that she asked out loud whether John could hunt or fish. "Is he good for anything?" Marulia wanted to know.

"Maybe soon," Anne Girl said, and she pulled at the flap again. She looked up into John's eyes and felt the unexpected urge to pull him down on her so that his long, narrow figure would suffocate her loss. And when her body was mashed up against his, she would enter a space where the restlessness would finally subside. Where she could find quiet and breathe again. Anne Girl traced his waistline with her finger. "The net loft is warm year round. I know another way to get in there. But keep your arms close to you, so you don't get cut."

Afterwards, they lay side by side on top of stacked nets, exhausted and breathing hard. Anne Girl rolled over and smelled the mixture of fish and sweat. John's hair was frosted with scales that glimmered in the darkness, and she picked them off one by one. "Frederik will wonder what you've been up to," she said, and began to giggle. "Make sure you tell him that you were working hard."

Five

M*y Girl, how did we get here? What the hell did I just do?*

Anne Girl agreed to marry John the following summer, only after her mother's death, after she burned Marulia's clothes in a great fire on the beach that made all the village women come down and watch. They circled the flames, telling spirit and ghost stories until the driftwood burned down to glowing chunks. It seemed as if every woman on the bluff—young and old—crawled out of their homes to join the fire on the beach. Anne Girl's closest friend, Alicia, stood next to her and made sure that nothing of Marulia's remained intact.

When the bottles of booze began to be passed around, some of the women wanted to keep the flames high and made a move for the skiff, which lay on its side at the grassy edge. It still needed work to float again, but at least it was no longer suffocating under John's double ender.

"Not the skiff!" Anne Girl yelled. She positioned herself between the woman and the boat. "It's all I got left."

"Com'on, it's nothing but dry wood."

"Burn your own damn boat." Anne Girl patted the bowed ribs. "This one's still good—once my Norwegian learns how to wood work."

The women laughed and muttered among themselves that Anne Girl was probably drunk to think John would fix that heap of wood.

Anne Girl could breathe easy standing on the shore with the women who had known her mother better than she did, but didn't really know it would be alright until she saw a raven perched on the ridge of her mom's roof with berries tucked in her beak. She then saw her mother fly toward Dillingham with a sleek black coat and wings clipped at the edges. Her largeness eased Anne Girl's worries. Her mom was already eating good.

Somehow word about John's inability to pick a net or handle a tiller must have traveled to the cannery, because that summer he couldn't find anyone interested in hiring him on. Often during low tides, he would go down to the docks and talk to fishermen who were waiting for the tide to change. The fishermen would laugh a little and become guarded as soon as they learned his name. "I see now," they said, while grinning. "You've had a little experience with sailboats, huh? Whatever happened to it?"

Sometimes Anne Girl joined John at the dock, hoping that maybe her presence would convince the thick-skinned fishermen that John was worth at least one high tide, maybe two if she could talk fast enough. Most of the time, she and John sat on the dock with their legs swinging over the side as they shared leftovers from the mess hall or smoked fish with the fishermen. It was a rough season, the fishermen said, when they saw Anne Girl. Or some would hint that John looked a little skinny to be pulling a sailboat. Once she almost convinced a stocky Norwegian to take John. "He is your cousin," Anne Girl said. "Looks just like you only with thinner fingers." The fisherman laughed as he crawled down the ladder to his boat. "Next tide, huh?"

Anne Girl couldn't tell, but perhaps the Norwegian felt sorry for them, because when he reached his boat he jumped over the bunched up cloth, rummaged through a wooden crate, and tossed a bottle to John. He nodded at them both before bending down to his net pile.

"Ooh, good times," John whispered, and held the tan bottle before them. "I haven't had this brand in a long while."

Anne Girl took the bottle from John and saw that it was wine. She licked her lips slowly. "We aren't sharing this with nobody," she said. She stood up and brushed the wooden splinter from her slacks.

"Maybe we should just come down here and beg for food. We'll be like seagulls."

Yet without work, Anne Girl wondered how they were going to pay for the next food order that was to arrive on the barge. He insisted on certain foods from the barge, like cheeses and jellies, yet he didn't seem to think about how much it cost. She smoked extra fish and gathered berries until the pads of her fingers felt sticky and hot. At least they would have fish, she figured. And when she returned home, she watched John haul water and gather driftwood, as if that's all they needed to get through the winter. And he would stack the wood ever so neatly against the house, laying the sticks against one another in perfect order. It made her want to spit. She shook her head and wondered if she could teach him to shoot a caribou, or if she would have to do that herself.

"Where you going?" he asked, when Anne Girl picked up her berry bucket as soon as he walked through the door.

"Up past the bluff, the berries are ripe," Anne Girl answered, and she continued putting on her boots. She wore a *qaspeq* that hung down to her knees. "Going berry picking with Alicia."

John stared at her mouth.

Anne Girl looked up. "What?"

"You picked yesterday. Why do we need this many berries all the time? For just the two of us?"

"Ahh, you want to come?" Anne Girl smirked. She picked up her berry buckets and her *naivaa* cup, still grinning. She ran her tongue across her lips, teasing him.

John bit his lower lip, but his face was beginning to redden. "I think you should sew."

"Sew? What does that have to do with berries? I don't have enough berries. And we need a lot in the winter. You'll crave them just like you itch for coffee."

"Why don't you sew more? We could bring your furs to the trading post in Dillingham."

Anne Girl stared at him and rattled the buckets against her legs. She was thinking, placing his statement about the furs against his strong frame that was good for nothing but water and rotten wood. Once her mom had asked if this John man could grab the air with his hands and guide a fishing boat, or was he just good for crashing up the beach.

"Sew? Sew what? You going to go out there and trap me some mink and beaver?" She laughed. "I see you now, on your knees calling out to the poor bastards, because you don't know how to set a trap line."

"We could sell fur parkas, you know," he said, his voice rising. "We could do that together, if you would just sit still and start sewing. We're broke."

A line of color crept up his neck, but Anne Girl shook her head as if it wasn't her problem. "I must've married the wrong man then." And then she motioned with her head toward the Killweathers' house. "Go ask your Frederik. He knows everything. Maybe he can teach you to work."

Anne Girl stopped in the doorway and tapped the handle with her finger. Her expression had transformed into one of impatience and disgust, as if looking at him made her want to vomit. "Are you going to just sit there?"

"I didn't mean that you should sew for us," John paused. "For me."

But she had already walked out the door with the two buckets clanking against her legs.

"Go pick then. Pick your damn heart out until you have enough to feed the entire village!" John yelled after her.

Outside, the wind cut through Anne Girl's *qaspeq* and she shivered. She felt the noise of the cannery settle on her skin, and she stopped mid-stride. She took in a long breath. "Ha, the entire village," she muttered as she turned back toward the house.

John was staring out the window when she returned. He didn't move when she opened the door, even after a gush of wind flapped the curtains. Anne Girl saw that she missed a chunk of hair above his left ear during his last trim. Maybe he would let her cut it now. Real quick. She stood in the doorway, and it seemed like the new moon had come and gone before John looked up.

"I'm eating nails," Anne Girl said and met his gaze. "Sorry. Winter gets to me, you know."

The corners of John's mouth turned up slowly until he looked something like a spotted seal, grinning at her. "You *are* nails," he chuckled. "You just now figure that out? I knew that the first day you flung that damn salmon at me."

"If it wasn't for that salmon . . ." Anne Girl paused as she realized that John wasn't angry at all, that he had forgiven her that easily. Just like that—he forgot, and for a brief second she understood that happiness can exist. "Come with us." Anne Girl tossed one bucket toward him. "Them long legs of yours will be good for the hills. Please."

"Nah, you go," John said. "It's too fine of a day for me to hold you back. That pilot that flies in packages for the mission is at their house. He says it's a good time to be flying in the bush now. Good time."

Anne Girl's hand went to her mouth, "Ooh, you can be one of them pilots." She giggled. "My mom loved a pilot—probably my father. Then he flew away," she said. "Couldn't get far enough, I bet."

"Now the truth comes out. What else do you have hiding under that hood? A pilot? A boat captain? I don't believe a word you say."

"You shouldn't," Anne Girl said. "My dad was probably a fat beluga."

"Don't believe that either," John countered, and he stood up to stretch. "You would have eaten us out of the house by now."

Anne Girl took all of him in. "Hmm . . . a flying Norwegian." She traced the grains in the door with her fingernail, trying on the idea of living with a pilot. She almost liked the sound of it. All the places she could go. "Hmm . . . we can fly to Anchorage. I want to see a movie there. Pray, if Frederik says that will help."

John chuckled. "Don't get too ahead of yourself. I got to learn first. Might have to go to Anchorage for that." And he motioned toward the bluff. "Get out there. I know you are dying to go. I'll tell you all about it when you get back. We want five buckets!"

Jumping up, Anne Girl gave him a quick kiss on the cheek. "Listen real good and tell me if Frederick talks to himself. Alicia says he does!"

Across the village, past the grassy bluff where the land rolled into gentle, soggy tundra, Anne Girl, Alicia, and her cousins trudged through the soft ground, their eyes fixed on the horizon, searching for the pale pinkness of salmonberries.

Anne Girl watched the younger girls run up and down the trail, and she remembered a time when she had sprinted through the tundra. She wasn't much older than they were, but her mother's death and her marriage to John had changed her. She felt the weight of responsibility in her blood, slowing her down. Now she picked for food, not to play. Yet it was nice to feel the breeze that skipped the surface for a thousand miles brush her cheeks. It was good to breathe again. No one warned her that living so close with a man would be like sitting in *maqi* with the stove door open, heat clinging to her flesh. He was always clinging, like a girl.

"You girls watch it, uh. You might be stepping on berries!" she hollered. But a smile played on her lips. She couldn't help herself, no matter how much she wanted to be serious.

"Don't go too far. The *carayak* will get you." Alicia joined in, although she laughed, because no one was worried about ghosts.

"You always say that."

"Well, how else we going to get them to listen?" Alicia answered. She stopped and cupped her hands around her eyes, so that she could see only the patches of salmonberries. "We need to go this way," she said, and pointed to several rolling hills toward the village of Ekuk.

Anne Girl picked up some tea leaves and stuffed them in her pocket. She would show John how to make some good tea. She looked up and spotted a lone figure lumbering in the distance. "Is that Sweet Mary . . . or a bear?"

Alicia's head snapped toward the direction of Anne Girl's finger. "Better be Sweet Mary. You see it roll? Hmmm . . . looks like Mary. A bear would have caught wind of us by now."

"I don't know," Anne Girl said. "Sweet Mary won't leave us any berries, you know. Probably planning to feed the cannery with them. All them cannery men. One by one."

"Well, someone has to," Alicia answered. "She will not let one starve, if she can help it."

Anne Girl watched the figure and tried to determine whether it had a long braid trailing behind it. That was Sweet Mary's pride. When she was finally convinced that the round spot wasn't a bear, Anne Girl looked down at the green carpet beneath her feet. She jumped a little to feel the marsh quiver around her. "Better her than me. That's too much damn work," Anne Girl laughed. And then she felt bad. Everyone in the village loved Sweet Mary, who would give her last meal to anyone who needed it. Yet she was a busy woman, making a name for herself at the cannery. When they were younger, Marulia had told Anne Girl to stay away from Sweet Mary, that the larger woman would cause stories to stick to her legs. The whole village would know, Marulia had said. But it seemed silly now.

"You like it up near that church?" Alicia asked.

"Yeah, it's good."

"You lie."

"No, it's good when the cannery is closed. Quiet. I don't have to haul water as far," Anne Girl said. "Actually, I don't have to haul water at all. It seems that's all John likes to do." Anne Girl wanted to say more, but she stopped herself. She knew that he was talking to Frederik right then, and she didn't want to say anything to Alicia just yet. She didn't want Alicia to make up any stories about her, because the woman would talk once she gleaned enough information. That was the one thing that she missed about her mother—she knew the difference between stories and gossip and never went so far as spreading any of the latter. Her mother had said gossip was as bad as the coughing disease that went through the village many years ago and took her parents.

"Except," Anne Girl said. She grabbed Alicia's arm and pulled her close so that she could smell the faint odor of smoked fish in her friend's hair. "Except, sometimes I hear them singing."

Alicia's eyes widened. "Who?"

"The neighbors," Anne Girl said. "I think they have thin walls."

"You mean during church you hear the singing? Damn, I heard they liked their music. Didn't know they did that every day."

Anne Girl smiled mischievously. "No, I mean at night."

"Really? Who would have guessed that they sing in bed?" Alicia threw back her head and laughed. "Really that loud, uh? If Nora only knew, she wouldn't be inviting you over so much. I could just see her ears turn red if she knew you heard them."

"I know. I know." Anne Girl laughed.

They veered off the trail, both following their own sense for the berries. Anne Girl took a deep breath, feeling the fresh tundra soak into her lungs as she looked around. These same hills were brown and lifeless just a few months ago before spring took root. And now everything was ripe, spilling into seeds. Moss and lichen with emerald-colored leaves formed a carpet around them. Few low brushes with the buds of cranberries and blueberries waved in the breeze. The tundra was out of hibernation and ready to give back sweet berries.

As if a part of them had finally awakened to the moving land, the women got to work. Alicia sat down with her legs sprawled in front of her, and Anne Girl squatted into a perch. Close to the ground she smelled the green of the tundra, its moist moss and fresh flowers. She heard the wind rustle through the low brush and the grass as it followed the slope of the land. She ran her hands through the brush, feeling the leaves tickle her palms and the ripe berries stick to her touch. And then Anne Girl began to pick with a determined fierceness that rose from the pit of her stomach. She picked a handful of salmonberries, dropped them in the bucket, and then picked another handful. Her fingers became sticky as they guided her. She picked quickly and rarely raised her head to catch her breath. Yet, once when she looked up toward the direction of the bluff, Anne Girl's eyes caught something. She couldn't be sure and blinked twice before seeing a black-tailed ermine scurry by her. He stopped briefly and turned to Anne Girl with beady black eyes. He stopped only long enough to wave and then dashed toward the brushes. Anne Girl turned back to the green before her, and she saw the bright salmonberries sparkle as if they popped up from the ground only for her. And for the first time since her marriage, since her mother's death, the knot in her stomach loosened a bit.

Six

Changes come and we aren't prepared for them, such as this tide. Normally, I know when the tide switches, unless the moon is tilting the wrong way. Then the tides move sideways and not even the best fishermen in this bay can outwit them. So I told you the war would come. And it did. Right when no one was expecting it, the Japs landed on Attu and Kiska islands. Up here, in Bristol Bay, it didn't matter so much. The village women say there was an order to cover all the windows from here to Bethel, but not everyone listened. Your Nan didn't listen to anyone.

Anne Girl lay in a silent sweat, struggling to give birth. She sucked on a dishrag and gave only the faintest groans. She didn't want Alicia to tell everyone that she screamed too loudly. Only *kass'aqs* were loud and attracted attention when in pain. Feeling her bones rip from the sockets, the flesh convulsing around her groin, she gave one last push, dimly saw Alicia pull a sheet over the window, and passed out.

Years later, Anne Girl told Ellen that she had been too lazy to make her way out, that she was a stubborn one headed for trouble.

Ellen, lighter skinned but with round cheeks like her mother, always had a reply. "And why didn't you help me?"

Anne Girl pulled the girl close, so that she could braid her hair. "I did, but you didn't listen." She tugged hard on the long hair, and

Ellen winced. "You never listen. You wanted to stay forever where it was warm, so that you could be lazy."

"Then you should have been nicer to me," Ellen answered.

Still holding Ellen's braid, Anne Girl angled toward the window and saw John heave himself out of his plane. "Look at him," Anne Girl huffed. "Always wiping like it's going keep him in the air. We're going to starve because of that thing."

He pulled out a rag from his jacket and began to wipe the propeller in slow circles until the sliver metal gleamed in the afternoon. It was a ritual that he never failed to miss, shining his plane and checking the wings and rudder for damage. Anne Girl wondered if he did that just for show, so that all the people at the cannery would know that he was the pilot in the village. Her pilot, anyway.

She yanked on Ellen's hair. "Now you moved again, and I have to start over. Can't you keep still for a minute?" She began to loosen the knot, yet not her grip, so Ellen had to stand with her head tilted backwards. "Look, you're nearly eleven and you can't braid your own hair. We should probably shave it."

"Shave your own head." Ellen turned to her mom, her eyes bright. "Let's both cut our hair!"

"Enough now," Anne Girl said and pulled on Ellen's shoulder.

Anne Girl listened for John's steps in the front porch and his typical rattle of the door knob and felt a smile play on her lips. He's home, she thought, and took in a long, slow breath. Yes, he's finally home.

"Papa, did you bring me anything from Dillin-ham?" Ellen tried to run to him, but Anne Girl held on tight to the braid and pulled her back.

"*Usuuq*, I'm not done yet." She pulled the ponytail again and Ellen yelped.

"Mama! Stop."

"Just a minute now." Anne Girl looked at John and surveyed him with black eyes that were just as sharp as they had ever been. "You fly good then?"

When John was learning to fly, he was full of promises about flying to Seattle and around the territory. Everyone could fly in those days, John included. And it sounded good to be married to a pilot then. Even Alicia was envious, saying that she wished Amos would do more than fish and hunt. But the war changed it all. The stories coming from Dutch Harbor were enough for her to want to tie down the plane herself, and getting a pilot's license was easier than ever. She didn't even bother to hide her delight when John returned after being dismissed from the recruiter's office. She giggled and couldn't wait to tell Alicia that flat feet kept him from flying for the war. She had always known something was wrong with how he walked, and those big officials proved her right.

But she knew John wanted to fly, could feel it at night when his left leg twitched and shook the bed. And when he secured a minor contract with the Postal Service and some mining camps in north, Anne Girl bit her lower lip until she tasted blood. Didn't they know he flies like he boats, with one eye closed and muttering the whole time? Although the villages were close enough to make several trips in a day, they were just far enough apart for him to die in the middle of nowhere if he crashed.

Very few villages had decent airfields until the end of the war. Pilots created their own runways, and sometimes a sandbar was the best thing in sight. And Anne Girl had a feeling that if John needed to make an emergency landing, he would miss his mark, the same way he crashed his boat into her life. When he started his first run, she had stood near the runway and watched every take-off and landing, every dip into the wind, and she knew that sometimes he turned too sharply before landing. Sometimes she stood and stared until she couldn't tell the difference between the swooping seagulls and the wings of his aircraft.

"Yeah, yeah," John nodded. "The flight from Togiak to Dillingham was a bit bumpy, but we made it alright. The ceiling was low around Togiak and it seemed like I kept getting sucked in the clouds." John motioned with his hands, and he talked until Anne Girl got up from the table and went to the kitchen.

"So what have you two been up to?" John reached out and pulled Ellen onto his lap. "You've been helping Mama?"

Ellen frowned and began to unravel the braid.

"Don't take it out! *Assiipaa*. Look now," Anne Girl threw up her hands. "You ruined it. Well, when that rat's nest gets caught in the brush, we're cutting it. Yep. Right there."

"You know, all the girls at the Sunday school wear their hair really pretty," John said.

Anne Girl shot him a warning look. "We talked about this already, uh. She's not going to that missionary's place on Sunday too. School is enough."

"You mean our neighbors?" John pointed out the window. His voice was even and calm.

"Yeah, yeah. Our neighbors, your neighbors. You just want to go listen to the radio with Frederik. No one cut off your feet. You can go anytime." Anne Girl put the kettle on the stove. She wiped her hands on her shirt and stared thoughtfully at John's backside. His back was a washer board, straight and uneven. She could see the bumpy knobs of his spine as he bent down to hug Ellen.

"At least you aren't dead this time," she muttered.

"I bet you I won't be dead next time too," John answered. "If I am, I won't ask about Sunday School . . . maybe."

She could feel the grin in his voice. It was contagious, and Anne Girl tried to hold onto her anger like it was her last berry. He always did that, made her momentarily forget why she was mad.

"How long you going to be here before you have to fly out again?" she asked.

John kissed Ellen on the forehead and whispered in her ear. "I brought you something from Dillingham. Go play outside for a while, and you can have it tonight after dinner."

Ellen glanced at her mom to see if she heard before running out the door. But Anne Girl was elbow deep in the kitchen. She was loud as she took out pots and pans from the shelves and banged them against the counter.

"When you flying again?" Anne Girl repeated. She needed to know how much time she had until her nights became long again. Their separations tugged on her and made sleep impossible. Even Alicia had asked if she was well and needed a *maqi* to cleanse herself. She never wanted to be the kind of woman who waited for her man to return to her, but it seemed that's all that John left her to do. And while he could pick up where they left off, Anne Girl had to quell the anger that had risen in his absence.

"How long would you like for me to be here? I can be here forever."

Anne Girl knocked a pot of water onto the floor and stared at him. The water pooled toward the direction of the door. "John, how long?"

"A couple of days if the weather holds up," John said, as he picked up the pot and reached for a towel.

"Good, I'm gonna need some wood for the smokehouse. You can get some when you're not doing nothing."

"Come here, you. Don't get yourself all worked up about it. I'll get all the wood you need."

Although Anne Girl tried to dodge him, John pulled her close and wrapped his arms around her. "All the wood you need and more."

Anne Girl let herself relax and buried her nose in his chest. She inhaled and could practically taste the mixture of engine oil and sweat coated on his shirt. She inhaled again and again until she realized she was shuddering.

Seven

"A*mpi*. Come now, Ellen. You're too slow," Anne Girl said, and she walked down the beach to check on the smoked fish. She turned around to see Ellen dragging her feet in the gravel and occasionally picking up rocks as she walked. She would roll the rock in her hand before tossing it ahead of her. Anne Girl clicked her tongue and wondered if this girl would be like her father. No doubt Ellen was on her way to resembling him, with long arms and a sense of idleness no one should have. Yes, Ellen was John right down to her toes. "Clumsy," Marulia would say.

The thought brought a smile upon her face as images of her mother seemed to appear like lingering morning dreams when she was on the beach. Once her blood began to move and take in the salty air, her mother's words always came to mind. She pictured all the times they picked fish in the skiff and how after her mom became weak, she would bend like a sharp angle over the cork line until her nose practically touched the wooden corks as if she were smelling them. Somehow it seemed that the dead woman wouldn't leave her alone. And now as she looked out toward the bay, toward the deceivingly calm water, Anne Girl wondered what these images were supposed to mean. After all this time, she was beginning to believe that maybe she had forgotten to burn something. She stopped and waited for Ellen to catch up.

"Mama, I *am* walking fast. Why you running?" Ellen answered when she finally approached her mother. "Always running here and there."

Ruffling Ellen's hair, Anne Girl conceded. "Ha, you haven't seen me running. Now the little people. They run so fast that we can't see them. But if you ever see one, then you'll be taken away to where they live forever."

"Why?"

"Because they'll be angry that you saw them and might give away their secrets."

"Nuh-uh."

"Yeah. That's why the Sams' kid disappeared, before you were born though. But they go the church all the time, thinking he'll come back from the little people. He won't though."

Nancy and Gil Sam became religious when their son disappeared one summer while hunting caribou. Parents told their children that it was a *carayak* or maybe even a little person that took him away, even after they found his partially eaten body in a bear cache. But of all the villagers in Nushagak, the Sams were the most faithful. Some said that Frederik promised that their son would make it to Heaven if they prayed hard enough. Others clicked their tongues and muttered, "*Akleng*, they must hurt still yet."

A thin trail of smoke filtered through the door crack and air vent as they approached the smokehouse, and Anne Girl chastised herself for forgetting to plug the door seam with a cloth. The smokehouse was old, blackened by years of smoking and the occasional flood that rusted the tin walls. When her mother died, Anne Girl had thought about asking John to build one closer to their home, but somehow she could not give this one up. She liked the idea of smoking her fish in the same black walls where her mother had smoked her own strips. Anywhere else, and the fish would likely overheat and cook instead.

"Stand back now and don't breathe in the smoke. Go get some driftwood to get this fire back started—small, dry pieces."

Ellen shrugged at the thought of gathering wood. "Let's look for the little people," Ellen said. Her eyes were good, she knew. One time in the fall she saw a ptarmigan on the tundra when even her mom couldn't see its brown stripes.

"Enough now of the little people. I'm gonna need some leaves too—dry ones!"

Anne Girl ducked through the door and was immediately greeted by warm, dry air smelling of sweet alder trees. Most of the smoke had cleared, and she knelt low on the ground until the rest of the smoke had moved out. It was a chore, checking the fish every few hours and making sure that the fire wasn't burning or cooking the strips, but Anne Girl loved the rhythm. She pulled off the fire pit lid to find that she hadn't made it in time. The smoke had promised a fire, but there was nothing but dying embers.

"*Usuuq*. Get me some of those pieces leaning against the building over there. Small ones. That's a girl."

Ellen brought two pieces of wood and crouched next to the opening. "Smoke's gone. I'm coming in now."

"Not yet. Give me some more, some with leaves on them. You need to keep gathering wood," Anne Girl answered. She stood up and inspected the fish. It was still too early. The flesh of the fish was still bright pink. Not until the meat was dark red and dripping with grease would they be ready.

She had hoped that they would be ready in time for next week's potlatch, which the village was holding at the community hall. All were invited, including those from the cannery, and all were expected to attend and bring their favorite meal. There would be *pateq* bones, caribou stew, seal oil, strips, *akutaq*, and Spam from those who could afford canned food. Anne Girl thought that maybe she would bring some fish strips. Hers weren't too salty, just right. Otherwise, John would want to fly to Dillingham and get canned soup that made her stomach swell larger than a sea otter. Anne Girl pinched a piece of the meat and felt its moist flesh between her finger tips. She should have made the strips thinner, she thought. These ones are too soft and still pink.

She didn't see Ellen sneak through the door and walk to the back of the small hut. She had brought in a stick and batted at the strips hanging above her head. Fish oil sprayed in tiny droplets around them as the strips swung violently from the poles.

"Oh, the girl has ears but can't hear," Anne Girl said when she saw Ellen in the corner. "You know what happens to girls who don't hear?"

Ellen stopped and looked at her mother, her mouth open, her eyes wide. "What?" she demanded. "I got all the wood. Go see."

Anne Girl resumed her work. She gathered the dry leaves and the small twigs and placed them carefully in the fire pit as if every twig had its rightful place to burn. She looked up and saw that Ellen had dropped the stick and was crouched across from her, waiting impatiently for the story.

"Little girls who have ears but don't listen lose their ears. I remember when this old man and woman had two little girls in that village over that way." Anne pointed toward the rising hills across the bay. "The woman was once young and beautiful with long black hair that she braided just like yours. But she was old and slow when she had these girls. They wore *qaspeqs*, pretty ones that their Mama made for them. Their *qaspeqs* were bright red and orange, made from fabric from up town. Their Mama told them not to play in the mud flats, because she saw how the tide changes its mind quickly. How the current becomes strong on its own. She told them that if they were good, she would make each girl another *qaspeq*. But the girls didn't listen." Anne Girl paused and then continued, speaking low and adding her own thoughts to the story that her mother had once told her. She added the part about the *qaspeqs*, because she knew Ellen loved playing in her *qaspeq* and wanted another one. "They come home and their *qaspeqs* were full of shit mud. All the people in that village knew they played in the mud flats and were surprised to see them come walking back with mud in their ears and around their hair. Their Mama told them again not to play in the mud flats. Their Papa too. But when the tide rolled out, the girls walked out in the mud flats, and threw mud balls at each other. They even went mud slicking, just how you like to do. And then the tide changed and water took them under. The village knew what happened. And so did their old parents. But they found their ears floating nearby. And a seagull swooped down and ate them."

Anne Girl lit the fire and motioned for Ellen to follow her out. "The strips will be done in a week or so, just in time for the potlatch."

"The seagull didn't eat the eyes first? Don't they like eyeballs?"

"Not this time. This time, they liked ears. See what happens when you don't use your ears. Come, we got to get water. Your Papa's going to be flying in soon. I feel it in my gut." Anne Girl grabbed Ellen's hand.

They began walking toward their house, and the outline of the cannery and the stilt-legged homes, bony and sharp, came into view. Anne Girl could see the cannery men milling around the buildings like ants, getting ready for the fishing season. She was pleased that she had put up most of the fish for the winter already. Next they would go duck hunting. She figured that if the season was good, they would make a little extra so John wouldn't have to fly so much in the winter. She worried that one of these days he would try flying with ice on his wings. Anne Girl and Ellen hiked up the beach as a single-engine plane curved right and landed bumpily on the dirt road near the cannery. Anne Girl knew instantly it was John and that he had once again missed the runway.

The Nelson family arrived at the potlatch with a bag of strips and a jar of seal oil just as the elders were beginning to make their way to the long table of food. The hall, a circular room with benches along the walls, buzzed with conversation. There was a pregnant hum in the air, the anticipation that something good was about to happen. People were standing and sitting, talking about fishing and about the weather, wondering if anyone had spotted the herd of caribou way past the bluff. This wasn't the potlatch of the old days. Nearly everyone in the village was there, including the Killweathers and some of the cannery men as well as the cannery superintendent. People from the surrounding villages of Igushik and Ekuk also arrived with their children in tow. Although everyone from all over the bay was busy putting up fish for the winter, they didn't mind taking a little time to eat and share while food was plenty.

From across the room, Alicia waved frantically toward Anne Girl and pointed to an empty space next to her. Anne Girl turned to John and said, "You watch Ellen. I'll be over there. Let's stay long this time."

"We can stay as long as you like," John said. "As long as you like."

Alicia moved over to make room on the narrow bench for Anne Girl. "Sit your butt down right here. Lots a good food, huh?"

"Yeah."

"There's going to be dancing once this meeting gets over with. Unless they start drumming. We should go up to my place after, huh? Amos needs a good drink before he stores himself in that boat. You know what this meeting is all about?"

Anne Girl frowned. "You forget, I don't hear nothing over that way but the cannery talking, so don't ask me."

"Yeah, we never see you this way anymore. I've missed you. You need to come more and *maqi* with me sometime. We'll have good hot ones."

"I'll bring the girl too." Anne Girl nodded and looked at Ellen playing across the room as if she was seeing daughter for the first time after a long separation. Sometimes Ellen was an afterthought, something she had to remind herself to check as if she was checking on the smokehouse. But the girl was always there, under her feet, never allowing Anne Girl to forget.

Alicia pointed to Frederik and John talking on the other side of the room. "How are your neighbors? Still noisy? Too bad Nora never had any more kids," Alicia said and laughed. She leaned forward and peered at Frederik. "Is that a Bible he's giving John? Probably one of them Yup'ik ones. Nancy loves them, even though she can't read any of them words. She thinks she can read."

Ann Girl scoffed. She didn't have much to say about the Killweathers and their Bibles. Although Anne Girl had managed this far without saying more than a few words to either Nora or Frederik, it seemed as if they took up residence in her kitchen. Nearly every time John returned from up town or from flying, he talked about the bits of news that he thought Frederik would like to hear. And sometimes he stopped at Frederik's first. That burned Anne Girl more than anything, because she knew they both had their ears to Frederik's radio. If she saw his plane tied down near the runway without any sight of him, she refused to cook and sometimes dumped out all the drinking water before he arrived home. For all she cared, he could talk about all the news he wanted on his way to the well.

Once, shortly after she heard his plane land, she looked out of the window to see it sitting empty on the edge of the runway. There was no sign of John walking in his buttoned-up jacket toward her. She had sniffed the air and tried to find a hint of his sweat and raw engine smell. Nothing. Something then inside of her shattered, like dry wood popping in a fire, and she had marched out to his plane, loosened the rocks holding the wheels in place and climbed into the cockpit. She started pressing buttons, shifting rudders, anything to get the motor started. She was going to drive that piece of metal into the drink. From the corner of her vision, she saw John running toward her, pulling at his unbuttoned pants. He opened the cockpit door and slammed it against the wing frame. The entire plane shook with his anger.

"The hell you doing!" He was shaking all over, gripping the door until the tendons in his forearm looked as if they would snap. "Don't mess with anything. I'm already low on oil. You could break something. Jesus!"

"Going for ride, you want to come?" She smiled at him.

John's jaw was tight, and he bit his lower lip as he had tried to calm himself. "No, no. You said you don't ever want to get near this thing. Get out."

She looked at his pants and realized her mistake, but it pleased her to see him get riled. She didn't want to stop now. How far could she push him? How far would he let her? "Were you in the outhouse? Let's go for a ride now. You know how you always want to take me up in the plane. Let's do it now. I'm ready. I'm ready for Seattle."

"Jesus, Anne," John said. "Just get out. Just get out now."

He had reached into the cockpit and pulled her out with a strength that she didn't know he possessed. His fingers dug into her waist and thighs, and her shins hit the rim of the door as he dragged her out.

She wondered where this man, this strength, had been all this time. He was always so gentle and tender, even in bed, that she had begun to think he didn't have anything else to give. He set her down on her knees next to the plane wheel, and then twisted the lock on the door.

"I didn't think I would ever have to lock it from you, Anne. The village kids, yes, but not you."

He had left her there on the ground and headed back toward the outhouse. She kneeled there, resting her head against her knees until Ellen had sat down next to her and said that the fish head soup was boiling.

The sounds of the meeting and Alicia's elbow brought Anne Girl back to the hall. She always wondered if John had wanted to hit her then. The thought kind of pleased her, because then maybe he would act more alive and possessive. Then she could hit him back for always leaving her. Even if she wasn't successful, she tried to remain calm or indifferent when he went over to Frederik's for a game of chess or for the news. She at least tried. It was the least she could do for him, she had decided.

"You letting Ellen go to the Bible camp this summer?"

"Nah."

"You should. That Nora's a good teacher, real quiet, you know. Not like some. Ellen will just be in the way for fishing. I'm letting my June go. Phil's going fishing with Amos. And I won't be able to watch her all the time. It'll be good for them to learn a little something."

"A little nothing is what," Anne Girl said, and she took a bite from her strips. She worried that Nora in her womanly ways would soften Ellen so that the girl would never learn to fish and hunt and take care of herself. Her hands would become soft and her fingers tender. And then they would be useless. Anne Girl couldn't let that happen.

While Alicia listed off the benefits of allowing Ellen to go to Bible camp, one of the most respected elders, Old Paul and his son, entered the hall. Old Paul, named after his Russian father Paulvnskii, a fur trader at Hooper Bay, was one of the oldest in the village. He was a young adult before the cannery pounded piles into the beach and declared the settlement to be a fishing village. He was so old that it was rumored he was a shaman, a good one who knew how to stretch his years from one century to the next. The old man, hunched over, leaned on his son and walked slowly toward the table of food. His thinning white hair glistened in the light like a full moon. Although most of the children didn't pick up on the sudden tension that weighted the air, Anne Girl could feel something. And she watched Old Paul and Frederik closely.

Frederik nodded to Old Paul and took a few steps backwards. Years ago when Frederik arrived fresh from the States, it was clear to everyone in the village that he believed all would want to follow the peaceful ways of the Moravian Church. And because the Killweathers had a radio and medicine from doctors, most joined the congregation. Others, like Marulia, avoided the missionaries because it took too much energy to explain why they didn't want to sing on Sunday. But Old Paul had walked right up to Frederik's face and told him to leave Nushagak, that he wasn't wanted in the bay. Half the village, including Anne Girl, saw Old Paul do it. He barely reached Frederik's shoulders, but he stood as if Frederik was a child with a pair of glasses too large for his nose. Anne Girl had expected Frederik to reach for his Bible and quote something in tongue, but he only turned and walked back toward his side of the village as if his truth would eventually find a way into Old Paul. That's when Old Paul began his own preaching. He told stories. It made Anne Girl laugh that Frederik still didn't seem to know that he couldn't touch the stories repeated during *maqis* and over tea, those stories that linked the young with the old.

When Old Paul sat down, there was a sense that the potlatch had finally begun. Shrieks of laughter from the children echoed in the rounded walls while the low hum of conversation renewed itself.

Although most people came for the potlatch and the dancing, few came for the important issues facing the village. The cannery superintendent had a list of grievances, ranging from children playing on the dock to the broken windows at the mess hall. He stood in the center of the hall and paced in small circles as he listed each one. But the council members listened and agreed that kids shouldn't be on the docks. One of the members, Sweet Mary, with her rolls of flesh, stood up and said, "Parents with children on the docks will be fined." The council then announced that Sunday Bible camp was being held by the Killweathers this summer. There were murmurs of interest and glances at Nora and Frederik as people ate. Between strips of dried fish and stew, the villagers agreed on nearly every issue at hand as they waited impatiently for the dancing and drumming to start.

The drums began their thunderous beat as soon as the door closed behind Frederik and his family. An elder, a tiny and wrinkled man, rose and walked to the center of the room. He meant to tell a story, one that would catch the beat of the drums and ride with the chanting of the singers. All ears, young and old, turned to the old man, and he began a mournful song. The children, knowing that it was time to listen, pushed each other as they crowded toward the center. Ellen was among them, clasping June's hand and pulling her close.

A few people sitting along the wall began to sway with the beat as the elder began to dance. He tossed his arms in the air and flung them about. Anne Girl had a bottle of booze in one hand, and she held it loosely. With her eyes on the dancing elder, she rocked, gently swaying from the waist, freeing herself from the confines of the village. The vertical crease between her eyebrows relaxed as her lips curved into the gentle shape of a skiff. She felt a pair of eyes on her and looked toward the doorway to see John gazing at her as if trying to break down the scene in pieces. She knew what he was thinking. He was summing it up, understanding how separate they were, even when lying naked side by side. Anne Girl felt goose bumps rise along her neck, and she looked away. She leaned back into the drumming and tried to forget that John was probably right.

On the following Sunday, a storm blew in from the North. Unshaven fishermen stood in their rain gear at the cannery dock, shaking their heads as they watched whitecaps curl toward them. It was an off-shore wind that blew the salmon farther and deeper in the bay. Too deep for nets set off the shore. Those who had fished Bristol Bay for several seasons understood that this storm may have been the run, their food in the pocket while they perched on the dock watching it go by. Those who didn't know the ways of the bay paced the wooden planks impatiently, not understanding that they had no choice but to watch.

Likewise, a storm that had been brewing beneath the roof of the Nelson house swooped in like a gale of wind when John told Anne Girl that they were invited to have lunch at the Killweathers', that Nora asked if Anne Girl liked lentils. Anne Girl's shoulders bristled.

They argued, each drawing lines in the sand until they found themselves defending what they didn't believe. John tried to explain that he liked Frederik's company after a long day being cramped in the air. And Anne Girl had no reason to dislike them. They had lived in the village too long to be treated like outsiders.

But the Killweather name set Anne Girl's eyes aflame, and they argued until they had nothing left. Their heated words gave way to the sound of rain drumming on the window pane and Ellen's voice, as she played in the back room.

Too exhausted for words anymore, Anne Girl scowled as she pulled on a pair of rubber boots and a raincoat. Shit on friendship, she thought. She felt the anger still breathing fire as it moved from her voice to her shoulders. She had meant every curse from her lips, even the Yup'ik ones that John didn't understand. Now she would pull the net farther up the beach, because even if there were no fish, the day promised a high tide. Her mother's ghost was probably sitting in the kitchen, laughing at her for marrying the clumsy *kass'aq*.

"*Ampi*, Ellen! Let's go pull in that net before the anchor rolls. Like we have time to sit around and drink tea and worry about lentils." She motioned with her arms. "Lentils."

Ellen walked in from the bedroom, wearing the only dress she owned. On one foot was a blue stocking; on the other was black one. She ran past Anne Girl to find her coat. "No, I'm gonna go to Sunday school today. And June will be there and Matty. And we are going to eat cake like they do during the week."

Heat rose to Anne Girl's face. Her eyes fixed on Ellen's socks, and her lip slightly curled as she saw that the girl had knock-knees like her father. It looked like she was going to have his sense too. "Fine, you go ahead then. Play with that June and don't come back whining to me about being bored when Nora makes you sit with your legs crossed." She pulled her raincoat close to her body and braced herself for the wind.

Because John couldn't find a pair of pants that weren't stained with engine oil, he and Ellen arrived late. With the benches full, the small chapel seemed even more compact, like one of those crates stacked against the cannery net loft. People huddled next to one another, knee to knee. There were even some fishermen who came in wearing rain gear spotted with silvery scales. Water dripped off their clothes, giving life to a small stream of water that steadily flowed toward the center of the room, where Frederik commanded their attention. He began to sing. His coarse voice was off-tune, but his eyes were closed as if every word emitted from his lips evoked the Holy Spirit.

As soon as they entered, Nora took Ellen's hand and led her to the back room.

"I am glad you could make it this morning, Ellen," she whispered. Her breath was warm and smelled of crackers. "We were just beginning to play a game."

Children who Ellen knew from the village had already made a semicircle around Kristen. The room was no bigger than a closet, but its walls were plastered with sheets of children's art and scripture lessons. Seeing the other children and the walls of pictures and Bible verses, Ellen sighed as if she had finally found a place for herself. She wanted a picture on the wall. She wondered how it was to be Kristen, wearing long dresses and leading in games that her mother made up. The only game that Anne Girl ever played was to see who could pick berries the fastest, and she never let Ellen win.

"Kristen, please show Ellen where she can sit. Perhaps next to the girls her age."

But Ellen saw June's black, sleek braid and pointed to her friend. "No, I'll sit by June." She said this with such determination and loudness that Nora paused in mid-stride and stared at her.

"Your mama here too? Mine is." June hooked her arm through Ellen's.

Ellen shook her head. "No, she wanted to come, but she feels sick today. Next time, she and Papa will come together." She traced the wooden floor with her finger. "She really wanted to come too."

As Kristen began to give instructions, the rain pelted against the roof—insistent, and demanding the attention of the churchgoers. There was a pause in both rooms, a communal appreciation before the voices continued with a new and louder fervor than before.

Farther down the beach, Anne Girl walked. Instead of going toward the bluff to check the net, she meandered in the opposite direction toward the cannery. The argument had left her tired and her mind weak. To hell with the net. She needed something more than just a net to relieve the tension in her arms. It was rumored that some of the younger cannery men sold whiskey and tobacco to each other. Maybe they would sell a little to her.

Anne Girl pulled the hood over her head and walked briskly past the chapel, not daring to look in the window. Not wanting to find a set of eyes that could see right through her. She told herself that it wasn't a big deal, and when John cooled off they would laugh about it later. He would tell her that she was being silly, sneaking past the church as if she had something to hide. And she would agree. She was being silly.

Eight

Look how the sandbar has grown now. We can probably jump out and walk home. Walk on water. That's what Nora would say and then the whole village would think you were magic. Or God. The tide has gone out pretty fast. It does that once in a while, and you will learn to notice it.

I used to think that the sandbars in the middle of the bay were pieces of land we should move to until the cannery whispered stories about storms and turnovers. Who knows how many drowned or became fish food. No matter how many times they were warned, it didn't matter once the nets were full of salmon. Salmon came first for everyone, even your Nan. She would shove you out to sea before letting the run go by. You laugh, because you think I am joking.

It seemed to Anne Girl that she was in constant search of time. And when the cannery men left for the winter, she was always reminded of how little of it she had. The first signs were in the fireweeds. When they took root along the trails on the bluff, their long stems flowered into petals of deep fuchsia until the entire stem was splashed with purple warnings that the land would soon brown and die. By this time, the red and silver salmon had furiously beat their tails up the bay and laid their eggs in clear water streams, and if Anne Girl wanted any more fish she would have to wait for the smelts to hit the beach.

Then cannery generators that never seemed to sleep shut down, and the windows were boarded up as the cannery workers left. Soon the cannery, with its gray-blue wooden buildings with white trim, sat like a ghost town at the edge of the village with only faded memories of fishermen walking in its alleys. Its silence made Anne Girl restless, and all she could do was worry for the winter.

Anne Girl and Ellen hiked the path behind the row of houses and fish racks on the bluff. Anne Girl's gait was quick, and Ellen ran in spurts to keep up. With a kiss on Anne Girl's forehead, John had left early in the morning for a long cargo flight to the north. Watching his plane climb and point toward the mountains across the bay left Anne Girl restless, as if her smokehouse had suddenly collapsed and needed replacing. The knot that stretched in her stomach had awakened with such a force that it took all of Anne Girl's patience to wait until the sun crept over flowing tundra before leaving the house. She had stood at the window long after John's plane was no bigger than a mosquito and contemplated the day. The knot was either him or the house with its dark walls rising around her like a lurking bear. But instead of waiting to learn which was more real, Anne Girl pulled Ellen out of bed, saying that there was much work to be done.

The village was still asleep, and with the empty cannery, the high grasses rustled a new tune, a promise of quiet in the open air. Occasionally, Anne Girl stopped and picked a stalk of wild celery. She peeled the outer skin before biting into the inner meat of the plant.

"Where we going?" Ellen asked.

"Getting ready. Have to put away the net and rope for winter. Need to secure the skiff so it don't float in a storm. Can't leave things out for everyone to see." Anne Girl looked at Ellen thoughtfully. Seeing the sleep in Ellen's swollen eyes, she added, "And we can see June too."

The answer was enough for Ellen, who copied her mother and picked the flowered end of a celery plant. She bit into it and immediately spit it out. "*Ik'atak!* I don't like it."

Anne Girl laughed, took the long stalk, and ripped off the flowered end. "Not that end. Peel it like this."

"See that pond over that way," Anne Girl said, and she gestured in the direction of the grassy land farther inland where brownish pools of water trickled between the tall stalks. White cotton balls drifted in the breeze, making the morning seem like a miniature blizzard under the blue sky.

Ellen jumped up and down to see over the grasses. "Where? I can't see."

"See that pond, see how brown and ugly it is?"

"Uh-huh."

"That's where your grandma and my grandma used to live."

"In the water? Why would you live in the water?"

"Who said anything about living in the water? Listen, before you let your mouth tell stories. Before there was water." She paused. "Gee. Here sit down, and I'll tell you. Before we had all this"—Anne Girl waved dismissively toward the houses lined up behind them—"Nushagak was Saguyaq, a real summer village. People lived here in the summers, hunting and fishing. They lived in homes made of dirt and moss near there, so they could walk up the tundra easy. You know, they had to pick lots of berries. More than I pick. More than anyone picks now. People were always thinking of food. You had to then."

"With your mom?" Ellen asked, and she frowned. "I don't believe you. Show me where you lived in that marsh."

Anne Girl grunted. She didn't like to be interrupted. "You talk too much. Listen now. I'm not telling you again, uh. Your grandma, my mama lived there. But then the ice didn't break one spring, and when the tide came, the water rose and rose. They had to leave on their *qayaks* and move to higher ground, over that way."

Her voice rose and fell as she added to her story, strengthening it with images of the rising tide and the frantic scramble to move up the hillside. The story was only partially true. She left out details of the sudden illness, which spread like tundra fire and killed the majority of the villagers before the flood buried their homes in an eternal grave. Anne Girl's mother was the only one in their bloodline to survive both, and she had relived her loss daily until she was finally placed in the ground. Anne Girl decided that she would fill in the blanks when Ellen was ready, when the girl learned how to listen.

Although Ellen had one ear tuned into her mother's voice, her attention had turned to the fly crawling up her leg, which balanced itself on the ridge of her shin bone. She prodded at it with her finger until Anne Girl couldn't stand the sight any longer. She pulled Ellen's chin toward her with a bony hand, her fingertips digging into the soft skin.

"Listen now. This is your history. And now it's in that swamp right there. You want that happen to you?"

She heard herself, high and shrill, like a squawking seagull over rotting salmon, both announcing and defending its find. But she wanted Ellen to understand that this was her beginning, where her blood was rooted in the soil. She wanted Ellen to remember.

Anne Girl loosened her grip, embarrassed. "Here, look again," she said softly, and she pulled Ellen close. She pointed once more to the hollow of swamp, to the patches of bright pink fireweeds that circled the pond like a memorial to the sunken homes. "See those fireweeds. They always grow first, they come back first. Once they spring from the ground, then everything else follows. You understand now? Come, let's go to Alicia's."

Anne Girl took Ellen's hand, and they continued through the deep grasses toward the bluff. Alicia's cabin was tucked under a blanket of sod and grass. Except for the times when the sun began her journey behind the mountains across the bay, the house was practically invisible under the waving grasses and furry moss. Only when the sun hovered behind the peak known as Aamaq Mountain, for its nipple shape, the front window glared loudly, revealing the quiet home among the wild.

The path narrowed and the grasses seemed to tower above them as the ground dipped and curved. As they rounded a corner, a glistening gray head, bobbing slowly among the green, could be seen. Anne Girl immediately recognized Old Paul, who had recently returned from his travels in the North. She wondered how he traveled so much this time of the year when there was so much to do to get ready for winter.

"*Cama-i*," Old Paul said with a toothless grin. The edges of his mouth were brown from chewing *ikmik*.

"*Cama-i*. What you doing now?"

Old Paul spoke in Yup'ik as he bent toward Ellen and touched her cheek with rough and dry fingertips. "Look just like you when you were young. I bet she'll be good, yeah," he commented as he examined Ellen.

Ellen held onto her mother's hand while he and Anne Girl talked about the coming winter. She stared at him, at the eyes that must have seen the flood swallow her mom's grandma's house and thought that he must have been really old. He smelled like he had been living in the smokehouse, and Ellen figured that's probably where he had been stuck all this time.

Old Paul thanked Anne Girl for the salmon she had left at his door over the summer. He was glad that they were not as salty as the ones last year. The Sams always gave him salty fish that made his mouth burn, and Old Paul wondered if Nancy knew what she was doing. But Gil Sam had seen a few caribou way past Etolin Point a few days ago. And although they were late running this way, he was going hunting soon. And without many more comments, Old Paul patted Ellen's head and said that he must go. There was so much to do and the days were only growing shorter.

His departure left Anne Girl quiet, contemplative. She watched him shuffle down the path toward his home, slow and deliberate. She had offered to assist him, but he had refused, saying that the air was just right for a slow walk in the morning.

It was still disputed among the villagers whether Old Paul was a shaman. He didn't, some said, have the great powers like the shamans of the old days. Even if he was the last one to live in a subterranean house with dried smelts hanging along the doors, he couldn't curse or protect you if he wanted to. It was the 1950s. No one had those powers anymore. They disappeared with the big death and the new stories of the missionaries. He didn't know how to use spirit powers or how to talk to the little people and the seals, some said. And then they argued that this was because there wasn't a *qasgi* anymore. There was no place for the men to sweat together. But Anne Girl ignored what was said. Old Paul did not have powers, but he had time wrapped in his pocket. Her mother had always told her that Old Paul knew about their family from the time they were trading furs with the Russians at Aleksandrovsky Redoubt, but he had disappeared for many years after the sickness and flood, taking those stories with him. Once, Anne Girl had even heard him speak about her grandmother, saying that she was always the first one to pick berries in the summer, sometimes while the berries were still hard and bitter. Anne Girl fiercely believed that Old Paul knew more but had locked all her family's stories inside of his bent body. And she wanted them.

His stories made her mind reel, and while she thought about how maybe she could ask him more about the old village before the flood, she led Ellen down a path that was a shortcut between Alicia's and the main dirt road. She thought she had seen some of the children use it, their black heads streaming through the tall green stalks, chasing one another. That was one thing she never wanted to see Ellen do, running without a purpose when there was much to be done. Their parents let them have too much Bible school and not enough work. Anne Girl was thinking this when her foot slipped into a hole, twisting her ankle. White pain shot through her foot as she fell onto the mounded grass humps.

"*Akeka!*" She landed with a thud.

"Mama? You okay?" Ellen shrieked.

Anne Girl swore under breath. "Yeah, yeah. Gee, Mama's alright. Help me up." She reached for Ellen's hand but quickly saw that Ellen was too small, just skin and bones. Anne Girl sighed but was almost tempted to just sit and listen to the grass move around her. "Go to Alicia's and tell her to come. *Ampi* now."

No sooner than when she heard Ellen's feet thunder down the trail did she hear those feet return, louder and with less bounce. Anne Girl opened her mouth, ready to spit out a string of words at Ellen, when Nora, with her long swaying dress, came into view and blocked her vision. Anne Girl gritted her teeth at the way Nora walked, slow and careful as she watched where she stepped. Her long skirt swept the ground behind her. Only someone from the outside would drag good material from town through the mud, Anne Girl thought. They never seemed to worry about the winter, about the seasons.

"Why, Anne, are you okay?"

Anne Girl nodded stiffly and tried waving Nora off. She didn't need this woman to go telling stories to all the other church-goers about how she had to help poor Anne Girl out of the grasses. She could practically hear Nora speak in that slow, serious tone of hers as she poured tea for her listeners. She would probably even tell them how she managed to convert Anne Girl as well.

"Yeah, yeah. I'm good."

Nora knelt down and inspected the ankle, which was already swelling. "It's not too bad, just need to soak it in some cold water for the inflammation. I'll help you home." She extended her hand.

"Weren't you going somewhere? You don't want to be late."

"Oh, it's no trouble at all. I was going to have tea with Nancy and Sweet Mary."

"Sweet Mary?" Anne Girl blinked. "Since when does she sit and drink tea?"

Nora smiled. "Yes, you should join us sometime. We'd love to have you."

"Cannery all clammed up," Anne Girl murmured to herself. "Tea time this time of year."

Anne Girl wanted to laugh and cry—laugh at the absurdity of Nora's offer and cry from the sharp needles pricking her ankle. Sweet Mary, the lover of all war heroes and cannery men. Who would have thought that Sweet Mary liked to cross her legs and drink tea like a real woman?

"Come on, I'll help you home."

Anne Girl protested, irritated that of all the people in the village, the only one awake was this thin-skinned woman. "Ellen's on her way. I can wait for her."

Taking Anne Girl's arm, Nora hoisted her up. Anne Girl was surprised by the firmness in Nora's grip, which held her upright easily. Her foot didn't even touch the ground, just hung there like strips on a rack. Perhaps Nora was more than just a shadow of her husband after all.

"Nonsense. Ellen will know you made it home."

There was no use arguing. Nora was practically carrying her through the grassy trail toward their home. Anne Girl wondered how it looked with her leaning on Nora's shoulder as if they were sisters soaking in the cold sun and contemplating how many buckets of berries they should pick. John would have enjoyed that image, would have thought that Anne Girl broke her head to allow Nora's arm wrapped around her waist. Anne Girl choked on a giggle and snorted. She imagined Alicia peering from her window, her mouth open like a caught salmon. How tongues would fly.

John didn't need to know about this. If they arrived home before Ellen made her way back from Alicia's, no one would know. But then, Nora would talk. She'd probably been dying to see the guts of their cabin so she could compare it to her own, which was most likely decorated from all that church money they brought in from the States.

"Uh, thanks," Anne Girl managed to say when they arrived at the cabin. Nora offered a few tips on how to wrap the ankle, but Anne Girl didn't listen.

The front door swung listlessly from its hinges, and the front steps were gray with dry rot. Since John was flying more this summer, he didn't have time to keep up the porch. She would have to tell him to order paint from town. And now Anne Girl saw that Nora would want to come in. She had to put a stop to this.

She grabbed the door handle and stood firmly on one foot. "I got it from here." And before Nora could do anything, Anne Girl slipped through the front door and shut it. She breathed in heavily, felt the dampness of the porch enter her lungs before limping to the kitchen chair.

As soon as she sat down, the front door opened and slammed. "I can't find Alicia, Mama. She must be berry picking or something," Ellen said, as she entered the kitchen. Her cheeks were blotched red, and she was breathing heavy.

"You came back all this way to tell me you couldn't find Alicia?" Anne Girl snapped. "What good are you?"

"I got Nora," Ellen said. She pulled Nora from the porch by her hand. "She was standing outside anyways. She must have knew you needed help, huh, and was right here waiting for you."

Nora squeezed Ellen's hand and smiled faintly. She immediately set to work, picked up Anne Girl's foot, and took off the stocking. "Let's get this foot up or it's going to look like a purple onion. Ellen, run down the beach and get some water." She turned to Anne Girl. "You need something cold to keep down the swelling."

"No. Ellen, put water on the stove," Anne Girl said. "I need hot water for my head."

"Really, some cold water is best. It's already bruising," Nora said.

"Make it boil, Ellen."

Ellen hovered in the doorway and stared at both women, who locked eyes with each other. "*Usuuq!* Which water you want?"

Anne Girl sighed and motioned for Nora to sit down. "Shit, you might as well sit down and have tea. You were going have tea up that way anyways." She turned to Ellen. "Kettle on the stove."

Anne Girl had once believed that Nora had only two expressions. But Nora's frown shaping itself into a half smile wasn't one of them. Was it triumph? Relief? Anne Girl couldn't tell. She gritted her teeth until the nerves in her jaws rattled. As Nora found a chair, Anne Girl marveled that she had the preacher's wife sitting in her room. Sitting there, smelling like a lilac branch. Was that lilac? Anne Girl was not sure, but she counted only ten hairs off the top of Nora's head that could be out of place. The rest were combed back neatly and twisted into a tight bun.

When Ellen brought in a hot cup, Nora wrapped her arm around Ellen's waist and pulled her close. "Thank you, Ellen. This is much better than walking back to Nancy's. I will just have to tell them—"

"That you got sick," Anne Girl interrupted. "Tell all those women you got sick."

"She looks good to me," Ellen said. "So happy you can stay for tea. We got strips too and Pilot Boy crackers and jam. Stay a long time."

"I will tell them that we'll have tea another time," Nora said slowly. "Nancy will try to stuff me with food to make me feel better." Nora patted her belly. "And as you can see, I don't need any more food."

"Getting sick sounds better," Anne Girl muttered. "*Akeka*. Ellen, you gonna stand like a girl at the cannery begging for candy or get me some tea too? Boiled. Not that warm stuff you just gave her."

Anne Girl waved her hand over her head like she was mixing stories above them. "Here's our home. Don't mind the blankets for doors. I know you got doors. Nice ones too, I bet."

Nora blinked. "We should get your ankle wrapped."

Anne Girl pointed to the doorway. "We got blankets for our doors, but I washed them . . . last year. Probably need a good washing again."

"The house came with the doors." Nora paused. "I guess . . . they are nice."

"We can't afford that kind here," Anne Girl said, and she clucked her tongue. "John's a lazy pilot, flying when he wants and sleeping the rest of the time."

Although Anne Girl continued to point out items in the front room, she noticed Nora's back stiffen and that the taller woman tried to hide her discomfort behind the cup of tea. And then Anne Girl felt sorry her. It wasn't Nora's fault that their home came with painted doors and windows that weren't cracked. She probably didn't even like the color. Anne Girl changed the subject.

"Remember when this house was haunted," Anne Girl said.

Nora laughed, showing a straight line of teeth. "That's right! Everyone was saying that before John arrived. And then he wanted to move in."

"Yeah, we were saying he was crazy to move here."

Anne Girl recalled the time when the bluff side of the village saw the heaps of building material stacked outside and heard the hammering of the wood. They had pointed toward the building and speculated on how long it would take before John heard Old Henry's spirit, who forced out Aaron Sting from the house the last winter. Everyone knew that it wasn't the dark winter that made the poor man leave, but that creepy Old Henry who was still looking for his clothes that were probably tucked in the attic.

When John was nearly finished with the repairs, Anne Girl had decided that she needed to see her new home. She entered the cabin unannounced and surveyed the room as if she were surveying the tundra for a patch of berries—quick and unblinking. She held a small bag, keeping it close against her chest.

"Come on in, I'll show you around." John motioned for her to enter. He was grinning from ear to ear, clearly proud of his handiwork.

She watched John take two steps backwards and realized that he didn't know about Henry. How long would it be until he felt the spirit, Anne Girl wondered.

John pointed toward the newly plastered back wall and the kitchen shelves he had built himself. "The roof must have leaked all summer long, because the entire wall in the back needed to be replaced. It was warped from water."

"Aaron, the person who lived here before, left in the middle of the winter, didn't even close the door on his way out. I never seen someone run so damn fast."

Anne Girl moved to the window to see the waves coming toward the shoreline. She figured that John didn't know about how to keep warm, that all windows and seams needed to be covered to keep the heat in, that sometimes you had to sleep in your parka just to keep the blood moving in the right direction.

"You need to cover your window." Anne Girl tapped on the glass. Maybe if he covered them, Old Henry would be fooled and not return. Maybe he would walk right by John's house and go to the Killweathers instead. Wouldn't that be a sight to see? Naked Old Henry asking Nora for tea with honey. Anne Girl wondered what the Killweathers thought of him.

She had wanted to say something more and tell him that he should come to the next potlatch, but she could only think about getting ready for winter. It was as if she was always getting ready, planning for the snow, for the summer, for someone to die.

John scratched his forehead. “Yeah, I know. I can make an order now and maybe some material will arrive on the next barge. There will be one more barge before winter, right?”

Anne Girl walked past him, trying not to stare at the blueness of his eyes. She wondered if they hurt in the sunlight. They were so light, so fragile.

“The barge comes before the snow,” Anne Girl answered. “But we got some good caribou fur that would keep in the heat. It’s better than the store stuff. Lasts longer anyway.”

“You think I should move to the bluff side then,” John said. “Aren’t bears over that way?”

“Bears here too. Soon one might want to crawl into bed with you—just to get warm,” Anne Girl answered, and then she bit her tongue. Maybe he thought she didn’t want him to stay at all. But she didn’t know what she wanted, just that he wasn’t too close or too far. “No, no, no. This is good for you—you wouldn’t want to be too close to my mom. She bites.”

An awkward silence passed. Anne Girl still held onto her small bag, and John’s arms dropped to his side. Standing side by side, John towered over her with long, skinny legs.

“Just put up some dried fish, brought you some,” Anne Girl said.

She had handed John the sack and stole a glimpse of his smile. As her eyes lingered, searching the contours of his face, the tingling in the pit of her stomach shot through the base of her abdomen and spread like fireweeds across her groin. And Anne Girl had decided that she would someday marry this man.

Anne Girl saw Nora staring at her, hanging onto every word, and she frowned. She said too much. She should have just stopped with Aaron running to the cannery store to buy matches in order to set the cabin aflame. “Yeah, well, now here you are sitting on that broken chair he thinks he’s too busy to fix. Don’t get too comfortable in it.”

“*Akeka!*” Anne Girl reached for her ankle and signaled to Ellen. “Go get some cold water.”

Nine

You see that seagull toward the direction off of our bow? Yeah, that one—the one that is bobbing in the waves. She is mocking me. She will mock you too. Are you prepared for that? I wasn't. She still throws me off guard, with her black eyes following me here and there. I bet she is just waiting for this skiff to sink so she can scream at us. You see, she thinks this skiff is hers. When the tide is out, sometimes she sits on this skiff and preens herself. And then I come to a skiff full of bird shit.

I know a bit about gulls. They tend to come in and out of my life like paraluqs on rotten fish. It will be the same for you too. And no one will believe you if you say you are being followed by a seagull. I would keep quiet about that for a while. Unless you want to be called crazy. Then I'm sure a few people will want to put you in the front row at church. And I would have to let them.

The winter of '53 would be remembered for its length and its sudden arrival in Bristol Bay. Within days after the last moose hunts, a fury of snow and hail pelted the land. The bay heaved and sighed, threatening the villagers as it climbed up the rocky beach. When the waves calmed and receded, leaving a frozen scar around the village, a crystallized type of coldness settled between the village homes.

Anne Girl leaned her head against the window and watched John's plane lift above the runway, its tail rudder barely missing the snow bank. Its blue belly glowed against the gray light of the afternoon. Before long, darkness would descend again and Anne Girl would welcome its presence. Once she could no longer see John's wings, Anne Girl exhaled, realizing that she had been holding her breath. His flying always seemed to do that to her.

"Ellen, get your parka, we're going fishing." She had heard that Gil Sam had caught two large pikes, long, slender ones that he had to beat over the head to kill. Anne Girl couldn't be sure, because it seemed a little early for pike. But there could be smelts. She felt them turn into the bay the other day when the tide shifted. She dug in the porch for those two fishing sticks and netted pole that she had made earlier. They weren't as sturdy as her mother's poles, but they would do for now. No doubt Ellen would lose interest once the hook dropped in the water. The girl was turning out to be too much like her father.

"This thing is too tight—going to squeeze me to death," Ellen said, once she pulled on the previous year's parka, with her arms poking out of the sleeves like wooden poles.

"You've gotten too big already, huh." Anne Girl suppressed a smile. "Not that one. I put your new one near the stove, so it's warm. Wear that one."

Ellen ran her fingers slowly through the fur of the parka, feeling both its softness and warmth. "Aw, it's perfect, huh. *Quyana*."

"Here." Anne Girl took the coat. "Let me help you put it on."

It was a squirrel and beaver parka, which Anne Girl had sewn over long nights, squinting by the kerosene lamp. She couldn't count how many times she pricked her fingers. Although her stitch wasn't nearly as tight as her mother's, Anne Girl was pleased that it fit. Ellen allowed Anne Girl to help her into the parka and boots without a fuss, her eyes steadfast on her mother's dry hands as they tightened her *mukluks* into a warm bundle around her feet. Her fingers tied quick knots, weaving and weaving so tight that Ellen had to hold her breath. When Anne Girl reached for the hood, Ellen placed her hands on her mom's shoulders and looked at her. "Mama, he's coming back tonight. He said so."

Startled, Anne Girl looked up, her face a messy *akutaq* of anger and sadness, like that of the berry mixture coated with oil.

"You think you know, huh?"

Ellen nodded, her chin high.

"Well then. You know if we are gonna catch anything today?"

"Yep."

"You're good for something after all," Anne Girl answered.

Outside, the cold jumped at them. The air was unmoving and silent, as if the wind had decided to quit for the day. Yet it bit at them, gnawed at their lips and noses, sucking all heat and moisture from their cheekbones.

Large ice chunks bobbed along, like lost ships looking for land. The beach extended itself far out into the bay with layers of thin ice that were too weak to stand on, so Anne Girl and Ellen walked around the cannery spit to where the mouth of a small creek met the deep salt waters. The cold was no less harsh, but they squatted low to keep their heat from leaving them.

With a pick, Anne Girl hacked at the hole until sweat crystallized along her brow. When the hole was wide enough, Anne Girl looked up to see that they weren't the only ones fishing that day. Bodies along the creek's edge, reminding her of the little people, were crouched between snow drifts, all seeking to snare that long, toothy pike. Seeing them warmed the numbness that ached her stomach so much lately.

"We can't be lazy even in the winter," Anne Girl said, pointing toward the other villagers. "Just because it's cold doesn't mean that it's time to stop." Anne Girl dipped her hook in the water and jigged it a little as she began to tell a story.

"So in that village across the bay, people were getting lazy. Lazy, how? All these cannery men built a nice barge landing for them, so they ordered lots of food from Seattle. The people in the village forgot to hunt. You hear me? When the fish came in the summer, they sat on the beach and watched the belugas chase the reds up toward the river, but they didn't catch any for drying or smoking. They just shrugged their shoulders and said that the barge would bring canned fish and that other canned meat that's way too salty. You don't want to eat the canned kind, you hear? It goes bad."

Nodding, Ellen carefully crouched closer to her mother so that her leg touched her mother's without leaning against her. Her mom didn't like to be leaned upon, didn't like to have more weight against her body. Ellen waited for her mom to pause, before interrupting. "My feet hurt," she said.

Anne Girl didn't seem to hear Ellen's protest as she continued with her tale. "You listening now? You don't want to eat the canned fish when we got the whole bay to feed us." Anne Girl waved her arm out toward the bay, its waters frozen under chunky layers of ice, a cold desert between the village and the western mountains. "So guess what then? One winter it snowed lots and the wind came from the north and south, confusing anyone who tried bringing food to the village. So the village sent out their young men and told them to go trap ptarmigan. But those men were lazy, used to the warmth of the stove and forgot how to trap and fish. You can't forget like that here."

Anne Girl jiggled her stick after she felt the end tug toward the earth. She was pleased with her story, although she should have added something about the little people in it. Next time. Ellen liked the little people.

Ellen heard her mother's satisfied sigh and watched it rise from her mouth in misty clouds until it disappeared above them. She didn't care about the village across the bay, because her feet ached so. The boots were too tight, and she wanted to tell her mom that the blood in her toes had stopped moving. The village across the bay may have forgotten how to fish, but at least their toes were warm.

"We eat good tonight," Anne Girl said as she pulled out a long, thin pike from the ice hole. "There's gonna be a potlatch tonight. The village up river is coming. We'll bring some fish, uh?"

Anne Girl saw Ellen poking at her feet with a stick and figured that Ellen's boots were crowding her toes. "*Akleng*, you got big feet like your dad. Your toes are cold, huh? Maybe we've been out here long enough." Anne Girl would have liked to get another pike, but one would do for now. "Let's cook your toes and have some tea. Maybe June and Alicia will drop by for some too." Anne Girl became quiet. "That would be nice."

Despite what Ellen said, Anne Girl knew John wasn't coming home when the sky darkened from gray to black and when she saw the faint glow of the kerosene lamps flicker through the Killweathers' window. Nora must be knitting herself to sleep now, Anne Girl thought. Peeking out the window, Anne Girl sighed and felt the heaviness of winter hit her straight on, like a wave of cold water covering her body. The days full of the darkened moon on the horizon were consuming her. Her hands shook, and no matter how many times she squeezed them just to feel the blood warm her fingers, she craved a drink or something to make the anger fade.

"We going to the potlatch?" Ellen asked.

"Yes . . . no, not tonight."

"You said that we were."

"Not tonight. I'm tired." Anne Girl folded her hands and tried to calm herself. She thought that if Ellen went to bed soon, she could make it to Alicia's house for a drink.

"But you said so," Ellen answered. "June and Matty will be there. I told them we were going to be there. You want me to tell them you made me lie?" She kicked at an empty water bucket. It rolled on its side and underneath the stove.

"Ellen," Anne Girl warned.

Ellen spread out her palms just inches above the stove so that she could feel all the heat it had to offer. "Papa probably didn't want to come home tonight anyway," she said. Looking directly at Anne Girl, Ellen kicked the water bucket again and felt the metal rattle her bones.

Anne Girl threw up her hands. "Goddamn you, Ellen. You were crying earlier because it was too cold to fish. Make up your mind." She pointed toward the dark window. "It's too cold for even the moon, and you want to go outside."

When Anne Girl saw Ellen's eyes narrow in disbelief, something snapped inside her. She opened the porch door, and the arctic air rushed into the room. She threw Ellen's parka and boots onto the floor. The squirrel tails lining the front pockets fanned out like feathers on dance fans. "Go then. Here, I'll help you. Just go." She slammed the door and went to the kitchen area, banging pots against the counter. Leftover soup and water sprayed all around. "You think that I am here just for you, just to keep you warm? You think that, don't you? Well, as your father would say, I have a news headline for you. I'd be free without you sticking to my side like a goddamn mosquito."

Anne Girl motioned with an iron pot toward the parka on the floor. "Go to the potlatch then."

Tears flooded Ellen's eyes, and she blinked to make them stop, but it was no use. Years later, she would recall her mother's bent wrist and the crooked fingers as they curved around the pot handle as if holding on to it kept the tide from shifting and shifting around them. And Ellen would remember how she felt two-faced when she saw the tight-jawed expression of her mother's and replaced it with Nora's easy smile. She saw the skin lighten, her mother's straight black hair become brown with a slight curl around her forehead. The lips became smooth with a touch of pink rose that Nora used on Sundays. And she would remember how since that moment, she pretended Nora was her mother.

Ten

With the arrival of spring, the earth tilted toward the warmth of the sun, and the days grew long, and break-up began. Icy chunks from the inland rivers sailed to sea, taking the same route around the Nushagak Peninsula that the Russian fur traders took a hundred years ago. No sooner had the ice receded than the cannery men, imported from the Philippines and China, arrived with their duffel bags. Once the store opened, men from the village began to sit on its porch or at the dock, hoping to be taken on as a fishing partner. There was talk among the villages in the area that the fishermen might be able to use motorized boats that summer instead of the heavy sail boats, but all the surrounding canneries were protesting against it. At the time, only the canneries were allowed to have power boats, so they could tow the sailboats when it came time to fish. They said it would be unfair to the fishermen who couldn't afford a motor. Some fishermen agreed, but most wished they could just set sail.

Whenever she could, Ellen watched the cannery come to life once again. Nearly every high tide, a new barge would arrive with more supplies for the cannery—lumber, boxes of food, paint, hammers, and nets and dories with green trim. Before the barge would leave the bay, hammers began their pounding and the frames of new sheds and warehouses began springing up on the spit until it seemed as if the cannery was working its way to the bluff.

Ellen sat on the bottom step of the front porch, not paying any attention to the breeze blowing tantrums around her face, her eyes fixed on the commotion at the end of the spit. With her mother's voice like a song in her ear, Ellen made up stories about the men who looked much like the villagers. Many times she overheard her mother and other grown-ups say that these men were Filipinos or Chinamen, and she wondered if they felt lonely being so far from home. She watched the wiry ones catwalk up and down the boats, and she imagined they were born on boats way past Cape Constantine. She had never been there, but she heard that the waves rolled higher than the fish racks, and one had to be faster than the swells to survive.

"*Elli-ak*, there you sit." Anne Girl came up behind her with heavy steps. She carried a basketful of wet clothes. "Why you always look that way?" Anne Girl peered over the railing and saw the men walk from one building to another. She spotted the cannery superintendent with his black cap and button-down shirt, the chief of those people who feasted briefly on the Nushagak waters but never stayed long enough to allow their feet to settle in the mud. He walked stiffly with his shoulders thrown back, and Anne Girl felt in her stomach that it would be a good year for the cannery.

"These clothes need to be hung." Anne Girl set the basket down as June walked by on her way to the Bible school camp. She waved at Ellen, who returned the greeting with a giggle.

A few days ago, Anne Girl had found herself again face to face with Nora, who hinted that Ellen would be more than welcome to join the group. Only that time, both of Anne Girl's feet were working. As she rushed by Nora, she let the light-footed woman know that Ellen had much work to do that summer. Too much for Bible time.

Anne Girl pinched Ellen's arms, feeling for muscle. There was talk among the villagers that the salmon season was going to be a good one. She heard Gil Sam say that he caught such a big king it almost pulled him overboard. Even if Gil liked to tell stories, she felt it in her bones. The cannery was planning for a good season. They were extending the length of spit with fractured rock from the bluff side to support the new buildings. There was word that they were making room for a men's steam bath and a clinic. The men were going to have a *maqi*. Finally.

"*Akeka,*" Ellen yelped.

"Stop that. You're strong enough. This year, you're fishing with me. We gotta put up lots this year."

"In the skiff too? I want to go in the skiff this year."

Sizing her daughter, the crease in the middle of her forehead deepened so that a river could run down between her eyes. The girl was too clumsy yet, she thought. Just today, Ellen had nearly caught the house on fire when she left the broom leaning on the stove. If Anne Girl hadn't been there to take it off, who knows how long it would have taken for the house to burn. And John was flying a new route this summer, so someone had to watch her. Anne Girl would die a cold death before she would let Nora fill Ellen up with silly stories.

"Yeah, in the skiff," she conceded reluctantly. "Shit, we need to patch it up. It's starting to dry rot. Maybe we can get your dad to get us some paint."

Anne Girl squinted. "But you got to work fast and no *naanguartuq*. The water will suck you under if you play too much."

"No water is going to suck me under."

"I'll be mending the net. We got a big hole it in." Anne Girl made a large circle with her arms. "A seal must have got through. Once you're done hanging those, come to the smokehouse. Good time for you to learn to mend," Anne Girl said, as she walked down the beach.

The clothesline was strung high between the corner of the house and the outhouse so that Ellen had to jump several times before she could take hold of the string. Ellen threw her papa's pants and her mom's long *qaspeqs* over the line and loosely pinned them on. They flapped like sails of a boat ready to take off whenever a breeze rattled the line. She was halfway through the basket when June peeked from behind a long nightgown.

"Hey you," she said, grinning. Her black hair waved wildly about her face.

"What you doing here?"

"I left school. They talk too much today." June jumped up and grabbed the line and held it for Ellen.

"Nora teaching today?" Ellen asked. She tried not to sound hopeful, but once it came out of her mouth, the question just sounded silly. Of course Nora was teaching. Sometimes she imagined going to Bible school too. Once in a while June would stop by and show Ellen new drawings and projects. As much as she tried to avoid it, a tinge of jealousy poked at her, and she imagined herself sitting in Nora's hot living room with the other girls. And Nora would be so pleased to see her, just like the time her mom rolled her ankle. Ellen would have hugged Nora then if her mom wasn't sitting there chewing on her lip.

June rolled her eyes.

"You wanna go to the cannery? There's a store over there, one like in Dillingham. You never been there yet, huh? I got some money for candy."

"Yeah. Let's go then." Ellen dropped a shirt back into the basket. "I'll get these later."

It had been a long time since she had a piece of licorice, and that wasn't even from her dad. The last time was from Sweet Mary, who declared that she was feeling rich and bought all the kids at Sunday school long, sticky pieces of licorice.

Leaving the half-empty basket next to the line, Ellen and June hiked to where the beach narrowed into a spit. Along the way, they pulled out long stems of grass and sucked the juice from the ends. They walked the sandy beach between the pilings of the stilted homes, and the closer they were to the cannery, the thicker the pilings became. At every turn, there were more and more of them until it was like they were in the middle of a forest. Neatly tied to one piling was a small net with a rotten flounder and salmon caught between the gills.

"Ooh look, someone forgot to pick his net," June said. "Who do you think keeps a net under the dock so no one can see?"

"Maybe Old Paul. I seen him sneaking this way one night at low tide. He follows the seagulls this way."

"Nah, he's too old. He can't hardly move. Maybe his son."

"Yeah, his son," Ellen agreed, and she imagined Old Paul's son running through the pilings at night, cutting out fish to bring home to his father.

Above the girls, the life of the cannery grew loud as heavy trucks rolled over the wooden planks and rattled the pilings around them. Shadows flickered through the cracks, and Ellen saw how each beam seemed to sweat and shake under the weight.

"Eeee, are they going to fall on us? Come, let's go to the store now. I got to hurry before my mom is done with her net," Ellen said. She wondered if the wood was strong enough to take all that noise, or would the pilings fall and crush them?

June took Ellen's hand. "You have to follow me. I've been there before. We have to take the ladder up right before the mud starts and then walk the alleys," June commanded, making sure to walk slightly ahead of Ellen.

As they neared the ladder, the sounds of the cannery rang in Ellen's ears. Its music of generators and grinding steel ricocheted off the pilings, making the whine of the seagulls seem like chimes in the wind. Ellen's stomach jumped, and she laughed, knowing that her mom would pull her ears off if she found them here.

"Why didn't we just walk down the boardwalk?"

"Cause they can't see us this way. Nora would have a fit and tell my mom if she knew I left. Have you seen Nora get mad? It's like a teakettle on the stove. Steam comes out of her head, you know?"

"Nuh-uh." Ellen tried to picture steam coming out of the woman's ears but couldn't make Nora red enough.

"Yeah-huh."

After they crawled onto the boardwalk of the cannery, June and Ellen walked single-file through the maze of buildings, because June said it would look like they belonged there. They passed several cannery workers, men in dirty overalls with mud and grease up to their ears as they carried equipment and tools. They walked by one tall white woman whose skin reminded Ellen of the transparency of a seal's gut. She wondered if she could see all the woman's veins if she was closer. The woman didn't notice them and ran her fingers through her hair as she entered one of buildings.

Ellen knew instantly which building was the store, because the door was plastered with small advertisements for flour, sugar, and gloves. There were also signs nailed next to the ads in large capital letters: "GOOD FISHERMAN NEEDS WORK" or "PARTNER NEEDED THROUGH SILVERS." But to Ellen, the store was the most beautiful place in the village. It had a small covered porch with a wooden bench next to the door, which slapped shut every time a person passed though. Men walked in and always came out with something colorful in their hands—orange gloves or cans of food or packs of cigarettes.

The girls sat down on a wooden stump across from the store, so that they could get a good view. They waited to see if someone was going to come out with candy or not. Men in overalls and boots passed by without seeing them. Some old trucks that the cannery purchased from the army after the end of the war rumbled loudly, kicking up dust and shaking the earth. Except for the one truck the army had left near the runway, no one on the village side had one yet, not even the Killweathers. Ellen wished they would quit driving by, because they interrupted her view and they were too noisy.

Ellen gave June a little shove. "Why don't you go in there? See what they got."

"You! Go in and ask them how much for licorice."

"No, you. You been inside before," Ellen said. "Why you so scared now?"

June shrugged. "I haven't been by myself. Last time Matty went in by herself, she got yelled at by the clerk." June whistled. "She's a mean one, that one."

Neither girl budged. Ellen imagined that there were shelves stacked only with candy. Rows and rows of chocolate bars. June's father fished on a boat, and he gave her money when his boat was at the dock. But he was out getting ready now. They decided that they would hold hands and go in together.

Just as they were about to weave across the crowded walkway, Ellen felt a sharp pinch digging into her shoulder as if someone's claws were cutting into her skin. She went rigid when she heard her mother's icy voice booming in her ears, even more deafening than the cannery generators.

"This . . . this is where you've been, uh?" Anne Girl demanded. Her brows were knitted together in a tight weave. She looked as if she could spit. "I've been looking all over for you. I come back to the house to find our clothes draped over the lines and clumped together. And you were nowhere to be found. My bloomers, my bloomers were just waving for the village to see!"

Anne Girl breathed heavily. She couldn't get her words out fast enough. "Forget the bloomers. What you doing down here? Don't you know that they run over little rats like you with that noise? Those guys aren't watching out for you two. Gee, if the superintendent saw you . . ." Anne Girl stopped as she thought of the superintendent and how every year he complained that too many village kids were at the cannery, getting into trouble. And if he saw Ellen, Anne Girl would just die.

"No one saw us," Ellen finally answered defiantly, daring to look into her mom's eyes. "We walked the beach and ended up here. Someone has a net under the dock. Did you see it too? There is a red in it. We think it is Old Paul's. What you think?"

"You know what they say about kids hanging out at the dock," Anne Girl stated, taking both girls by the arms and guiding them toward the village where the sun and the tide ruled the rhythm of the day. "You know what they do, don't you? That cannery super doesn't like to see kids playing over there. It's for work. Never play." Anne Girl talked herself out of a rage and into a story. Word got around in the village, and the grown-ups and the elders branded any child seeking attention at the cannery docks as "no good" or as "dirty."

"Dirty?"

"You'll be a used rag and no one will ever want to touch you. That's what happened to Nancy Sam before she got religion. We all remember that! And poor Gil was the only who wanted to marry her, even though everyone knew about her living at the cannery. Up there, *uyug*-ing for everyone to see. No one will ever see you the same. Their eyes will know what you've been up to, sitting at the docks and the net lofts," Anne Girl said. "You don't want to be a dirty girl, do you?"

"I took a *maqi* two days ago," Ellen answered. "Maybe June didn't."

"I steamed! What you saying?" June protested.

What was so bad about being dirty, because Ellen got mud caked in the lining of her clothes all the time? Sometimes at night when Ellen undressed, her legs were dusted with the grayish silt from the bay, and she never knew how the mud found its way between her toes and under her knees. She decided that she would be careful even when playing on the beach.

"What you doing down here too, then?" Ellen asked.

It was brief, but Ellen saw a vertical line deepen in the middle of Anne Girl's forehead as she was on the verge of telling a lie. Ellen knew it was going to be a lie by the way her mom's mouth twitched, as if searching for the right words.

Anne Girl's fingers dug deeper into Ellen's arm until she was sure her mom found bone. She winced. "Looking for you. What you think? I just wander that dock like a lost seagull?"

June giggled despite Anne Girl's tight grip on her arm. "We just wanted licorice. *My* mama said I could buy some if I wanted."

"June!" Ellen hissed. She didn't want June to witness the anger that made Anne Girl sound like a seagull, screeching for attention. She didn't want June to see what her mom was really like.

"And you," Anne Girl turned to June. "Aren't you supposed to be at Bible School? Does Nora know you want to be dirty too? Nora doesn't like them kind either. At least that woman has something right."

But June didn't seem to notice or care. She shrugged and walked with head high as if she wasn't pinned to Anne Girl.

They walked in silence, and as the sound of the drumming machinery receded, Anne Girl talked. "I went to the boat graveyard near where the Chinamen are buried."

"What for?"

Anne Girl sighed. "There's a good cleat still on one boat back there. No one scavenged it yet. Thought I could get it, but I need a saw. Your dad should get it for me. And why not? He broke mine to begin with." She clucked her tongue and reflected. "Man, it's a good one. I hope no one gets it first."

"He doesn't go near the skiff," Ellen said. "How did he break it then?"

"Oh, him and that skiff." A smile played on Anne Girl's lips, although her grip on both girls remained just as tight. "He's too scared he'll wreck it again."

"You talk to the dead Chinamen then? Did you say, *Quyana?* What they say back?"

June pulled at her eyelids and made a face before Anne Girl yanked her. Ellen laughed.

"Maybe I should just send you both to get it instead," Anne Girl said, and she gave them a little push down the beach. "Leave you there. Your mom won't mind a little scare for you, June."

Anne Girl spun around and headed back toward the cannery, taking the girls with her. "Yeah, I think that's a good idea. Since you both like the cannery so much, I'll let you wait there while I go search for a toothy saw."

"I'm not scared," Ellen said. Although as she said this, she felt Anne Girl's nails dig deeper into her shoulder.

"Yeah, me too." June joined in. "But—"

"Not buts. That skiff is no good without a cleat—can't tie up or nothing," Anne Girl's voice rose. "If I can't tie up, I can't deliver fish. Then we can't get money. Then we starve. You want that, don't you?"

Ellen looked up and noticed that strange stare her mother had when she was focused on getting angry. Frowning, Anne Girl didn't blink but stared ahead until looking at her made Ellen's eyes feel scratchy.

"We won't go to the cannery again," Ellen said quickly.

"Yes, we promise."

It no longer mattered. Anne Girl couldn't hear either girl. Darkness descended upon them as they entered the alleyway between two warehouses. The smell of fish found its ways to Ellen's nostrils once more, and she wrinkled her nose. Cold tickled the back of her neck, and it seemed like autumn rested in the shadows of the cannery. The path was a tricky left turn, past the laundry room, the mess hall; right turn, past the Chinamen hall, the water storage tank; more turns. Ellen couldn't keep up. And it was difficult to pay attention as her mother was reciting the history of the skiff.

June sighed and looked quizzically at Ellen.

". . . that cleat, I have to use the ridge of the wood for the knots and it warps every time I tie up." Anne Girl clicked her tongue. "Dry rotting on me. We just want that skiff to last as long as we can. It used to be your nan's and it will be yours someday."

Ellen allowed her mother's words to settle in her gut as she tried on the skiff in her head. The high bow and wide rails rode the waves without a hitch when it was anchored. It needed painting.

The three turned a corner and the dark opened up to the Chinamen's graveyard—a couple dozen crosses and mounds scattered between the tall grasses.

"Bet the tide cleans them bones once a year," Anne Girl said.

"I'm gonna paint the skiff when it's mine."

June nodded and added, "Blue I—"

"That boat there!" Anne Girl let go of her clutch of the girls and pointed to a heap of wooden boats and scrap material. Some were piled on one another as if one large wave picked up each boat and set them down into one mashed-up puzzle. A strange mixture of pepper and cinnamon hung in the air. Apparently, when a fisherman was done with a boat, he threw out the kitchen too. "That's the one! The only one left."

Anne Girl eyes swept over Ellen and June. She pulled at the ends of her hair and seemed to see them once again.

She sucked on her teeth. "Stay here while I go snatch a wrench. Maybe a hammer. Don't you dare go anywhere."

June's eyes grew to the size of tea saucers. "But what about being at the cannery?"

Anne Girl appeared not to hear as she turned on her heel to the darkness they came from.

"Where are we?" June asked.

Ellen shrugged. "Don't know. I've never been this way."

Eleven

Pushing the knot from her stomach, Ellen forced herself not to think about her mom or being left in the middle of the cannery. She couldn't think about her mother right then, much less explain her. Instead, she became suddenly aware of the boats hiding in the graves. Every breeze seemed to shift a piece of wood or rusted plate, but Ellen wondered if the Chinamen were walking between the boats.

She jerked her chin toward the graves. "You think they are . . ."

"Awake?" June whipped her head around. "Nah. Maybe after the cannery closes at the end of the summer. That's all those women say during the winter, you know."

Ellen's legs felt heavy, yet she wanted to move. Needed to move. She needed to move. "*Ampi*, let's find that cleat."

Tin metal rattled. Wood creaked. June jumped. Ellen remained still. The noise in her head overpowered the cannery generators. A gust of wind and the smell of pepper filled her nostrils. Ellen held her breath. Which boat? Her mom would be so proud if she and June got the cleat. Ellen could hear her telling Sweet Mary and Nancy that Ellen's joints are greased good too. And they were! Just in time for fishing.

Faintly, the sound of an engine coming from the direction of Dillingham wavered over the cannery generator. It had a rhythm that was similar to crashing waves; every few seconds, the buzz seemed to be really loud before receding into the wind. She knew that tune like she knew her mother's screech. Her father was just north of the village, probably two spits away. Ellen exhaled.

"*Usuuq*, she's going to come just now. Watch," Ellen said. "Going to forget all about that skiff. Like she never had one."

No sooner than she said that did Anne Girl appear from the dark alleyway. Her hair was a wild mess and there was a streak of black oil across her cheek. She motioned to the girls with her forefinger.

"Forget the damn cleat now. Your papa's home. *Ampi.* "

After the cannery incident, Ellen saw little of June and more of the backside of her mother as she followed Anne Girl from one side of the village to another. She picked up on Anne Girl's quick gait and no-nonsense sway so easily that she soon mimicked her mother's walk from several feet behind. It seemed to her that Anne Girl marched as if the tide was going to change now and that all hope for picking fish would be lost unless they were at the net, wrestling with the salmon. It wouldn't occur to Ellen until many years later that most villagers followed a different rhythm when it came to the seasons, and not the anxious bustle of always getting ready that Anne Girl practiced. Always getting ready, planning for the next flood or blizzard until her fingers were numb and stiff. She thought that if being grown-up meant that you had to run from one place to the next, she didn't want any part of it.

The days between John's leavings and goings went by more quickly for them during the summer, because when they weren't fishing they picked berries and gathered driftwood. Clouds often lingered like thick, gray pillows over the bay, and Anne Girl could read the movement of the wind and the visibility for flying better than John, and would know whether or not he was coming home or if he had to stay overnight in Dillingham or Bethel. Anne Girl sensed it in her body on the days he returned. She felt the smooth rumble of the engine in her stomach, heard the propeller spin noisily, and finally could taste the salty sweat that formed in crystals on his sideburns.

On good days, mornings when the water was like glass with few ripples, Anne Girl took Ellen out in the skiff to pick fish. Ellen sat in the bow and picked out flounders as Anne Girl yanked out salmon after salmon from the net. With each hard pull, the small skiff rocked and Ellen moved with it, feeling the movement in her stomach until she felt sick. Yet, the sick feeling couldn't erase the sense that she had her mother all to herself, that even if Anne Girl sucked air through her teeth with impatience, she couldn't leave Ellen.

"See this one here," Anne Girl huffed as she pulled and dropped the fish on the floorboards. "It's a female. Already eggs coming out."

"Already dying. Even as it swims." Ellen bent down and poked at the eyeball with her pinky.

Anne Girl caught a glimpse of Ellen's sad face and laughed. "Get up. It's not dead yet. On its way to croak, though." Once salmon began the long journey to spawn, their bodies began to rot from the inside out. Their skin, the silver luster that reflected the light, reddened and became waterlogged until it peeled off, taking chunks of meat with it. Some salmon were lucky if they even made it to the spawning grounds with their flesh still clinging to their bones.

She pulled on the cork line to bring more net into the skiff. "Quit playing with your food, or those fishermen out there are going to think something's wrong with you."

Ellen's head snapped up and she scanned the bay—a stretch of green water lay before her. She saw two skiffs and only the shape of bent backs. They were shaped like large mushrooms underneath their gear as they hauled in fish. "Nah. They don't see nothing." She threw up her hands. "We got enough fish. Can I go play now?"

"You think I am going to pull us back to shore for you?" Anne Girl huffed. "We can't stop when the fish are here. You wanted to work on the skiff with me," she reminded Ellen. "I can easily get Matty or anyone at the cannery to help." She loosened another red salmon from the web, dropped it into the growing pile, and pulled on the net for more. Her face was a mask of hardness, yet she blushed from the exertion.

"I didn't say I didn't want to fish with you," Ellen said. "Just that we have enough food."

Anne Girl shrugged. "You've never been hungry before."

She became silent and thought of the winters before missionaries and the yearly barges from the south, when they weren't sure they would have enough to last until spring, and how her mom chewed on fish skins, her jaw working in constant circles to keep the hunger from biting her insides.

Ellen touched her own cheeks, her fingers cold on her skin, and wondered if they reddened like that of a king salmon too. She decided that they must have, because her eyes were dark brown like her mother's. She wished they were blue like Nora's eyes. Her dad had blue eyes. She asked Anne Girl why she didn't get blue eyes instead. Why was her dad stingy with his blue eyes?

Laughing, Anne Girl replied, "You're mixed with the both of us." Anne Girl wiped scales from her face. She took off her gloves, reached over, and brushed the hair from Ellen's eyes. "You have my eyes and round face, but I think you have your dad's hair. You were almost blond when you were born. Yeah, you were. You were born during a blackout when all the houses on the beach had to cover their windows because the Japs were bombing down on the chain. And then you come along, pale as a ghost with light brown hair."

Anne Girl pulled her gloves back on. "You have your father's ugly hands, though. Those fingers didn't come from my family."

Ellen stretched out her hand in front of her face. "I like them."

"Good. Yeah, all mixed up, so better get used to yourself. Probably with too much of your father. Sorry about that," Anne Girl said at last. The thought made Anne Girl sniff the air to sense him out. "He'll be home in a little bit. Had to stop in King Salmon first for Frederik's medicine."

On days when Anne Girl saw June and Ellen playing behind the house, she hurried over to the bunkhouse above the cannery store. She climbed the steps two at a time, knowing that if she was gone too long, Ellen would look for her. There, in the hallway of the bunkhouse, one of the cannery workers left a small paper bag next to his locked door. She had rarely seen the worker, but they had an agreement that she would slide her money beneath the door and he would leave a paper bag for her. Inside the bag was a six-pack of beer that she would gulp in large swallows before John came home with more for her. She wondered if he ever noticed her breath or the lightness of her voice when he walked in from a long day of flying. She couldn't remember how all this started, how this cannery worker even came up with the booze. But it helped, if only for a little while. More and more, Anne Girl felt like jumping out of her skin. It itched, and she knew it was either John or the house that she was allergic to. She wanted to talk to Old Paul. He would tell her to drink more tea, and he would tell her what to do. Until then, her visit to the bunkhouse helped her get through the empty days.

Anne Girl slipped the few dollars underneath the door and picked up her bag. She twisted the cap off one bottle and took quick, long swigs until her throat ached from the rush of the fluid. She leaned against the wall, painted clean and white, and looked down the empty hallway. Rows of freshly painted doors were lined, giving the feeling of cleanliness that contradicted the slime and muck gathering at the docks. She could live here for a day or two, if she had to.

She heard footsteps climbing the stairs, and she quickly finished off the bottle and threw it in the bag. She ducked her head and hurried down the stairs, not looking at the guy who passed her on the landing. But she felt his eyes on her, felt him survey her body and his effort to determine which room she came from. Anne Girl gripped her bag and rushed out of the building and ran directly into Nora and Kristen.

"Why, Anne, what brings you down this way?" Nora asked, and her lips curled into a pleasant smile.

"The store," Anne Girl said, breathlessly. She wondered if Nora had seen her running down the stairs of the bunkhouse.

"We are too. Ran out of dish soap and forgot to tell John about it before he left," Nora answered and nodded toward the small bag she carried. "And they have good chocolate too."

Flustered, Anne Girl took a step back and tried to collect her thoughts as she clung tightly to her sack. John had never mentioned taking shopping orders for the Killweathers, but it sounded like something he would do. Hell, if he could, he would ask the entire village if they needed anything while he stopped in Dillingham or King Salmon. And here this woman was talking about chocolate.

"Chocolate?"

Nora smiled and reached into her bag. "Yeah, can you believe that? It's like shopping down in the States." She paused as her grin faded into the paleness of her face. "Well, almost. Here, give some to Ellen. I know she has a sweet tooth."

Frowning, Anne Girl took the bar of chocolate and stuffed it into the bag. She wondered what Nora had been feeding Ellen during those Sunday services. But as much as Anne Girl wanted to tell Nora to quit fattening her girl, the pressing weight of the bag made her fingers tingle and her mouth water.

"*Quyana*. Thanks, I'll give her it." Anne Girl bowed her head and backed away.

"We're going the same way, we can walk with you."

"Oh no. I better rush. You never know what Ellen gets into. Sticky fingers," Anne Girl answered and set off toward the edge of the cannery in a quick pace that she knew Nora couldn't match. She walked to the newer part of the village, where the homes were square and tidy and ready to be swept clean, but it felt like she was running toward the bluff side of the village, where the homes were worn into the ground from daily life. She felt her feet land on the gravel, heavy and hard, and decided that she must be running. That she was meant to run.

Twelve

In July, the summer heightened and the days grew so long that the sun never slept, and Anne Girl and Ellen fished until it seemed the days blended into one. They needed meat to last the entire winter, and Anne Girl was prepared to fish every tide, if that's what it would take. For the first couple of sets, Anne Girl distributed most of the salmon to some of the elders in the village, saving only a few for her family and the Killweathers. Not sharing would evoke bad spirits or make the fish flee, and Anne Girl figured that neither Nora nor Frederik knew how to fish anyway.

From the beach, she and Ellen watched the lines pull and tug as the fish hit the web below. Tail fins beat against the surface, splashing against the tide like mini-whitecaps, calling out to mother and daughter, promising them a good catch.

Ellen felt the hum of salmon in her blood as she watched the net and later as she tied the strings into knots for the strips. She felt the excitement, her mother's elation as if her whole life was meant to follow the fish. But when she looked at her mother, she saw that Anne Girl's gaze was set on the distant mountains. Her face resembled one of the masks used at the potlatches, with its mouth set in a frown and drooping eyes, as if trapped to tell only sad stories.

"What's wrong, Mama?"

Anne Girl didn't answer as she tried to listen to the knot in her gut. She didn't want to say anything to Ellen, but the other day a bird, a swallow which nests on the side of the bluff, flew into the window and fell to the ground with a thud. The bird twitched, its legs running in the air, before becoming silent. It was a warning, she knew. Someone she loved was going to die. Soon. Even though John was only flying to Dillingham that day, she knew that one day he was going to land on a sandbar. Maybe he was going to drown. She had tried to shut the thought out of her mind.

But yesterday a swallow had flown into the porch, flapping its wings emphatically as if urging Anne Girl with all its might to do something. Anything, those wild wings said, as the bird bumped against the walls of the porch before finding its way back out the door. As it flew out, a feather no bigger than her forefinger with a gray tip floated to the floor. Although she knew that a bird inside the house meant death, she wanted to see what Old Paul thought. He probably knew something about dead birds.

With her eyes fixed on the distance, Anne Girl touched Ellen's cheek. Her touch was so tender and smooth that Ellen hoped that her mom would wrap her arms around her.

"Yeah, we'll eat good now. Long day ahead to put up this fish. Get the buckets with the *uluaq*, and find a rock. We need a rock."

Ellen returned running and swirling in large circles. The *uluaq* rattled inside the tin bucket as she flung her arms back and forth. She dropped the buckets next to Anne Girl's feet and kept twirling down the beach.

"Elli, Elli, what you think?" Anne Girl asked. Her eyes followed Ellen. "We need to do something. You and me. Yes, we should do something, maybe before your Papa gets back. We should go somewhere." And she waved Ellen over. "Let's split these kings first and then . . ." Anne Girl's voice drifted. She couldn't collect her thoughts or make them straight in her head, yet they continued to eat her. "And then we'll go to Alicia's for a *maqi*. We stink."

It took all afternoon to split the kings and reds. They set up the cutting table on the beach, where the occasional breeze kept the flies from crawling all over them. Ellen imitated her mother as she glided the blade across the belly of each salmon. Her mother's hands were quick, and the insides spilled from the fish as if its guts were boiling over. Sometimes Anne Girl barely missed her fingers, but she never cut herself. The blade always missed, even when Ellen squeezed her eyes in fear that a finger would be left sitting on the table.

There was no need for words or directions. Ellen knew that once Anne Girl sliced the meat into long strips and shoved them to the end of the table that they needed to be knotted to a string and dipped into the brine. If the pile on the edge of the table became too high, Anne Girl grumbled a low warning.

While waiting for the fish to salt, Ellen's mind wandered down the beach. It seemed like no one else was trying so hard to put up fish. She looked out toward the bay and counted the few double enders trying to grab wind with their sails.

"They soaked long enough. Hang 'em."

Ellen heard her mother but didn't move.

"Elli, quit playing. Buckets need to be dumped," Anne Girl repeated. Her voice was low like the growl of a defenseless seal.

Ellen knew that tone, had it branded in her blood, and if she didn't listen, her mom would drop the *uluaq* and grab her by the hair.

She sprinted toward the cutting table before Anne Girl could repeat herself. She pulled up the strips from the brine, carefully placed them over a long pole, and counted the pieces. One fish, two fish, three fish.

With blood up to her elbows, Anne Girl scraped the innards from the king. Purple clots and lumps of organs plopped into the bucket where fins and other discarded parts lay. With the flick of her wrist, Anne Girl ran her blade against the rounded rock Ellen had found earlier. Without answering, she bent over a large tub of water where fins and heads broke the surface and pulled out a king as tall as Ellen. The skin was pink and smooth with scattered freckles along its backside. Anne Girl heaved and slapped it onto the table. She grabbed the *uluaq* and began slicing.

Something was wrong with her mother. Ellen felt it by seeing how Anne Girl jerked the *uluaq* across this salmon. She gashed and sliced into the skin without cutting the head and fins off first. It was all wrong. The fish wasn't supposed to be bruised, and yet there it was, gushing in blood. Bright pink flesh flared up from the wounds as if seagulls had pecked the skin.

"We keeping the heads?"

Her question was answered with silence and the cry of the seagulls.

"Mama, are we keeping the heads or no?"

Anne Girl looked up from the bloody table, her eyes shining as if they too sweat from the effort. She sighed with annoyance. "Now what you think? We always keep the heads. Gee, don't be getting dumb on me." She wiped her forehead with her arm. "Dump that and get those strips on the pole. They're gonna be too salty." Anne Girl waved her off. "I shouldn't have to tell you."

Her mother's voice beat in her ears. Yet Ellen stood unmoving, holding on to the bucket handle and staring at her mother, thinking that if she just stared long enough she would know what her mom needed. Maybe a better stone for the *uluaq*? Maybe this one was dull and made her sweat too much. Maybe her mom would look up from the table and see her. But Anne Girl had returned to the fish and no longer acknowledged Ellen by her side.

Thirteen

Ellen understood that the day was going to be different by the way the morning light bled through the window and danced on her feet. She heard her mom shuffling in the other room as there was scratching against the floor. Maybe she was moving the table. Or maybe she was pacing. Ellen couldn't be sure. Ellen squeezed her toes tightly and counted to ten. Ten seconds of warmth.

"Ellen!"

Almost twenty seconds.

"Ellen, get dressed. We're going for a walk."

It was that tone that didn't want or need a response. That much Ellen knew, and she rushed to pull on stockings and her shirt.

She pulled the curtain from her bedroom doorway to see her mom sitting at the table wearing three layers of clothes—her normally thin chest was shaped like a pillow, and both sleeves of her parka were stretched thin. Her frown was so tight that a river could flow through the creases down her forehead. In her hand, she held the sewing kit John had given her years ago. Ellen laughed.

"You look like one of them fat beavers."

"Let's go home." Anne Girl raised her arms. "Oofty, it's hot in here. Let's go."

Ellen surveyed the room and noticed that everything—salt, honey, and mason jars—was set carefully on the table, as if they were set for a still picture. She looked out the window, saw the shape of the waves against the blue sky, and wondered what bird had shit on her mom during the night.

"Home? We're home."

Anne Girl moved to the door. "He's flying, always flying here and there. Let's go where it's quiet."

"Why all the clothes?"

Anne Girl grunted and continued to gather small items—an *ulu-aq*, the rest of the eggs, and string. "It's cold at my mom's house. You should take some too, or your feet might rot off."

Ellen shuddered. "Eelie, *Carayak* live there!"

"Who told you that?" Anne Girl's head snapped up. Her eyes were sharp and beady, reminding Ellen of a seagull's stare. Maybe that's why her mom stuffed herself in all those clothes—to hide seagull wings sprouting from her armpits.

"Maybe June or Matty." Ellen rolled her shoulders. She thought everyone knew that her dead grandmother's house was full of haunted beings. How could it not be when every summer it seemed to sink deeper and deeper into the grasses?

"Stay here then," Anne Girl said. She wiped a trail of sweat from her brow. "I don't want you if you can't work anyway."

Her mother's words stung, and Ellen scraped her mind for reasons why Anne Girl should take her. She didn't want to be alone waiting for bears while her father was flying about. "You can't leave me here. Papa's never home."

Anne Girl didn't respond but walked out the door, saying nothing. She moved stiffly as the many layers of clothes seized her joints. Ellen rushed after her, leaving the door open. She hoped her dad wouldn't mind.

"He knows where to find us?"

"How big you think this town is?" Anne Girl pulled at her collar. "Hot in here."

Ellen hoped no one could see her mother bobbling down the beach like Sweet Mary. But the beach between the cannery and the bluff side was empty. Not a soul in sight, unless you count the seagulls charging headfirst toward one another as they fought over fish.

"I told him we'll move back when it snows. Like it's fish camp or something. He can come down our way if he wants." Anne Girl said. "For now, you just need to work."

The women in the village helped themselves to Marulia's house when they found out that Anne Girl and Ellen were warming its walls once again. Ellen couldn't help noticing how they came in pairs, some with kids, some just with their eyes to take a look around. They too thought there were *carayaks* in the house. She pointed that out to her mom.

But all the visits were relatively quiet until Sweet Mary and Nancy fought to get in the door at the same time.

"Well, if you let me in, I'll open the door wider for your fat ass," Nancy huffed, pushing her body against Sweet Mary's. Her hip sunk into Sweet Mary's thigh until it looked like there was only half of her.

Sweet Mary backed up, taking all her weight with her, and muttered under her breath. But as soon as she took one step inside, she whistled lowly. "Feels like death in here." She pulled a small witch under her arm. "Got you a kitchen witch—Norwegian kitchen witch. From one of my men at the dock."

Nancy adjusted her hair, "I guess it's not doing you any good in your house. You and your men."

Sweet Mary grumbled.

"Ellen. Tea," Anne Girl said. Her eyes were bright and clear from the sudden influx of visitors, and Ellen wondered how long her mom would last before she locked the door. Anne Girl didn't like people after too long, and she wasn't afraid to push them out the door with a handful of strips. She waved her arm around the room. "Not much of a kitchen. Look—a good wood stove there. What you guys think? Still in good condition. My mom took real good care of it, wiping it down every night."

"You need to open these windows," Sweet Mary said. She took a sharp breath and heaved a window open. "Something's not right."

Light flooded the room and found corners Ellen didn't know had existed. And then, in one breath, she felt her history spill itself into colors around her—greens and grays, all in the shape of the beach. Her Nan was here. "Your mom is a raven, huh?"

Anne Girl's black eyes met Ellen's. "How you know that?"

"I told you," Ellen tapped her head. "*Carayaks*. This place is full of them."

Sweet Mary whistled again long. "Eelie, creepy one. She is."

Nancy stood next to Sweet Mary, her mouth open.

"Close your trap, Nancy. Bugs will crawl in there. She's fooling. I told her stories about her Nan and ravens. She's just full of stories. *Atem*, sit and let's drink tea and have strips." But Anne Girl was staring at Ellen in wonder as if she couldn't quite piece together what happened. She frowned. "Where's the tea? How many times do I have to tell you?"

"You don't feel it?" Ellen asked and pulled on her braid. She felt pricks on her skin.

"Maybe her monthly finally came," Sweet Mary added. "So sensitive your daughter is. I believe her. She knows more about your mom than you do. Probably knows where your mom sleeps during the winter. Huh, Ellen?"

Anne Girl colored briefly and then slapped her leg as she tried to recover. "She's not bleeding yet. Look at her. All sticks and bones. Good too. She won't be half a woman."

"Yeah, or you'll have to tie a string around her neck. Keep her from the dock." Nancy butted in. "What else you think she senses?"

Ellen groaned as she moved to the kitchen stove. "Quit talking like I'm not here. I'm right in front of you!"

"I remember those days," Sweet Mary said. "Never been the same since."

"Only you would say that."

As she stoked the stove with wood and placed the kettle on its surface, Ellen was aware of the prickly feelings around her neck and her back. How could her mom not sense it either? Yet, Ellen did feel her mom watching her as if she were keeping a record of Ellen's body—

the shape of her legs, hands, and hips—so that she could point out Ellen's faults later. It was like walking around naked, only without the protection of the steam in the *maqi.*

"You don't have your period yet, do you?" Anne Girl asked. She gazed at Ellen while a smirk played on her lips as if she was pleased she had Ellen under the spotlight. "Shit, ruined already?"

Ellen was aware of the heat rising to her cheeks. Even though the stove had short, stubby legs, Ellen imagined herself crawling underneath it. Maybe she would fit, and get stuck. But getting stuck would be better than here. And then she saw her mom's expression shift. She couldn't quite place it, yet Anne Girl appeared pleased with herself.

"You not going to answer?" Anne Girl asked.

"I thought we're having tea and Pilot Boy crackers," Nancy said.

Sweet Mary whipped her long braid around and began to unravel it. "Your skinny ass needs some of those. More strips too, or the wind will knock you over."

Ellen remained quiet and kept her face hidden as she selected a few cups and saucers for the older women.

"I should know these things," Anne Girl muttered. And as Ellen handed her a cup, she whispered. "I better not hear from Nora about it first."

Fourteen

Now that they were closer to the shadow of the bluff, Ellen expected her mother's wild stares and sudden marches up and down the beach to let up. Yet once everyone returned back into the rhythm of fishing and putting up fish, the darkness of Marulia's houses fell upon them, like a blanket of winter. At times Ellen wondered if Anne Girl was sick, or was she stuck with this new mother.

Anne Girl twirled a small feather between her fingers. "See this here. It will save us."

Ellen looked at the feather. The stem was like fur, but yes, it was a feather. "What bird is that? Swallow? Or that long whistling one? June has one nesting above her house. You should see it. We almost climbed high enough to look at the babies that hatched. We could hear them, though. Then one of them, maybe the mama or the dad, dived at us. It even had a piece of grass in its beak." Ellen laughed.

"You don't listen good."

Ellen sighed. Her feet were cold. "Talk, then."

If there was such a thing as being slapped by an expression, Ellen felt it right then. Anne Girl's eyes narrowed, and she showed her teeth. She held the feather up. "This is for you. This—" Anne Girl waved her hand around the room. "—is all for you. Just remember that. I'm trying to keep you safe over here." Anne Girl pulled on her stockings and pulled a dry pair of gloves hanging off the line above the stove.

"Aren't you going to tell some story about that feather?" Ellen asked impatiently.

"Nah, you don't want to listen. What good is that, then? Nothing matters if your ears are full."

Ellen pulled on her earlobes and found that she could hear the small rumble of a plane in the distance. She imagined her father's brows pinched together as he adjusted the flaps. "He's landing."

A brief look of pain washed over Anne Girl's face, so brief that Ellen wasn't sure what she saw.

"You should go see him, make sure he eats good tonight while I go to the net."

"Nah, I want to go to the net."

"I wasn't asking you," Anne Girl said, and left.

Running toward the cannery end of the village, Ellen felt the noise of the machinery grow beneath her feet. The cannery was rattling the earth again. It was prepared to sweep up all salmon in the bay if it needed to. And then she saw her father's plane tied down by the end of the runway and suddenly felt calm.

John greeted her at the door. "I already have a plate for you. You look like you have grown."

"Since yesterday?" Ellen rolled her eyes.

"Well, you could have. Some people grow a lot in one day."

"You sound like Mama."

John smiled. "Tell me all the news from over there."

This was the new and yet same ritual. John returned from his route, asked about home, and they talked or looked at catalogs. Ellen pinched down the pages that had shirts and pants she wanted, so she could show them to June and Matty later. John was gone so often that when he came home, he always thought that Nushagak had turned on its side since he had left. Ellen had to remind him that it didn't. The bluff was still grassy on that end. The cannery still liked fish. And yes, Mama was going to move back for the winter.

"I got the newspaper from up town and promised to bring it over to Frederik as soon as I was done with it. Looks like we might become a state soon. What do you think about that?" John asked. He folded the paper several times until it was a smooth square. Tapping it on the table, John met Ellen's eyes. "Kristen and Nora have been asking about you. Come."

"Why don't you come see Mama after we set the net?"

He paused. "Not tonight, Pumpkin. I need to fly out early tomorrow."

"Please."

"You worried that I want to see her, since I didn't move to fish camp with you both?"

She avoided his eyes, picked up a cracker, and began to spread honey over it. Now that he said it out loud, it sounded silly to be worried. They were just down the beach.

"You want to come with me?" John asked.

Ellen shook her head.

John tapped the table with the newspaper and rose to leave. "Bring your mom those apples. I got them for her."

From the window, Ellen watched her father walk to the Killweathers'. Unlike her mother's step, his was slow and resigned, as if his shoes were filled with lead. When he reached their porch, he stopped, brought his hand to his mouth, and turned toward his plane. He stood there tapping his mouth with his fingers for so long that Ellen wondered if he was going to climb back into the silver wings and take off. Her Mama always said that he liked to fly away when there was work to be done, when she needed him. She saw the wings shudder in the breeze and observed how he leaned forward as if being pulled to the plane. And she understood then that if he could, he would live in the air.

When she couldn't see his shadow through the Killweathers' kitchen window, Ellen headed down the beach to see villagers, mostly women, getting their nets ready to fish. Some fishermen were launching their sailboats, yelling and hollering at each other over the sound of the wind. The tide was coming in quickly, but there was still time to set the net. She kicked at the rocks and watched them tumble in front of her.

As she neared the bluff side of the village, Ellen saw Alicia and June crouching on the beach. A long string of net, corks, and web was spread out in front of them. Alicia's head was bent in concentration, grunting as she strained to tighten a knot.

"Gee now, it's you. You scared me for a moment. I thought it was that Jap from the cannery coming to ask me to mend his damn net too. I'm not mending no more nets," Alicia said, and laughed. She surveyed Ellen's dirty face and clothes. "Come to help your mom? She's down that way."

June stood up and began to run toward Ellen. "Wait, Ellen, I'll come with you."

"June, you stay with me," Alicia ordered, as June tried to sneak away.

"Shucks! Come back when you're done, uh," June hollered. "Let's go look for needlefish."

When Alicia wasn't looking, Ellen nodded.

Ellen approached her mother's site carefully, trying not to disturb the still figure kneeling alongside the shore. A net was scattered in front of Anne Girl, who kept the lead line taut. Her mother's hands were magic once again, wrapping twine around the end of one line to prevent it from fraying. They moved again and again before fastening a tight knot.

"Where you been? Tide's coming in. Food doesn't take that long to eat." Anne Girl pointed with her bent finger to the lead line. "Get the cork line and let's set it."

Anne Girl stood up and heaved the anchor over her shoulder while gathering as much of the lead line that she could. And then she walked down the beach, toward the gray mud. The wooden corks clanked and bobbled over the rocks with each step.

Ellen placed the apples next to the grasses and skipped over the webbing that was being dragged across the beach. She was careful not to trip as she picked up the cork line. Anne Girl wasn't waiting and was already halfway down the beach as Ellen struggled with her half of the net. She felt clumsy, as if her hands had their own thoughts as they found ways to wrap themselves into twine. She followed her mom as she stepped across the threshold between the rocky beach and the mud.

It was cold and up to her shins within the first step. And then she realized she had left her shoes on as silty water filtered through her stockings. And she swore that the silt was made of fingers, because each step was as if someone were pulling on her ankles. And if she was too slow, the mud formed a suction cup and held her in place. But Anne Girl kept moving forward, and the tide was coming at them, so all she could do was follow and hope her mother didn't find out about the shoes. Anne Girl was already ten paces ahead and the line between them grew taut. She looked back at Ellen and tugged on the line. "*Ampi*. The tide is coming in."

Anne Girl waded to her knees in the water before throwing out the anchor and giving it a jerk. She grunted loudly and pulled on the cork line to straighten it. Ellen dropped her section of net and lengthened the webbing as well. Already the water was lapping at her feet, and Ellen watched how it filled the holes in the mud first before finding another trail to follow.

"What you looking at?" Anne Girl ran by Ellen, all the while pulling on the net. As the water rushed closer, the swells took hold of each cork, and they bobbed in the water. "Hold it until I get it tied up the beach. Don't you dare let that net go."

"Yeah, yeah. I know."

Ellen felt the shift in her mom as strongly as she felt the near freezing water suck the warmth from her toes. Anne Girl was her own tidal force coming at her. Fishing did this to her mom—turned her into an angry seagull looking for food.

The web Ellen held was still knotted and wrapped around the corks. And around her fingertips, so tightly, she couldn't feel anything. She pulled at the net to separate the web from the corks, so that it would float evenly when the waves picked it up. But it was tangled, and with the mud on her fingers, Ellen couldn't grasp the thin string of the web. She couldn't even feel it.

The water was reaching for her knees. Anne Girl was already up the beach tying off the other end of the net. She wiggled her toes. They could still move. She pulled one leg, but it was trapped beneath the weight of the silt. Stretched ahead of her, she saw each cork bobbing with each swell like miniature boats. She tried to get each foot loose again. Panic set in.

"Mama!"

Anne Girl was still turned away from her, bent down and yanking at rope. Her arms were moving in wide circles. A gust of wind kicked up, and her *qaspeq* ruffled and long hair appeared like a fan around her.

"I'm stuck!"

Ellen picked at the web but could only feel the slow creep of water move up her thighs. The force of the tide was taking hold of the net as well. And the line pulled against her with each wave. Colder and colder. Ellen tried to move her foot, but the silt still refused to give. She picked at the web. But water was cold and pulling on her. Drown. She was going to drown.

Ellen dropped the tangled net and let the water take it as one lump with the web and lead line tangled around the corks. She watched as the bunch rode each swell. She leaned and pulled on one leg, hoping to set it free. Move her toes. She just needed to move her toes. Her teeth began to chatter.

Maybe her words found ears, because when Ellen looked up she saw Anne Girl's arms waving violently as she ran down the beach and into the water. She was a sea lion splashing toward Ellen. No. Those were seal teeth coming her way.

Anne Girl pushed Ellen aside. Her feet suddenly broke free and she fell forward. Icy water stung as it found every crevice in her body. Her skin was instantly numb as she struggled to stand. She choked and coughed.

"*Caa Una!* Quit playing!" Anne Girl yelled. "This gotta go out straight. Or we get no fish. You know that. The hell were you thinking? How could you let everyone see our net go out like this?"

Ellen coughed and her eyes stung. Her mind was cold and slow. But as she watched Anne Girl unknot the line, Ellen's throat tightened. She lost her shoe. And she was aware that to her mom only the fish mattered. Her mom would dive for salmon if she had to. Maybe if she drowned, her mom would have noticed, but then Ellen wasn't so sure.

"My feet got stuck."

"Quit *naanguartuq* and walk instead," Anne Girl said. She dropped the line and set for the beach. Ellen followed.

"I wasn't *naanguartuq*."

"Let everyone see our net like that," Anne Girl muttered. She examined Ellen up and down, squinting until a horizontal crease across her forehead appeared. "Oh, your shoes! What were you thinking?"

Ellen looked down at her feet. One leg was blackened by silt, and somewhere underneath that mess were her toes. The polished ends of the shoe were barely visible. Ellen shrugged. "You can drown on a teaspoon of water. Nora told me that once."

Anne Girl sucked air through her teeth.

Hugging herself, Ellen trailed Anne Girl up the beach toward the path that would lead to Marulia's house. She spotted both apples near the grasses, sitting side by side—two red bulbs. When Anne Girl wasn't looking, she took a bite of one and tossed them both into the grasses.

Fifteen

You feel cold? I feel it. The temperature is dropping. There is a saying in the village that if it can get worse, it will. It's getting worse. Maybe you can't tell, but we might freeze and turn blue in the lips before we get a chance to drown. I'm not sure which one is worse. If we sit below the railing and block the wind, that will give us more time. We still have a few more hours.

Sometimes the current fools you into thinking you are going in one direction when really you aren't moving at all. I thought maybe the tide had changed and then I would be free of you and this story.

When the salmon didn't hit the beach, people panicked. Like a tundra fire, word spread about the lack of fish until even Anne Girl felt the worry settle in her blood, and she began to think about food all the time. The cannery continued to murmur that the salmon were sure to come, yet few people caught enough to even fill their fish racks. Anne Girl lost sleep along with the other villagers and often stood in her skiff, peering over the side to see if she could catch one by the tail. Just one, she thought. Just one more.

Sipping tundra tea and booze, the villagers talked about whether the smelts were going to arrive and who was the latest to shoot a caribou. "Where's them damn caribou when you need them?" they asked each other. Others wondered out loud if anyone was planning to fish at another bay. "There's none here, anyway. Who knows what happened to them fish? Go ask Old Paul, he might know," some said.

It was because Old Paul knew things about the earth that most had forgotten. He knew the weather and the omens better than anyone on the beach, and so when Anne Girl found the strength, she walked to his house with the feather tucked in her *qaspeq*.

Before she knocked, Anne Girl stood in Old Paul's arctic entry and took in the rich smell of the smoked fish and dried meat. Little light spread itself along the darkened walls of the porch, but she could see the dried strips of caribou and salmon hanging on nails. She thought of her mother flying in the form of a raven and wondered whose turn it would be next. She breathed in deeply, filling her gut, and tapped on the door.

"Come in, come in. *Kita*," Old Paul pointed toward the table where hot water steamed from two cups. "Sit and drink some with me."

"You look good," Anne Girl said, after she hugged him. "You catch any fish?"

Old Paul shook his head. "Not much out there now. They probably went to the other side of the bay. You know, too much noise or something on this side. You know salmon get tired of all the noise, so they change direction once in a while just to make a point." He ran his hands through his white hair and peered at Anne Girl. "But you want something else. You came for more than just tea, yeah?"

Anne Girl pulled out the swallow feather, which seemed just as sleek as it ever did, and placed it on the table between them.

Old Paul clucked his tongue. "The bird came inside, didn't it? That's not good. Not good at all. It was a young one, huh?"

"Yeah, young."

"Had lots of life yet to give, you know."

Anne Girl nodded and reached for her cup. "Yeah. Probably fell and knocked its block."

Old Paul shook his head slowly but didn't say anything. He didn't have to, because Anne Girl knew. Someone close to her was going to die. She could just tell by how he didn't want to say it and licked his chapped lips instead. There was no way she and Ellen could move back with John now. How could she protect Ellen from what was to happen? Death was at their door.

Anne Girl watched Old Paul reach for his teacup and tip it from side to side. And then he spoke again, "It's going to be a tough winter. Fish and hunt lots, so you don't get hungry. Tough one, but things will be good in the spring," he said, and he raised the glass to his lips.

After speaking with Old Paul, Anne Girl rolled up her clothes and walked over to Alicia's *maqi* for a bath. Together the women talked about the coming winter as they threw water on the rocks.

"Yeah, Amos hardly caught anything." Alicia poured water into a basin for herself. "Well, not enough to get some things from town. And the kids are getting so big, they need new shoes and clothes. Remember how good your mom used to sew? She'd sew for me, for you, for nearly everyone in the village. Her fur coats were the best." She touched Anne Girl on the shoulder. "Okay. Yours are good too, although you haven't touched her needles since—"

"Yeah," Anne Girl answered. "I stopped."

"Amos said that the fish didn't come near the mouth of the bay then?" Anne Girl asked. "I just thought that they all went across the bay to Igushik." She was comforted by the thought that she wasn't the only one hit with poor luck. For a while she wondered if the lack of fish meant something else, like a punishment for moving back to the bluff side. But the air grew heavy with the thought, and she knew that her bones couldn't take the worry. It gave her headaches, imagining him in a downed plane, against a snow bank or sandbar. She could see it over and over again in her head, playing out like a growing image underneath the story knife.

She threw water on the rocks and listened to the stove sizzle into a hot steam, sucking all the bad juice from her skin. She breathed deeply and so did Alicia, both feeling the air burn their lungs, a burn that was good and refreshing. The heat reminded Anne Girl of how much work she had ahead of her before the ground turned to stone.

The first couple of times she put out her net, she had caught enough to fill her smokehouse. Fish strips were hanging sweetly off the drying rack, gathering oil and taste in the wind. A couple of days later, the clouds grew thick over the bay, and the wind shifted as the rains came, soaking her strips. Spoiled, her fish were spoiled. And Anne Girl felt her work drain from her body. Her arms ached, and she found herself walking with her head down toward the cannery, thinking about the store-bought drink she was going to get. A couple of the cannery men never let their closets go dry. And they always seemed happy to sell her bottles of booze, as many as she wanted. She didn't tell Alicia about her cannery friends, though. Alicia didn't need to know those things.

"No, there's just no fish," Alicia broke into her thoughts. "I don't remember a time when the fish didn't come. You?"

Anne Girl shook her head, picked up a ptarmigan wing, and began slapping herself on the back. She felt the deep muscles of her shoulders loosen with each beat and thought that maybe she could beat the alcohol out of her veins.

"No, my mama talked about it once, but that was before the big flood and death."

Anne Girl laughed a little. She recalled how when the coughing started in the village and around the bay, the missionaries suddenly appeared. It wasn't Frederik and Nora at first, but another couple who ran a mission near Goodnews Bay. They came with medicine and blankets and thick books. People were in awe. Now they were going to have to burn those black books just to keep warm this year.

"Yeah, that was a long while ago." Alicia watched Anne Girl hit herself.

Anne Girl hit herself once more and passed the ptarmigan wing to Alicia, who began slapping herself with the same fury, as if the feathers would sting all the sweat from her body. Anne Girl watched her friend's flesh jiggle in waves as her arm moved, and she couldn't help wondering about the caribou. There hadn't been any sightings yet, and by this time there was usually already a small group sneaking up the coast. "I can sit in this forever," Anne Girl said and leaned back against the wall.

"When you going to shut your mom's place up for the winter? Should be soon, huh?"

The heat was a strange thing, and Anne Girl felt it stick to her head and seep through her skin. Maybe it was making her brain watery, Anne Girl didn't know. Part of her wanted to sleep where there was more than just driftwood to keep the stove going. She wanted to give in once.

"Nah. He thinks so," Anne Girl said. "You try live on that side and count how many times he almost misses the ground."

Just the thought of returning to the other side of the village made Anne Girl's skin turn cold. He had waited until her mom died before he trapped her like a tundra rabbit. Well, that's when John convinced her to move to his cabin and the newer side of the village where the buildings were sturdy and safe from floods. Even though John had all the perfect reasons, that the house was newer, it was protected from the high waters during break up, and it had windows that weren't boarded up, Anne Girl resisted the idea. In all her years of living in Nushagak Village, Anne Girl never imagined that she would live among the starched buildings on the other end of the beach. Somehow they seemed too clean for her. And when the fishing season was in full swing, the area was too busy. The fishermen were like flies on a dead carcass, crawling up and down the streets of the cannery and dock. She felt silly, but she missed the thick grasses and knowing that the shifting tundra was just a few feet away.

But she didn't like John at her mother's house either, because his eyes roved the walls as if he was searching for Marulia in the plaster, even after she told him that she had burned all Marulia's clothes. She even told him that Marulia was a fat raven probably living on top of the bluff, that there was nothing to worry about. He became like a scared pup in Marulia's four walls, which made her want to pinch him. Yet, he tried. So when he gave her a new kit for sewing furs and a carved ivory needle as part of a promise that she didn't have to change for him, Anne Girl became quiet. She held the kit with her palms open and stared at John as she did the first time on the beach. She could sew furs now. Marulia had sewn furs. Now she could too. Shortly afterwards, Anne Girl arrived with the few belongings she had—her *uluaqs*, an old mink fur, her new sewing kit, and a couple of *qaspeqs*. She slammed the door twice to make sure that it shut right and to announce her arrival on the cannery side of the village.

Alicia splashed water on the stove, and Anne Girl was suddenly aware of the heat.

"*Akleng*, that must be too much. What you going to say to him?"

Anne Girl sucked in hot air. "I'm not. I'll just let him think maybe next week and then the next."

"And the next? God, you're tough. You should say something at least. Have Ellen run down that way."

Anne Girl grinned slightly. She felt Alicia's frustration bounce off the walls, and somehow that made her calmer. She couldn't make Alicia feel the knots, and she couldn't explain to her how it hurt to breathe through them. It was no use to even try.

"When our moms are done taking steams, let's go, huh?" June said. "The smoke is still going hard. And we need to beat my brother, Phil, to it. He'll use all the water."

June was at Murlia's house, standing on the chair peering through the window. With each breath, the windowpane fogged and cleared up.

Ellen wasn't listening. She was thinking of ways to get June to go home so she could leave herself.

"You hear me?"

"Yeah, you saw Matty go to the cannery with her mom."

"I never say that."

Ellen looked up at June and tried to separate her mind in half. On the chair, Ellen saw June age before her eyes—her hips wide and her lips full. She could see laugh wrinkles that would form at June's upper lip. And she felt sad—sad for June, because she was going to end up with big hips like Sweet Mary. But mostly sad for herself, although she couldn't quite place where that ache was coming from.

"What you say then?"

"*Maqi*. You stink."

June jumped off the chair. "There's no food in this place. I'm gonna eat first. Just come when there's lots of smoke out the chimney. I'll put wood in it for you."

The porch door slammed against the wall, and Anne Girl thundered in. Her eyes scoured the room, pausing at June before landing on Ellen. The light coming from the window seemed to pause on her face, making her jaw and nose sharper than usual.

"You told, huh?" she said. "Why you tell?" she yelled.

"Anne Girl, I thought you were in the *maqi* with my mom," June said. "I didn't see you come this way."

"Go home, June," Anne Girl said.

Ellen backed up to the wall and wearily watched Anne Girl.

"He was going to find out soon enough."

She hadn't meant to say anything at all to her father. It just happened when John suggested that the three of them fly up to the lakes before the summer was over. They could go berry picking. He wanted to know if Anne Girl would come.

"I think I will go home now," June said. "Yeah, good time for me to go."

June skirted between Anne Girl and Ellen and closed the door softly behind her.

The tides between Anne Girl's emotions played on her face, and she fell to the floor like a bucket full of fish, flopping this way and that. "Why you do that?"

The wall had ribs, Ellen thought, and they were poking her spine. She shifted on her feet and stared down at her mother. For a moment, she felt both sad and annoyed. "Why you cry? Get up."

"It was better for him to die not knowing. Better that way."

Ellen's skin became cold.

"Die? He's not sick. You haven't seen him in weeks. He's not sick, Mama."

Anne Girl put her hands on her temples and talked into her lap, muffling her voice. "*Akleng*, you don't know nothing. He's going to. The bird flew in the house and died."

Ellen slid to the floor, feeling the wall push against her spine like a mallet. She smelled the beach on the floor. The smell of fish and salt barely covered the earthy odor of the wood. She thought she caught a whiff of alcohol off Anne Girl, but probably the air was playing tricks on her nose again. It was too much for Ellen to take in.

"How you know I said anything?" she said finally.

Anne Girl tapped her forehead. "I know things, more than you think. I can't be there to see him die that like. Nancy would, though. She would sit by the stove and watch her husband go cold."

It was hard to know what to believe. Her mother read the tides and the coming of the run just by the way the waves curled to the shore. And Anne Girl was usually right when it came to the wind. Her heart beat in her ears.

"We gotta go home," Ellen said. "Mama, you hear me?"

Anne Girl's head snapped up. The hole she had dipped into had passed, and she jumped up like a bear over a moose. "Like to see Sweet Mary move this quick. Don't think she could, you? Don't you cry." On her way to the kitchen stove, she paused over Ellen and pointed so that her forefinger was inches from her daughter's nose. "Don't even think of it. We need wood. I want the whole porch full before the seagulls fly away for the summer."

Ellen left Anne Girl at the kitchen stove, muttering to herself. She was supposed to be wandering down the beach for driftwood, yet she chose another path. She took the grassy trail back to the cannery side of the village, because it was longer and hidden from the wind and the eyes in the village. Weaving through stalks, Ellen felt an ache well within her and felt both longing and guilt. She paused once and saw a swell of smoke rise from Alicia's *maqi* before the wind took it. June was probably causing steam to pour from every crack. They made her think of her Papa. He wasn't home yet, but if she got a good fire going, she could have tea ready for him. Maybe she could eat at Nora's.

Sixteen

When the ground hardened, but before the snow arrived in white storms, Anne Girl arrived on the steps of her old home, carrying a shoulder bag and a distant stare. She stood behind the smokehouse and waited until John's plane had left the runway. She watched the plane rise and rise into the distance and wondered if today would be the day the bird omen would come true. It had been four months since she moved into her mother's old house, but she felt as if she had been hungry since the spring. She dressed in an old parka with new patches of fur on the elbows. She loosened the hood when she entered the house and examined the room, filling her eyes.

Seeing the bag, Ellen believed her mother was moving back home, and she ran to hug her. But Anne Girl mentioned no such thing. She acted strange, like a lost moose calf with nowhere to go. She walked around the small house, her eyes hungry, scanning the shelves for crackers, butter, and even canned meat.

"Mama, you want to put down your bag?" Ellen asked as she followed her mother to the kitchen. She attempted to take the bag from Anne Girl. "I can put it down and we can have tea. Papa will be home soon. He only flew to Naknek today. He's still alive. Your bird was wrong."

"The kitchen is clean," Anne Girl commented as she bent down and ran her hands along the row of canned beans and vegetables. She picked up a can of green beans, turned it over in her hand, and put it into her bag. She bent down and reached into the sack of potatoes and grabbed two. "Mama needs some butter."

"We have some. Papa brought some food from Dillingham. I can make us some crackers with jam too. Okay? And tea too. We have lots of tea." Ellen grabbed the water jug and began to fill the kettle.

Anne Girl didn't answer, but walked to the shelves in the back of the kitchen.

"You need to warm up from the cold."

"Ellen, get me some butter and some of those crackers too." Anne Girl began to tighten her hood until her face was practically hidden by a circle of fur.

"Let's have tea now." Ellen's voice rose. "You're going to stay, right?"

Anne Girl bent down and pressed her forehead against Ellen's. For the first time in weeks, she looked into her daughter's eyes, and in their darkness, she saw the same lonely path that Ellen would take living on the shores of the Nushagak. Her daughter would learn the seasons and sing the same stories, but she would also be alone and somewhere between this world and Anne Girl's world. Nushagak was going to change and the cannery was going to outgrow itself. More people would move onto the beach, and everyone would forget that fishing was for food and that hunting and trapping were for food. And they would forget, but Ellen would try to remember, and she would be alone. And then she would have to leave just so she could keep the memory. Anne Girl knew this, and she kissed Ellen on the forehead so that her daughter wouldn't forget. "I'll be back, okay? And you just remember about the little people. They will tell me if you are good or not."

"But you have clothes here still. You need them. And your *uluaq* is still on the window sill. Don't you want that?" Ellen motioned with her hands. "I sharpened it too!"

Not wanting to see Ellen cry, Anne Girl made her way to the door. "Don't tell your papa, okay? And I'll come back and visit," she said as she opened the door to the front porch.

Ellen ran to the porch after her and pulled at the gear on the wall. "You need them!" she yelled.

When Anne Girl shut the door between them, Ellen stood in the porch until her toes grew stiff with anger. She could smell the beach and the smokehouse lingering in the rain gear and gloves that hung on the walls—the scents of her mother sweating as she worked under the midnight sun. Beginning in her throat, her body filled with a longing that refused to settle, and she couldn't quiet. She imagined her mother returning to her, but no matter how hard she squeezed her eyes, she couldn't stop the tightness in her chest nor erase the image of her mom shutting the door.

Outside, holding the goods to her chest, Anne Girl walked away. On the beach, she saw Nora heading in her direction, and with the brown grasses frozen and flat, there was nowhere to hide. Anne Girl held her chin out and set her eyes toward the bluff, thinking that if she didn't look at Nora then the woman would walk on by without a word. The missionary's wife carried a small sack and was humming to herself. She was dressed in a long parka with fur lining along the wrists and hood. The material had to be from the village, but clearly Nora couldn't have made it herself. Anne Girl couldn't help but stare as she tried to determine who had sewn the coat.

"Who made that for you?" Anne Girl asked, and she pulled on the fabric of her own coat. The torn pocket and the new patches never seemed so obvious until right now.

Nora seemed startled to see her, and her eyes flickered as she looked Anne Girl up and down before making an effort to smile. "Isn't it wonderful?" Nora said and stretched out her arms. "Nancy did. Gil had trapped quite a few mink this year. So Nancy offered to make me one. What do you think?"

Anne Girl waited for Nora's arms to fall against her sides. The sounds of the ice-cold water hitting the frozen beach never seemed so loud. Talking to Nora was never easy. She was hungry, and Nora was showing off her coat. Anne Girl didn't care about how many mink were trapped to make it. But Nancy was good for something after all.

"You should come to the women's group," Nora said, and she reached for Anne Girl's shoulder, who jumped at the touch.

When Anne Girl didn't answer, Nora continued. "Next month we are planning a mini-potlatch with traditional foods at my house. There's always room for one more person."

Why did Nora worry about the women's group at a time like this? In that moment, a strange feeling boiled from within the pit of Anne Girl's stomach. She couldn't quite place it, but she became hot under her thin parka. Her skin felt like the *maqi*, and with Nora staring at her, Anne Girl felt sudden panic and anger. The feelings wrapped themselves around her body and tugged at her, telling her to do something.

"I know what you think of me, because I don't belong at your women's group. I don't belong . . . never could hack that kind of work." Anne Girl grabbed Nora's arm. She stared directly into Nora's eyes. "I know, but teach her—teach Ellen. To read, sew, cook for a man. She needs to learn like you, okay? I never got to learn to read. And Ellen needs to know. You understand?"

Anne Girl stopped talking but held tightly onto Nora's arm. There was more she wanted to say about Ellen. That her daughter liked to tell stories and be lazy. That Ellen just needed someone once in a while. Too much attention and the girl wouldn't turn out right. But Anne Girl couldn't even find those words, and it surprised her, because no one knew Ellen like she did.

Nora nodded and pulled away. She opened her mouth as if to say something but closed it again and left. She continued on her way to the chapel, and Anne Girl listened to her feet crunch on the ground. She listened until she could no longer hear Nora but only the sound of the waves coming toward her.

January never felt so long, and Ellen hated it. Hated how the ice clouds huddled close with only the promise of darkness, and how there was a strange quiet in the house with her father. On days that he didn't fly, he stared out the window and murmured something about frozen oil and daring the weather. Yet, he was quiet and still, and

Ellen hardly knew what to do. At least with her mother, she could predict the mood of the day by how Anne Girl handled the pots and the water jug. She could feel her mom's movement, even if she was in the other side of the house. Her father was different; because he stood at the window for such a long time, she never knew if he was coming or leaving. When he realized that Anne Girl wasn't going to move back in with them, he stood so long that she wondered if he forgot where he was. She couldn't tell anything about him, and that made January move like ice.

One morning, Ellen wandered into the front room to see John pulling on his boots with deep grunts. She rubbed her eyes and counted the buttons on his coat. "You're not flying today, are you, Papa?"

He gave her a parka. "Come outside, I want to show you something."

Ellen took the coat and slowly put on her boots, yet she refused to lace them. She wanted to stay inside, close to the stove. Maybe her mama would sneak in, hungry for more Pilot Boy crackers. She had placed crackers next to the stove to keep them crisp, just in case Anne Girl wandered to the stilted side of the village. How much she ached to see her! But her father was already dressed and waiting at the door. He had two layers on, and his hat sloped to the side of his face, but he didn't seem to notice.

She didn't know what to expect, but she followed her father on the snow-packed trail to the runway. The snow squeaked and groaned with each step, and Ellen bent her head down to avoid the wind cutting into her skin. She had to run to keep up, because his legs were long and so it seemed that he was barely moving them. It felt to her that she was always running after one of them—her Mama or Papa.

"You're flying then? In this wind? That's crazy."

"Not today, pumpkin."

"Then what we doing?"

John didn't answer, but he kept walking until they reached his plane. It was still dark, but she could see how it sat like silver on the edge of the runway. This plane was her father's joy, and if he had his way, every day would be good for flying. John gently patted the belly before he opened the cargo door and crawled inside.

Ellen peered inside and saw wooden crates stacked on top of each other. Crates of butter and Spam and other food items from Anchorage. John took the top crates and moved them to the other side of the plane. He grunted with each lift, and his breath rose in frosty crystals, filling the space with a pasty whiteness.

"Didn't make it to Egegik yet, but I will try tomorrow. The weather was no good, but I bet some families are still waiting for their flour and butter," John said, and he heaved another box off the stack. "You see, when you load a plane, it has to be balanced. The weight has to be perfectly centered between the front and the back. You can't have too much weight in the rear, because your wings won't catch air. But you can't have too much weight in the front or to the side. Your plane does like that either. You see that now, don't you?"

"You want me to help?"

"I had it loaded all wrong. All this flour was too heavy near the rear. I need some in the front with me so the tail doesn't drag."

Ellen felt the cold sticking to her legs and shivered. She looked back toward their house—a black shadow in the morning darkness. She wondered if her mom was up and moving yet. If she had some butter and honey set out on the porch, would her mom even come in? Maybe it was better to set Pilot Boy Crackers by the door, in case her Papa didn't go over to Frederik's today. But he always went over there.

"It's cold, uh," Ellen said.

"Your mama came by," John commented in a low voice. He dropped a crate and the plane drummed loudly. "She came by looking for you or for something."

The tightness in her throat kept Ellen from saying anything, but she felt her father looking at her.

"She comes often?"

"Once in a while. Sometimes she brings fish though."

She waited for him to yell, but he was quiet. He picked up another box and dropped it again. The plane rocked and sighed with the sudden weight shift.

"She doesn't need to come around here anymore," he finally said. "No more, do you understand? No more giving her food either."

Ellen nodded and felt her face burn. She was thankful that he couldn't really see her in the morning darkness.

Ellen imagined the tundra, despite the February wind that blasted from the bay and whistled through the door crack. She gathered the small driftwood and fed the kitchen stove as she saw herself looking into a sinkhole and seeing the secret world of the little people. She imagined herself with them, taking long *maqis* and eating *akutaq* with lots of sugar. Once the snow melted, she would go up to the tundra with her mom and find them, she decided.

The windows rattled and heaved. Ellen could hear Amos's sled dogs howling, and wondered if they saw something more than flying snow. Her father went to bed early, having arrived from Togiak red-faced and cold. She was placing twigs in the fire when she heard a tap at the door that sounded like chatter of squirrels. Ellen stopped and wondered if the *cayaraks* were finally set loose, roaming the empty trails and knocking on windows.

"Ellen, Ellen girl, it's Mama." A low whisper came through the crack.

"Mama?" Ellen almost yelled. No, it couldn't be her, and Ellen imagined her mother turning into a dark *cayarak* with a deformed head and mouth.

"Shush now."

Ellen knelt at the door and leaned her head against the wooden frame. A cold draft blew from under the door. She listened to the creak of the wood and imagined her mom bundled in fur, hugging herself.

"Elli-uk. Come, give Mama some food."

"Papa said no more food."

"Come now, give Mama some, uh?"

She heard rustling in the porch.

Ellen whispered through the crack. "Wait. Wait."

She grabbed some crackers and butter and slipped out of the house. The cold hit her like a slap and she waited for her eyes to adjust to the darkness. She could barely trace the shape of her mom—huddled against herself with the hood of the parka tied tightly around her face. Ellen felt her throat tighten. She pushed the crackers and butter into her mom's hands. "Come in and warm up."

"That's all?" Anne Girl spat. "That's all you're going to share? Nora would give me more if I asked."

"Yeah. That's all we got here," Ellen answered. She swallowed, trying to contain the urge to cry. It was there—wedged in her throat like a block of ice. "Just come home already. Your bird is wrong. Papa still flying good."

"I need more food. Next time. Save me more."

Ellen watched her mom leave, pausing at the top of the stairs before allowing the railing to guide her down the steps. Ellen backed into the house and kneeled on the floor. She stayed huddled next to the door long after the winds sailed around the walls and threatened to open the windows. She sat until her toes ached with cold and she was positive that they were going to fall off her foot into black pieces of meat. But it wasn't until later when she crawled under the blankets that Ellen felt her side ache, a gentle throb in her pelvic bone, and she knew that her mama went to Old Paul's to give her this pain. Only he knew how to make such hurt.

It was a hungry and long winter in the village. Violent winds and low clouds sucking their way through the Kilbuck Mountains in the north kept planes anchored to the ground. Without the planes, the villagers held mini-potlatches to share the little meat, dried fish, and frozen loafs of bread while they waited for the sun to peek through the clouds. They took *maqis* and talked of fresh seal oil and their beaver traps while they wondered if the salmon would return to the bay in the following summer. Although John always had food on the table, Ellen felt hungry—a deep, gnawing pain that rarely let up. It was present from the moment she opened her eyes until she curled in a tight ball under the blankets at night. In the years to come, Ellen would remember the hunger and how it carved itself in her chest and never left, even when she ate until she couldn't anymore.

Two weeks after her mother begged for food in the porch, Ellen slipped through the Killweathers' front door and was greeted by the warm smell of baked bread. The table was empty, except for a stack of bread piled five loaves high. Behind the curtain that separated the kitchen and the dining area, she heard a stove door open and shut as well as some rustling.

Kristen's head poked out from the curtain. There were blotches of flour on her temples and hair, but she smiled and waved at Ellen. "Hey you. Mom, Ellen's here." Even though she was few years older than most of the children in the church group, she rarely left Nora's side. And Ellen often heard Nora praise her daughter's patience and kindness. It made Ellen wonder if Kristen got into trouble, or if she ever wanted to throw rocks at her mother. Something wasn't right if you didn't want to once in a while.

"I'm so glad that you decided to come," Nora opened the curtain. She was breathless and her hair had fallen around her face, but it didn't seem to matter to her. Like Kristen, there were patches of flour on her clothes and skin. "I was hoping I could get your help. I believe that Matty, June, and some of the other girls will be here as well." She gestured toward the wash basin. "So wash up. We have a lot of cooking to do for the Girl's Club tonight."

Although they had sewn gloves during the Girl's club meeting last month, Ellen wasn't surprised that they were baking bread this time. With no planes flying, Ellen noticed more and more people showing up at the Killweathers' door and leaving with food tucked under their arms. One time she counted ten grown-ups and two children. They arrived within minutes of each other, but never together. Ellen wondered how Nora kept her house so warm when she was constantly opening and closing the front door. Every time her father came inside, it seemed that he brought winter with him, and Ellen had to stuff more wood into the stove.

Ellen liked Girl's club, mainly because there weren't any boys who shoved and dared each other to see who could spit the farthest off the porch. Whenever there was Girl's club, Frederik took the boys to check trap lines or visit the elders. Today they had left in snowshoes, tripping over themselves and each other as they raced down the trail. So Ellen knew that without the boys it was going to be a good afternoon once June and Matty turned up.

Soon the other girls arrived and took their places next to Kristen and Ellen as they began to make bread dough. Even Jill Wescoat, dressed in a thin *qaspeq* and gloves, joined the group. She was Kristen's age and lived far on the other side of the village, and there were always rumors of her being seen on the docks. No one seemed to notice or mind when she tore chunks of bread and stuffed them in her mouth and under her shirt.

There was flour everywhere, caked on the floor, the cupboards, and in everyone's hair. Ellen loved the silty feeling of flour between her fingers, but it took all her strength not to poke the dough when it rose. A couple of times, Kristen caught her poking at one and swiped at her hand.

"If you need to pinch something, pinch this," she said, and handed her a ball of dough.

When it seemed that everyone had been dusted with flour and that the loaves of bread could make a mountain in the middle of the room, Nora called for the girls' attention.

"Okay girls, listen to me." Nora clasped her hands together and motioned for the girls to be quiet. The bun which was usually twisted into a tight knot on her head was loose and speckled white. It was easy to picture her as an old woman, sitting in the corner and drinking tea with Old Paul. "You've done a good job. Messy, but good. We've made more than enough to give to the entire village. Jesus fed thousands, because he had compassion for those who were hungry. Each of you can take a loaf home with you, but I want you to go to every house and give a loaf to every family."

A couple of girls murmured about the cold. Others giggled and talked about warming their bread over the stove as they began to reach for their loaves.

"Listen," Nora continued. "Not one family left out. Go together and keep warm."

When Nora said the final blessing, everyone grabbed a sack of loaves and ran out the door. Ellen kept up with June and Matty as they ran toward the bluff side of the village that sloped under several layers of snow. At every house, they knocked and handed out a loaf. Everyone thanked them—the mothers nodded and smiled, the elders with missing teeth said *quyana*, and the poor fishermen who found themselves stuck in a frozen land blessed them in English or Norwegian. June and Matty were singing and Ellen joined in, feeling for the first time that she belonged. When they reached her grandmother's house where her mom lived, Ellen saw a faint flicker of light through the window. She imagined her mother was somewhere between those walls, keeping warm.

"Take one to your mother. Everyone knows she needs it," Matty said, and she handed Ellen a loaf.

"You're just saying that," Ellen answered. "She has so much food, she has been sharing with me because Papa has been grounded. Hell, I should just give you my bread."

Matty frowned and hit her legs to keep the blood in her legs moving. She looked hard at Ellen. "Why you talk like that? You're not living this way anymore. It's different."

Ellen turned the loaf in her hand, feeling its rough texture through her mittens. She patted the bottom and listened to the flat sound it made, like that of her chest when she tapped it—that empty place that never seemed to get full. Now she finally had a reason to see her Mama—and Ellen couldn't walk any closer. Her legs felt weak and heavy, and she fell into the snow.

"Ellen, go." June pulled her up.

The outer porch door was open, and Ellen stepped inside where it was dark and smelled of dried fish. She felt the heat of the house through the front door and listened for movement on the other side of the wall. There was shuffling, like that of snowshoes against the snow. Her mother was humming. It was definitely her mother—her mother, carrying a tune as if she didn't need anything else. Nora said compassion, but anger was easier. Ellen broke the loaf into two pieces. Steam rose from the center and crystallized onto the surface of the bread. She broke the pieces again and again, dropping them next to the door, until there was nothing left but bits scattered on the floor. It felt good to tear the bread to nothing, and Ellen hoped her mom would open the door right then.

She looked down, shocked at what her hands could do, and felt her chest tighten. Ellen bent down and tried to undo what she had done. She scraped the bits and mashed them together until they formed a tight wad of bread, sand, and snow and wedged it against the door. She rose to leave. But her mom had to know that she was here, and as she descended the steps, she slammed the outer door of the porch, shaking the house.

Ellen ran back to Matty and June, not looking back to see if her mom opened the door. Matty was smirking from ear to ear. Ellen wanted to hit her, grind her face into the snow until the grin rubbed off. But she smiled back, picked up her bag of bread, and said, "Mama said *quyana* and just in time too."

That evening, Anne Girl couldn't get warm. Dressed in her parka and *mukluks*, her bones still remained cold. She dragged in long pieces of driftwood with frozen limbs covered in layers of ice and set them next to her stove. She didn't see the bread until it rolled into the room with the wood. She took a bite and threw the rest into the fire. Another storm was making its way up the bay as the northern winds began to move once again. Although she had stacked piles of driftwood alongside two walls in her house, she worried that she didn't have enough wood. Once the wind began, it seemed to filter through every crack, making the house seem almost as cold as the outside.

"No, uh. Can't do that," Anne Girl muttered to herself as she put two pieces of wood into the stove. They fizzed and crackled as the moisture burned out of them.

Alicia had offered again, practically begged Anne Girl to stay with them until the ground thawed. When Anne Girl said that she believed her mother's old house had a couple of seasons left in it, Alicia just shook her head and said that Anne Girl was being more stubborn than a dumb moose, but her door was always open in case she changed her mind.

She thought about going to Alicia's but didn't want to arrive at her friend's doorstep admitting that she didn't know how to take care of herself. She rummaged through her shelves, through the cans of food, to see if she had anything left. There was a little bit of butter and some Pilot Boy crackers. But there in the back was a tall, green bottle of whiskey, one that she had been saving, although she couldn't remember what for.

The cool fluid ran down the back of her throat almost as easily as fish chowder. She perched next to the stove and listened to the wind begin to creep around the roof gable. It rattled the rain gutters until a metal symphony drummed all around her.

Soon Anne Girl felt hot as if her blood was boiling, and she took off her parka so that her limbs would cool. The more she drank from the green bottle, the better she felt. She stood up and began to move with the wind that beat in tune with the festival dances still held in the *qasgiq* sixty years before. With her eyes closed, she waved her arms as her body swayed from side to side. Her fists were clenched; her fingers wrapped around imaginary dance fans, holding the feathers as if holding on to life. The temperature continued to drop in the cabin as she danced and forgot to feed the flames. Dropped below freezing until ice formed shadows on both sides of the windows. But Anne Girl was warm. She was so warm.

Seventeen

When the village women found Anne Girl Nelson curled on her side, frozen, and cradling a green glass bottle, no one wanted to tell Ellen. But she knew the same way she understood it was snowing before she got out of bed. The deafening silence outside always meant that snow was creeping up the walls, but this silence was different, enveloped in hushed whispers.

She was thinking of all the reasons why she needed to stay in bed when a seagull bumped into the window pane. Her stomach knotted.

"Mom?" She sat up. "What you doing out there?"

The seagull, dirty white with gray-tipped wings, tapped on the glass with one side of her beak as if she were filing it. She shook her head as if trying to set her bearings straight, and then took off.

"Mama? Wait! I gotta tell you something. Wait for me!"

Ellen jumped out of bed, so she could follow the path of the bird from the front window. Running out into the front room, she was greeted by Sweet Mary, Nancy, Alicia, and Nora. They were sitting around the table, as if it were a normal winter day. Yet their faces were blotched and their eyes were swollen. Even Nora appeared like she woke up with a bad stomachache. Ellen sucked air.

"Mama's a seagull." Ellen said and opened the front door. "She flew by. You see her? She flew by. Just now."

Alicia jumped up from the table and reached for Ellen. She placed a cold palm on Ellen's forehead.

"Poor, she's got the fever, huh?" Sweet Mary said.

"Shut that door. No use eating the outside," Nancy snapped. "Fever or not, we can't all freeze now."

"I have no fever. You have the hot head," Ellen answered. "She's going to catch up with the others in the Aleutians."

"Creepy," Sweet Mary said as she wiped her eyes that were red. "*Akleng*."

Alicia bent down to Ellen's level and said that John was with her mom. And it took all of Ellen's effort to focus on Alicia's moving lips. They smacked, puckered, parted to show her crooked teeth, and then became tight as web knot. They kept moving like that, and Ellen couldn't match Alicia's words to their movement, and she gave up trying. And then her father arrived. As soon as he walked in the door, John picked her up in his arms, still smelling of cold. He said nothing, but his body shivered. Ellen wanted to cry, but nothing came out—no tears, no moans—so she held onto her papa's neck and felt his arms wrap around her.

People arrived at the Nelson home with black fish, *aqutak*, and small plates of cookies. They touched Ellen's cheeks and told her that she looked beautiful in her dress. Nora had arrived earlier with an old dress of Kristen's and helped Ellen get ready. She brushed Ellen's hair and talked quietly, telling her that if she was tired she could go lie down anytime. But Ellen shook her head. She had never seen so many people in her house. Her mom would say they were noisy ones, talking too loud. They talked around and above her, telling John how sorry they were for his loss, as if Anne Girl had been living with him all this time.

At one point, Frederik pulled John aside. "You know, even though we can't bury her until spring, we should hold a service for her. It would be my honor to do it for you, for her, for you both."

John wiped his eyes. "I don't think Anne would have liked that. She just wasn't that way. You know that, Frederik."

"I know what you are saying, but we're all children of God, in life and in death," Frederik said, wrapping his arm around John's shoulders. "Give her a proper burial. And when spring comes, we'll do it again."

Ellen looked up from the seal gut balloon she and June were tossing around, and heard John mumble something about a small service—one without frilly music. She heard her name, her mother's name, and locked eyes with father, who smiled weakly. He had aged years in a week, and Ellen decided that he would look better if he smeared flour in his hair, like Nora.

The village held two back-to-back services for Anne Girl. It began in the chapel under the booming voice of Frederik, who spoke of God's love and the afterlife. The villagers sat huddled next to each other in the small chapel room, riveted into a cold silence by his words. Frederik paced the room, soaking in their attention as if unaware that everyone was only waiting to go to the community hall where food and booze were being lined up on tables around the circular wall. When he closed his black Bible and whispered, "Amen," people sighed and moved toward the door, toward the dancing promised at the potlatch across the village.

At the community hall, the feasting began. People from villages all over the bay arrived with more dried fish and meat and whatever drink they had to share until the community hall was packed like ice. People danced and told stories. John and Ellen were surrounded by friends who kept the conversation light and didn't mention Anne Girl. Ellen wandered the room, allowing the debates about fishing to float above her. She wondered how they could talk about fishing and the cannery with her mother waiting to be put in the earth. It was a long wait until the ground became soft again.

"So it's true then. They are going to allow boats with motors in the bay?" Gil Sam asked. "Imagine, boats!"

Frederik cleared his throat. "Yes, they are talking about it. Maybe not this summer, but the next one. Who knows? It's all up to the canneries really."

"Took them long enough to make up their mind," Gil said. "We're the only bay that still has sailboats when there are planes flying around."

"Well, you boys will be able to go out faster, huh? Maybe, I'll take up fishing once we can use motors and follow you boys out to the line," John said.

Gil and Amos laughed. "Sure, sure you will. I would give money to see you set up with a double ender again."

"Just face it John, no matter what you want to believe, you have a way of letting the salmon escape. I've never seen anything like it before."

"Well, I just have a certain kind of talent," John answered.

When June and her family left the potlatch, Ellen felt the sadness and longing return with force. She took strips from the table and sucked on the meat as she searched for a quiet corner to hide. But the community hall was packed, and the front door kept opening to allow more in. People were laughing and patting each other on the back as they caught up on the news from across the bay and the territory.

"So this is where you've been hiding." Nora bent down to Ellen's level. Her usual pale cheeks were flushed red from the heat of the room. She smelled of lilacs when Ellen wanted the smokehouse smell of her mother. "We've been looking for you." Nora caressed Ellen's forehead. "You need to rest. Come, I'll tell your dad you're with me."

"I'm not tired. I'm not," Ellen answered.

"It's hard to understand, I know," Nora said and stood up. "It's always hard to know what to say. You want some tea?"

Ellen nodded, but didn't really expect Nora to return with a steaming cup and a jar of honey.

Shrugging, Ellen sipped on the tea. She didn't know what to think. The tea was so sweet that it made her wonder whether Nora always made it this way or whether it was just for today. Her mama's tea was always too bitter. She remembered how she often wished that Anne Girl were like Nora, and she wondered if her mama knew about that now. Could her mama read her mind now? Did she know how her chest ached and how she fantasized for Nora to take her home?

Ellen's mind was spinning, and she gulped down her tea, feeling the warm drink spreading down the space in her chest. Ellen looked up at Nora's hands, with her long, thin fingers, and was struck by a thought that would bother her for years to come. Did her dad see the mashed-up bread in her grandma's porch? If her mom ate a little bit, she wouldn't have drunk herself to sleep, Ellen wondered.

Eighteen

Although Ellen found a place on the Killweather porch steps to watch the cannery bustle the following summer, it didn't feel right, but instead like the chapel organ that was always out of tune and croaking out hideous songs. Nothing felt right. The noise of the cannery and the movement of the workers didn't match, and Ellen convinced herself that the cannery people and fishermen were not really there. She hadn't seen her mama dragging and cursing her net to the shore, so the men on the dock couldn't be real. She wondered if they too belonged to the little people, to that place where few were found under the tundra marsh and black lilies.

On days when her father was flying or helping out with the mission, Ellen wandered between her house and Nora's. Her dad told her to stay out of trouble, yet Ellen knew that he had asked Nora and Frederik to keep an eye on her like she was a scruffy mutt wandering the village. Even so, some days she just wanted to be near someone, even if it meant she was going to be put to work.

Even from where she sat, Ellen felt the hum that surrounded fishing that year. Motor boats were permitted in the bay, and fishermen were finding ways to attach nine-horse motors to the sides of their sailboats. Others sawed off the masts and burned them at the end of the spit in such large fires it appeared that the saltwater was feeding the flames. "No more of those monkey boats," they told each other, pointing toward the tugboat that had become permanently docked. "Yep, going to be a good year now. We can catch more. None of that waiting around for the wind." Men who normally didn't fish began taking out loans to buy boats, and before even the first king salmon was spotted the bay was littered with fishing vessels with engines revved for the signal to go. A new sound had entered the bay, the sound of motors coughing and grinding so loud that they could be heard over the rush of waves and wind and almost the sound of the cannery.

Nora stepped in front Ellen, blocking her view of the cannery. Up close with her hair pulled back into a tight bun, Nora appeared tall and wide. Ellen's eyes followed the curve of Nora's hands and saw how her veins were roots, crossing one another to get to the fingers.

"Ellen, dear, give me a hand." Nora lightly touched her shoulders. "I need the schoolroom straightened out. The children will be arriving in a couple of hours. I have a special activity for everyone today. I think you especially will like it."

Ellen stiffened and pulled away, simultaneously wanting to be touched and left alone. Sometimes the woman's hands made her skin crawl, and Ellen didn't know why. Since her mom died, Ellen didn't know what to make of Nora. It was as if Nora were trying too hard, trying to be kind when it seemed that her dark eyes didn't want to be. Her Mama once said that you can read a lot in how a person looks at you, and Ellen constantly searched Nora's expression, hoping she would find more than the simple brown eyes. But Nora's look was that of a nesting squirrel, always looking for ways to prepare her home for the service to the Lord. If she wasn't preparing meals for people, she was planning for Sundays and Wednesdays.

"Ellen," Nora repeated.

"Where's Kristen? She can help you, you know," Ellen answered and looked back at the cannery. Men were milling along the boardwalk, moving as if they had important business to take care of, as if they belonged there.

There was something in the way Nora stood that brought up the image of walrus ivory sitting in the kitchen windowsill. One time when she and her mom were cleaning dishes, Anne Girl reached up and ran her fingers along the smooth curves as if it would tell her something important. When Ellen asked why her mom kept fingering the ivory, Anne Girl bent down and told her about the ivory carver who left Nushagak Village years ago.

Back when men used *qayaqs* to hunt and fish, when dog sleds were faster than the winter sun, when the men sweated together in the *qasgiq*, there was a carver. He carved ivory and traded his work with the Russians for new beads. His wife liked to wear beaded necklaces and liked to sew them into her *mukluks*. She loved them too much; she told him that she needed more and more beads. So he carved, hour after hour, and polished his ivory pieces until the tips of his hands were raw. One day, though, he just stopped. He had piles of untouched tusks sitting in front of him, but he couldn't find the strength to carve anymore. He buried them on the beach and left in his *qayaq*, leaving his wife and her beads forever. Anne Girl's eyes gleamed as she breathlessly related this story, telling Ellen that they had the last piece of ivory from the carver.

Sighing, Nora looked away. "Okay, I'll let you off this time. But this"—she waved her hand at Ellen—"can't go on forever."

She turned and walked back into the house, and Ellen listened to her sweeping step fade into the groans of the building. She heard Nora speak to Kristen. Unlike Anne Girl's tone, which clawed and scratched, Nora's voice was smooth and without roots.

When the ground thawed, they had buried Anne Girl on the side of the bluff so that the body wouldn't be lifted during a flood. Frederik had led the burial, talking about his good friend Anne Girl. Placing a large cross over the raw earth, Frederik spoke of forgiveness and the need to move on. More than once, Ellen interrupted, saying that her mama wasn't dead yet but circling above them as a seagull, still hungry. Frederik had to signal to John to remove Ellen, because the women near the rear of the service were murmuring how this might be true since Anne Girl's things were not yet burnt. But Ellen continued to talk until Nora took her aside and said now wasn't the time to say such things. Ellen protested and screamed, and Nora held her by the shoulders and said to behave like Kristen, who stood silently behind the group of mourners.

Ellen laughed when, shortly after the burial service, the village women, still wearing their imitation dresses of Nora's, raided Marulia's house and started a fire. They burned Anne Girl's clothes, nets, baskets, and bed so that Anne Girl would no longer wander the earth. She wouldn't try to tuck herself under her blankets again. Just as the flames peaked at the old house, Frederik came running down the path waving his Daily Texts and saying that the Lord would save Anne Girl's soul in time. No need to burn everything in sight. Ellen could tell that her father didn't care if they burned everything—the smokehouse, the fish rack, or the outhouse—because he brought Anne Girl's clothes to add to the fire. Oddly, the women left the smokehouse. Nancy held up her hands and said she couldn't touch it yet. Sweet Mary told Nancy to quit flapping her arms like a choking fish and not to worry about the smokehouse. It would be useful when the kings came in.

The memory replayed in her head, and she felt an overwhelming urge to break into a run toward the bluff side and see her mom. Her legs stirred, and she ran off the porch, taking the grassy path behind the village so that she could not be seen. The grass stalks were still brown and stiff from the winter, but they moved past her as if they expected the summer winds to shake them into life once again. She thought she was going to the bluff to stand on the edge and watch the swallows dive, yet her legs took her to the grave markers. A swarm of seagulls scattered as she ventured to the newly turned earth. The rectangle area where her mother lay needed a blanket. The soil appeared wet and so cold. A wooden cross stood over Anne Girl's grave. Bird droppings, like white polka dots, were scattered along the wood, which made it seem like someone gave up painting the cross. Ellen kicked it, but the cross didn't budge. It made her want to push it down even more.

"*Akleng*, your dumb bird was right," she said, as she leaned against the wood. "But you were wrong."

Ellen pressed her back against the wood and held her breath as she pushed. It would go down, she was sure.

"Ellen!"

Ellen looked up to see Matty and June coming her way. She saw how Matty's hand was entwined with June's as if they were best friends. She even had her hair loose and falling around her face, like wild grass, like June's hair. Matty, tall and long-necked with rumors of her mother always urging her to be mean, squinted at Ellen.

"Don't just stand there gawking at me. Help me."

"The women will have your skin for breakfast," Matty said, and she brushed the hair from her eyes. She looked down the trail as if to see if they were being followed.

Ellen laughed. "Like fish skins."

June and Matty looked at each other. Suddenly Ellen felt silly as if she were caught naked in the *maqi* doorway. She pulled herself off the cross and wiped her hands on her slacks. But she couldn't bring herself to leave her mom's grave so bare. She pulled at the clumps of the long grasses and laid them on the ground, starting at the cross where Anne Girl's head would be.

"Help me cover her, anyway," she said.

June sighed but began pulling grasses. While June handed them to Ellen, Matty kneeled and placed her stalks carefully next to Ellen's. It wasn't long until the length of the rectangle resembled a light green bed.

"We're going up the tundra. Matty says that there's a trail at the edge of the bluff where there's a waterfall. Phil said that there was one too, but he can't show us it because they're getting ready to fish. Come with us."

Ellen patted the ground. "Now she looks better."

"Yeah," Matty said quietly and stood up. "So let's quit being sad and go."

"I know that waterfall at the end of the beach. My mama showed that one to me. The little people live there. Let's go down the beach way then."

Matty scoffed as if Ellen should know better. "Bears down the beach. And it's more fun on the tundra anyway." She held her chin out. "You would know that if you lived on the bluff.

"There's sinkholes up there, will suck you under." Ellen returned. She wanted to see the waterfall, but she had to be careful of the sinkholes when walking on the tundra, even when the land was still brown. They can swallow a person up fast if she's not careful. And then she would be buried underneath the ground forever. Didn't Matty's mom teach her anything?

"Okay, okay," Matty said, and began walking to show the conversation was over. "It's faster up the tundra."

The girls began hiking up a trail that winded its way up the bluff. Where they were now, the alders and grasses were so thick they could hardly see twenty feet ahead of themselves. But they knew that once they rounded the hill, the smell of the tundra would overtake them.

Matty stopped on the trail and raised up her hands. "You two bleeding yet? We shouldn't be up here if so."

"Not today," June said slowly.

Ellen was about to answer when Matty waved her off. "We know you haven't."

"No, I flow like the bay, Matty." Ellen snapped. "But not today. Today we are good."

"Boy, you two," June said and continued on. "Come, while my mom's still having seal oil with Nancy."

". . . Flow like the bay," Matty chuckled.

Soon the long grasses transformed into the deep tundra of low brush, lichen, and moss. The brushes were still bare from the cold spring mornings. There were only hints of buds and promises of the thin leaves of summer. Once the three found the trail, worn into a brown rut from passing berry pickers and hunters, they walked quickly away from the village, away from the heaving tides and the mountains in the distance. Every once in a while, one of them picked up different berry leaves and tried to sound like her mother by commenting on when she thought the berries would arrive.

"They are going to come soon this year, 'cause break up went real fast."

"Nah, not enough rain yet. They'll be hard as rocks."

"Well, I know where good patches are from last year. We went to the lakes and picked for days. That was after silvers arrived though. We'll go then, huh. Lots of bears, though."

But as they rehearsed their mothers' tones and mimicked their steps, in the back of Ellen's mind were the little people who lived at the edge of the waterfall. The little people lived in her, and every story she had heard until she was old enough to play story knife on the beach. A little person had magic in his hands and if one was caught, he would grant a wish. When the tide was out, the little people could run over the thick mud just as easily as if they were racing over the hard ground. If you saw one, then he could make you dizzy until you lost track of time. And hundreds of years entwined in one breath. The girls wondered what the little men and women looked like, if they would recognize them right away.

To Ellen, the little people seemed like her Mama's friends. She always spoke of them as if they were about to play mean tricks that only she would take delight in. Anne Girl warned her to be careful when looking for the little people, because they could keep you forever and you wouldn't even know it. The mountains across the bay could grow if you spent a day with the little people.

As Ellen walked by the gentle slopes, her feet squished into the unsteady ground and cold water lapped over her shoes. Underneath the layer of brushes and moss of the tundra was permafrost, and in some places, the entire surface of the tundra heaved and sighed with each footstep. One step had the rippling effect like water and the feeling that you could tilt the earth just by walking. Ellen wondered if the ocean felt her step. Soon the trail forked into two, one leading toward the bay and the other leading deeper into the tundra where the land kissed the sky in the horizon.

Matty stopped and raised her hands. "This is the one we want. This one goes to the edge of the bluff." She pointed toward the trail that weaved its way between low brush and long stalks of grass where the tundra seemed to disappear.

Seeing the trees and thinking of bears hiding near them, Ellen whispered, "You think there's bears?"

Matty sighed as if she were dealing with a child. "No. We'll know when we see one."

"Well, if the grass is all flat, I'm leaving. They say to always look for flattened grass." Bears were hungry this time of year, sleeping between meals and making nests on the bluff. Everyone knew that. Why did Matty pretend that she knew everything?

"We'll look for the grass," June said, as she took Ellen's hand and led the three of them down the trail.

The grasses, still brown from the dark winter, grew longer and waved above their heads. Ellen heard the sound of trickling water over the rustle of the grasses.

"You hear that? That's the waterfall where the little people live," Matty said.

"What wish are you going to ask for if you catch one?" Ellen asked.

"A trip to Dillingham. You?" June answered.

Ellen shrugged and agreed that a trip up to Dillingham would be a good thing to wish for. She thought that if she asked the little person to bring back her mom then the little person would laugh at her and tell her that she asked for too much. That she was too greedy. But maybe if she whispered in his ear how she dreamed of her mom knocking at the door, begging for food, then maybe he would know how often she stayed awake at night, straining to hear the wooden floor squeak, and wondering if each creak was her mother's footstep.

"Well, I'm going to wish for some new clothes to come on the next mail plane. I need new ones, like Kristen," Matty said. "You know where she gets them from, Ellen?"

"Nora makes them for her. They get mail from the States from someone down there. Nora said that she's going to make me a new dress too, if I can stay clean for a day."

"She's just saying that. She's really not going to make you dresses. You'll get what Kristen can't fit anymore. It's always like that," Matty answered.

"I don't care."

"What's it like when you are with them? They pray all day? I bet Nora makes you just want to take a nap. Sometimes she talks so slow!" June moaned.

"And Frederik talks to himself." Ellen said, slightly raising her voice, now that she had an audience. "You know how he moves his lips real fast in chapel, like he's going to say something, but doesn't?"

"Yeah."

"He does that all the time when he talks to himself. And sometimes Nora has to give him medicine to make it stop." Ellen lied, but at that moment it was what Matty and June needed to hear. She could imagine them telling their parents how Frederik talked to himself.

"Nuh-uh."

"Yeah, it's true." Ellen held up her hands to show that she had nothing to hide from them.

The slope grew steeper as the sound of the water became louder. In the village, this was the only area where trees had blossomed. Their roots were deep with branches that stretched wide, and on their leaves bees stopped to rest to look at the hidden waterfall below. It was as if the trees protected the water and the little people from the villagers and cannery men.

Ellen searched the grasses to see if there were any that were flattened, and she looked into the sky, because her mother once said that if seagulls are flying in circles, trying to get dizzy, then it means that a bear's getting full on something. Ellen's stomach caught in her throat when she saw a seagull swoop and dive beyond the bluff. But he was alone, flapping his wings toward the bay. She sighed and felt the fear drain from her limbs as she ducked underneath the alder tree branches.

Hiking down the hill, Ellen tried to be careful not to get her clothes snagged by the branches. Her Papa wouldn't care but she could hear Nora telling her to walk like a young lady and take smaller steps. Nora thought it was a good idea to dispense advice on how to behave now that her mom was dead. If she ripped her shirt or pants, Ellen figured that she would have to think of a good lie. And she thought she had done enough lying today.

The farther they hiked underneath the thin branches, the more closely Ellen listened for the heavy breathing and throaty growl of a bear. Every time they came upon a depression in the earth or a new grassy mound, she sniffed the air, because her mom said that you would know you were near a bear if it smelled like dirty socks and rotten fish. She said that you would know if you were standing in a bear's bed. So Ellen wrinkled her nose and inhaled deeply, but she could only smell the earthy limbs of the trees.

Matty held her hands up to stop their path. "You hear that?"

"What?" June whispered, trying not to sound scared.

"The little people. They're calling you, Ellen."

Ellen crouched low in the grass, feeling the coldness of the earth all around her. And it was true, between the rustles of the grass, she heard her name.

"Ellen!"

She peered into the brush and tried to capture something with eyes. Maybe the little people already knew about her wish. Maybe they thought it was more important than June's and Matty's. Her excitement spilled into her bones, and she ran past June to where Matty stood on the edge of a trickling stream. The water flowed noisily next to their feet.

"You see any?"

Matty cupped her hands around her eyes, and scanned the earth. A little person barely reached the knee caps of a normal person. "No, but we're close now. We're sure to see one."

The sound of water rushing grew louder, but so did the voice calling Ellen's name, both pressing against her. She began to run toward the water fall, jumping and tripping over the grassy mounds.

When she briefly glanced at the path leading back to the tundra, she saw Frederik marching toward her, as if following anger down the hill, swinging his arms from side to side as he tried to rush down the uneven slope.

"Shit!" Ellen said. "It's Frederik. Run."

"Jesus Christ!" Matty yelled and took off toward the brushes that were thick enough to hide under.

"Ellen! Get here now!"

Ellen stopped and waved the girls on. "Run and then go back the beach way. I won't say nothing."

As they ran, disappearing between the tall grasses, Ellen turned toward Frederik. He stood in front of her with his hands on his hips, breathing hard, his chest heaving up and down. It was so unlike the pacing preacher in front of the congregation that Ellen almost laughed.

"Ellen, where do you think you're going? Did you hear me calling you?"

"Nah, the wind was blowing loud."

Frederik wiped his brow and sighed loudly, as if trying to keep his anger under his forehead. But it formed in a thick, horizontal line that streaked across his brow. It moved and twitched as he talked.

"Did Nora say you can come here?"

"She didn't say no."

"Did you say where you were going?"

"She didn't ask."

Frederik raised his hand and pointed a long finger at her. "You need to watch your tongue and have respect for your elders, you understand me? Nora doesn't know that you're here, does she?"

Ellen looked down and saw beginning petals of a single black lily. They opened, facing downwards, as if the summer sun was too much light for them. It was the only one she could see on this side of the tundra.

"Who were you with?"

"The little people. They run real fast."

"Nonsense. Little people," Frederik huffed. "I saw some girls, maybe two or three, running. You can't just run off like a gazelle. What would we have to say to your dad when he returns tonight?"

"Gazelle? My Papa doesn't care where I am at," Ellen insisted. She was tired of talking to him. Any hope she had earlier while climbing the bluff had sunk within the permafrost. He ruined it, ruined her chance to get her wish. Her desire to bring her mother back wasn't going to happen. And Ellen felt the sadness well up from her throat and burn her tongue as she tried to hold back her tears. She squinted and looked away from Frederik and toward the slope, where she heard the rumble of the water moving away from her.

"Our Lord Savior doesn't like liars any more than he likes murderers or thieves." Frederik grabbed Ellen's hand and began the long walk toward the village. "He doesn't like liars," he repeated, more to himself than to Ellen. "You are going to apologize for making Nora worry."

"God lets people die," Ellen said quietly.

Frederik adjusted his glasses and coughed. "Your mom killed herself. God had nothing to do with that."

He continued to ramble on about what happens when you die, as they trudged back toward town. Ellen tuned him out and looked for seagulls. The sky was blue with bulbous clouds drifting farther away, but she didn't see any gulls. She realized that she would have to keep quiet from this point forward.

Nineteen

I have taken this skiff out once before, if you can believe it. It was when I first got the Evinrude that is now shit in the mud. It was such a smooth ride, you see, and I was fooled into thinking that all my skiff outings would be just as smooth. They would have been, if you didn't show up.

From the Nelson house the sounds of engines grinding and forklifts moving could be heard, even after midnight, when the sun teased the land with little light. In her room, Ellen lay with her eyes open, unable to sleep. The sun didn't set in the summer, just hovered over the mountains across the bay before rising again. Ellen liked to watch and determine the moment when the sun was neither falling nor rising, but sitting and holding the earth under a constant gaze. She thought that if she could find that moment and grab it, then time away from her mom would stop growing. Then she wouldn't forget.

If she hadn't been looking, Ellen would have missed it. Yet, there it was—her mom's skiff. It was lying on its side, against the smokehouse. It was of Norwegian style, with high sides that ran together into a sharp, aggressive bow. Layers of paint curled on the wood like miniature waves, and when Ellen ran her hand across the surface, she felt the paint and splinters poke at her skin. She smiled. Her father hadn't lied to her.

Before he left in the morning, Ellen asked her father where he left the skiff. She found him with his ear next to the radio, staring out the window and moving his lips. His eyes were dark and brooding, yet he didn't appear to be in the same room with her. John was somewhere in the sky, Ellen figured. It was easy to get information from him when he was like this, and Ellen asked where he was storing the skiff.

With her back, she pushed the skiff away from the smokehouse wall so that it landed on its belly. Dust and scales billowed in her face and she coughed. She looked up and down the beach to see if anyone noticed the commotion. By this time in the summer, the kings had hit the beach, and the village women were cutting and putting up strips along the shore. Their necks were bent, *uluaqs* raised, and forearms covered in blood. They didn't see Ellen and her new skiff.

She was still breathing heavily, but Ellen climbed in and sat down in the same place her mother had parked herself so many times before. Ellen closed her eyes and listened to the grasses rustle and the sound of the waves hitting the beach. Somewhere she heard or thought she heard gulls wailing along the shore, and suddenly an ocean of ache spilled forward. She cried, letting the tears and snot mess her face. When Ellen opened her eyes, she saw the cut-out holes in the wood her mom used for a cleat. The cleat! Her mom never got that cleat. How strange.

Ellen ran in the direction of the cannery. The gravel was difficult to run on, but she had never felt so strong. She passed her house, then the Killweathers', where she ran into Nora, and a basket of muffins flew into the air like shells. They landed heavily onto the gravelly beach.

"Watch it, Ellen!" Nora grabbed Ellen's wrist and pulled her. "For Heaven's sake, watch it. Ah, the muffins!"

"*Akeka*," Ellen looked down at the mess she made. "I didn't see you."

"Oh damn. It took me all morning to make those," Nora muttered and frowned. She was dressed in a long skirt and faded blue blouse she ordered from the catalog while Frederik was away. She had pulled back her hair into a tight knot, making her seem angry and tense.

"Sorry," Ellen said. "Can you let go of my arm now?"

Nora let go of her grip and sighed. "Where are you off to in such a hurry?"

Ellen looked up into Nora's eyes and smiled from within. "Going to get a cleat for my mama's skiff. I found it. And I need to fix it up now. I need paint, a good scraper, and a cleat."

"Oh dear, not another Anne Girl running here and there and into me," Nora chuckled. She looked toward the cannery, whose gears were already on, grinding away. "And where are you planning to purchase all this material?"

Ellen waved toward the cannery. "At the cannery, Nora."

"And your father knows about all this?" Nora said. "I don't think so." She pulled Ellen's shoulder. "Come with me, because you are *not* going to the cannery today."

It was useless to argue, because Nora was taller than her. The woman had a way of towering over you until you lost all your words. Ellen glanced at the cannery buildings and their newly painted gray tin roofs and felt her neck grow hot. Nora was wrong about her father. He didn't care if she marched down the main docks with her eyes closed. She would get that cleat.

Ellen followed Nora back down the beach trail she had just come from. She kicked at the gravel.

"Papa doesn't mind."

"We'll find that out later." Nora took Ellen's hand. "Now be a good girl and walk with me."

"Where you going now?"

"You know it took me twice to get that muffin recipe right. And now all those eggs are wasted."

"Let's go to the cannery to see if they got some," Ellen said. She tried to free herself from Nora's grip, but Nora's hand was firm.

Nora laughed. "You are Anne Girl's daughter after all."

Suddenly Ellen understood. Nora was on her way to see Jill and Penni. Everyone seemed to be talking about Jill Wescoat, who found a new lover at one of the net lofts in the cannery—a young man from the States. When the fishermen flocked to the cannery, the village tripled in size. Sometimes the cannery men came to the village side to drink and play cards. Other times, they stayed the night. And every so often, a young woman from the village would be seen walking the alleys of the cannery, drunk and naked. Sometimes a couple would be found, tangled in the net loft. Nearly every year there was an occurrence of this kind, and usually the favored place was the net loft. Sometimes the closets in the rear of the clinic, where thin, white sheets were folded, were chosen for lovemaking, but most ended up in the net loft where the cold, salty air never stopped rushing in from the bay. And the tongues would fly between the superintendent and the village council, blaming each other for the loss of control.

They passed by the village women putting up fish, their bent figures shaking over the cutting table, covered in blood. And their girls and boys were dipping the strips in brine and carrying the poles to the smokehouse and drying racks. She tried to remember what it felt like to have the cold meat against her fingertips, the sticky blood against her skin. And the damp smell of the smokehouse right before it was lit for the first time. Nora gave a faint nod to the group and tried to keep her distance from the blood, but Ellen stepped toward the women and breathed in the sharpness of raw flesh and slime. She counted the women, twice, to make sure her mother wasn't hiding somewhere in their group. Sometimes she felt that her mom could be everywhere at once. It was just a matter of finding her.

"Come on," Nora said. "And smile a little, won't you? It's a nice day out anyway."

"I'll smile when I have a reason to."

"Nonsense. There are plenty of things to be happy about. You're healthy and you have plenty to eat," Nora said, and she began to rattle off a list that included fresh vegetables and clean clothes—things that didn't even count for Ellen.

"How about my mom being dead then?"

"I'm sorry." Nora paused. "It's fine if you aren't thankful for that. God probably wouldn't mind."

"Maybe I'll thank him for not minding so much then, huh?"

Nora sighed. "Goodness, you are difficult."

"Why you didn't you bring Kristen? She's the one who's friends with Jill. Not me. They don't even ask if I want to go on walks with them anymore. But maybe I don't want to go with them anyways. They talk about the new Montgomery Ward catalogues."

"Kristen has work to do today," Nora answered, her voice sharp. "No need to bring her into this mess."

As they approached the bluff side of the village, the low houses stacked against the face of the hill loomed above them. They passed June's house and the remains of Marulia's house, where Anne Girl's body was found. There was a large semicircle of ash where the village women had burned everything of Anne Girl's. Ellen felt cold as they walked by. It was hard to believe that she lived there last summer, and now it was a mound of dust. If Nora wasn't clasping her hand so tightly, she would have sifted through the pile, just in case there was something that didn't burn completely. She reminded herself to do that later. Maybe June and Matty would join.

Like the other homes on the bluff side, the Wescoats' house was tucked against the long grasses, now green from the endless days of light. They swayed in the breeze as if waving to Nora and Ellen to come closer. Against the side of the building were a couple of long ice-fishing poles, dip nets, and a salmon net that was stacked according to corks and lead line.

Ellen tried to see if there was in any movement in the porch. The window was dark, covered by a blanket, to avoid the light outside.

"Now mind your manners." Nora bent down to Ellen's level. "Just keep Jill company, okay? She might be sad or embarrassed, so be a friend."

"Yeah, yeah," Ellen answered. She was still thinking about going to the cannery.

They entered the porch, Nora holding tightly to Ellen. In the center of the porch, two kings soaked in a tub of water. Their heads broke the surface and flies crawled along the glazed pupils and the black tongues. White specks of eggs were tucked in the crevices of the mouth and between the pointy teeth. Ellen leaned over, smelled the salt, and wondered if the black eyes could see her.

Just as she began to poke one, Nora knocked on the door. Ellen heard some rustling, and then a pair of feet dragging across the floor. Nora stood upright with a forced smile on her face as the door opened.

"Oh it's just you, Mrs. Nora," Penni Wescoat said as she opened the door. She tried to smile, but the dark circles under her eyes seemed to consume her entire face. She reeked of whiskey and smoked fish.

"Yes, just Ellen and I. You know Ellen?"

"Of course, Anne Girl's little one. My, you're getting big. How old are you now—thirteen?" Penni reached out and caressed Ellen's cheek. "She was a good woman, busy all the time though," she said as if the moment required mentioning Anne Girl. She returned her gaze to Nora. "Village girls are tough and wouldn't I know it." Penni laughed nervously.

Nora's smile was the same one she used when greeting people at the chapel—a stiff grin that seemed plastered to her cheeks.

"My girl must have taken after me, you know," Penni continued. And when Nora neither agreed nor disagreed, she opened the door wide. "Come in, have some tea and fish. I thought you were one of them talkers. Everything's a story about something or someone. Always something." Penni waved her hands around as if she saw flies.

"We would love to have tea," Nora finally said, and then she placed a hand on Ellen's shoulder. "We did have muffins to bring, but we had a little accident on the way."

Penni moved to the stove that stood in the center of the room, radiating out unbearable amounts of heat. "I was going to cut up those salmon out there, but then I saw Nancy Sam and that bunch walking down the beach with their *uluaqs* and string. They talk too much, you know? As if their kids are clean and holy. Shit. They are just foul-mouthed bastards is all."

"Well." Nora paused. "They are probably only concerned about Jill. How is she doing?"

"That little bitch. I think I'm going to have to tie her to a tree at night. But there are only alders around here. She still might get loose. And Jerry was so angry. I had to convince him to go ahead and fish, and I'll take care of her." And then a look of glee passed over Penni's face. "I think he beat the shit out of that fisherman, just a young good-for-nothing from up town. You have to watch these young men today."

While Penni ranted and Nora sat attentively, Ellen stood next to the table, partially listening. She looked around the single-room cabin, at the beds tucked in the far corner, and wondered what she was supposed to be doing. It was disrespectful to sit and listen to grown-ups, but Nora hadn't said she could go yet either.

Penni glanced at Ellen, and, for a brief second the hard darkness that lined her face softened. "You want to see Jill? She's out back washing clothes. You can go back there if you like while Mrs. Nora and I chat for a bit."

Nora nodded and slightly pushed Ellen to the door. "Please, don't get your dress dirty."

Outside, Ellen found Jill hanging clothes. "What you're doing here?" Jill asked when Ellen peered around the corner.

"Nora wanted me to come out," Ellen responded. She jumped up and pulled down the line for Jill. "You need help?"

"Nah," Jill answered, not looking at Ellen. "What they talking about in there?"

"Nosy Nancy and you."

Jill continued to pin shirts onto the line, stretching each time to reach the line. Ellen watched and noticed that her face was flushed as if trying to hold in all the emotions of the world. She waited for Jill to speak and wished that Kristen had also come.

"What they say about me?"

"Your mama's mad, says you shouldn't play in the net loft anymore."

A grin played on Jill's face, a secretive one, the kind Ellen would have been slapped for if her mom was still alive. "It was fun."

"Really? But don't you get dirty up there with all those smelly fishermen?"

Jill chuckled and shook her head. "It's not dirty when you're having fun." And then she stared at Ellen, her thin, black eyes grinning. "You'll know what I mean in a few years."

"Has Kristen been up there with you? You guys go beach walking all the time."

Jill laughed, long and hard, showing all her teeth. "Shit. She can't leave that house without having Frederik's four eyes following her. Oh, that just brought tears to my eyes, thinking of Kristen up the docks with me."

Ellen handed Jill a pair of pants.

"They think I'm pregnant," Jill continued and shrugged. "Or going to be."

The enormity of Jill's situation settled on Ellen, and she realized her picture of Jill in the net lofts needed some work. "What you going to do then?"

Jill smiled. "Wait and see."

Suddenly sadness gripped Ellen. "I wouldn't want a baby, because when I die it would be left alone. You should get rid of it."

Jill remained silent and continued to pin clothes on the line. A slight on-shore breeze moved the earth around them.

"I need to get that cleat." Ellen let go of the clothes line suddenly. "I forgot about that."

"Huh?" Jill shook her head. "Nancy wasn't lying when she said something was wrong with you."

"Funny, my mom said the same thing about her." Ellen peeked inside the porch and heard the rise and fall of Penni's shrill voice. And somewhere between Penni's pitches of fit was Nora's calm voice. Ellen couldn't be sure if she was agreeing with Penni or just quoting Bible things to make the other woman feel better.

Twenty

Ellen and her dad were late entering the chapel. Although services had already begun, Ellen felt the last-minute fury the Killweathers went through before guests arrived. The floors were polished and the hymnals were neatly placed on the wooden pews. And Ellen could practically see Frederik pace in the front, muttering his sermon in a breathless whisper. It made Ellen pat down her dress so that it was just perfect too. She didn't like the dress, but it felt good when Nora said something about it. That was almost worth the trouble of walking around with cold calves.

John kissed her on the forehead, and she went to the back room of the chapel where all the other village kids had gathered. Some, including June, had already started forming the usual circle around Kristen's chair. Next to June sat Matty, clinging tightly to June's hand as if their best friendship had been formed for life. Ellen didn't feel like forcing herself between them and sat down on the other side of the circle.

June never looked in her direction during the whole lesson. She sat as if completely enthralled with Kristen's story. She couldn't be, Ellen knew, because the story wasn't interesting at all. There were no ravens or little people in it, just a story about some man who talked a lot. And he gave people a lot of bread. Or something like that.

Ellen would have rather been outside, scaring the seagulls from the bloated fish.

When Kristen was done talking, the girls gathered in a corner and waited for Nora to pass out her usual snacks—Pilot Boy crackers and jam.

"June, remember when my mama caught us at the cannery?" Ellen said.

"Yeah, and then she left us there after all the yelling." June frowned.

Ellen laughed. "My mama would do that." She pulled and twisted her knuckles. "She never got the cleat."

June's eyes raised. "No? I thought she would have dragged your Papa to the cannery with a hacksaw to get that thing."

"Man, I wish I had been with you both," Matty said, and she pushed hair from her eyes. "I was probably home, waiting for my mom to sober up."

"And that took seven years." June laughed.

"Let's go to the cannery and see if that cleat is still over there," Ellen said. "I'm gonna fix the skiff up."

"You can't go anywhere," Matty said. She pointed to Frederik and John, who passed by, speaking quietly. Chapel services were over. Their heads were nearly mashed together. It made Ellen wonder if they were watching where they were going or if Nora was going to have to guide them. "You and your pop are staying for lunch, I bet. What you guys eat? My mom says it's *kassa'q* shit food, but you should save us some."

She could probably get away with it, especially if John decided not to have Sunday lunch with the Killweathers. If they stayed with the Killweathers', she would have to sit down and eat under the gaze of Nora. If she and her Papa went home, it would mean Pilot Boy crackers, honey, and a nap. John would pull up a chair in the front window and pull a hat over his eyes. And then Ellen was free to roam the beach. He never asked where she went or what she did.

"Papa doesn't care anyways. Let's go," Ellen said. "I could jump down a sinkhole up the tundra and he wouldn't know."

They headed in the direction of the mechanical noise, where the beach flattened and the boardwalks grew tall, holding the cannery above. Even though it was Sunday and the fishermen weren't out, the machines were going strong, humming and singing their own Sunday tunes.

As they approached the dock, a swarm of seagulls beneath the piers hopped and squawked at each other. Once in a while, one would put its head down and charge another for a piece of salmon remains.

"Oh shit," Ellen said and paled. "It's my Mama."

June turned around and stared up and down the beach. "Huh?"

"You seeing things?"

Ellen pointed ahead. She felt her mom in her gut before she saw her mom flapping her wings, her beak wide open. The gray bird appeared to be fatter than that winter. The black spots at the end of her feathers gave her away. "There. See her?"

Matty squinted. "You and your ghosts. I don't see your mama." She cocked her head toward the noise. "Just gulls over that way. Come on, I got some coins for candy before we go on a cleat hunt."

When they climbed to the top of the boardwalk, they made their way to the store, weaving between the fishermen who were leaving the mess hall with toothpicks wedged between their lips, smelling of fried salmon. Maybe the gull was trying to be secretive, but Ellen could see it following them, swooping and squawking its way through the crowd.

"You don't have to come if you don't want to," Ellen said. "I can look by myself."

"No way you're going without us," Matty said. "We're going to see the cannery!"

"We got the money, so you wait here," June told Ellen when they arrived at the store. "We'll be back real fast."

"Yeah, you go then," Ellen answered. Her eyes were on her mom, who had settled herself on the ridge of the store roof. "*Ampi.*"

It was break time, and men ambled from building to building, laughing and joking as they prepared themselves for the next shift. Ellen stood at the side of the building and watched men pass by, noting the odd things they carried—leather gloves or a wrench in the pocket. Once in a while, one would see her, and his eyes would rise ever so slightly, as if wondering why she was standing in the alley. Ellen kicked the side of the wall, trying to hold in her excitement. Which way was the boat graveyard, Ellen wondered. There were so many alleyways to follow. She peered down one, where she knew was the native fishermen's *maqi*. Maybe that way.

Ellen leaned against the siding, feeling the heat of the day and her excitement flow through her. More men walked by. A few of them entered the store, and the door clattered loudly behind them. One paused by Ellen and looked at her. He was greasy with stains patched up and down his jeans.

"Little girl, hello," he said. He stepped toward Ellen, not taking his eyes off her beige dress. A vein ran down the middle of his forehead, feeding the redness to his eyes. "You want to know how the cannery works? I can show you around." He looked at his watch. "I got some time. Wanna take a look?"

Ellen shook her head and stepped sideways. "No," she said and then remembered that Nora said to be polite. "No, thank you."

He shuffled forward and leaned against the wall, breathing heavy. He smelled of rotten fish, which made Ellen think of the bears on the tundra. He spoke quickly in a high-pitched voice that seemed to scratch the walls. "You see the fish are cut, salted, and put into cans. The cans go into a machine that seals the cap and sucks out all the air. And then they get steamed in the cooker." He paused and hooked Ellen's arm with his hands. "You should see the cooker room. Everyone likes that room. Steam room, cooker room, you will like it."

Ellen saw eyes popping out of a bloated fish with his grip and pulled away. Yet his hand was a like a snare and tightened when she moved.

"We don't have to go to that room," he said, and he pinched her arm as if feeling for muscle. His fingers lingered near her armpit, and she could smell oil. "The cannery has lots of warehouses."

Ellen sucked air and thought quickly. "What's the fastest way to the boat graveyard?"

The vein man's grip lightened slightly. He smiled, showing his teeth. "The graveyard, huh? What's a village girl like you want there? It's near the Chinamen Graveyard. I suppose we can detour that way."

He still held her arm, yet they walked down the alley toward the native men's *maqi*. It was shady and damp between the buildings, and Ellen suddenly felt cold. She twisted her head and looked for a sign of other workers. Yet the alleyway was now lifeless, and she wondered if everyone was still on coffee break. Even the roofs were bare. No seagulls were clattering on the metal tin.

"I just wanna know which direction. I can go myself," she said. The blood beating in her ears was louder.

"Oh, no, no. I'll take you there. Personal tour. Not many get a good tour around this cannery." The vein man spat. "All the Japs and Chinamen were buried back here near the boat graveyard. Should've just thrown them in the drink."

Up ahead a door opened, and out stepped a cannery worker. The vein man dropped her arm and nodded to the other worker, who stopped to roll and light a cigarette. For brief moment, Ellen wondered what to do. Run? Matty and June were probably waiting under the docks, eating the candy anyway. June wouldn't share if she didn't have to. Ellen took a deep breath. It was a cleat. That's what her mama said. A good one that someone left behind. Ellen breathed deeply. Everything that told her to run made her want to follow him.

"Where you work?" Ellen asked.

"Machine shop. Welding. After we see these damn boats, I'll take you there. No one thinks about what keeps a cannery running. Just fish. They only think about fish." He waved at the buildings. "You can't gut fish if your machines aren't working."

Once the other cannery man passed by, the vein man looked at her; his eyes were still like red flames. He cocked his head to one side. "It's up this way."

The shuffle he had near the store shifted into a brisk walk as he led her through a twist of alleys, past one warehouse after another, water towers, and a windowless building with black smoke catching the wind. Loose tin metal clanked against one another. She didn't realize the cannery was so large, yet with every step, she felt like she was treading deeper into the cannery secrets. A new odor, one she would remember for years to come, hit her nose and she coughed. It was the strange mixture of engine oil and bloated fish. Where was she now? She needed to remember how to get back. The turns. There were too many turns. How would her dad find her? Nora? Would Nora even try to look for her?

Ellen stopped midstride. Her stomach twisted into a knot. She pointed back toward the direction of the bay. "My friends are waiting. I gotta go."

"We're almost here," he coaxed, his voice soft. "Come on. I'll show you all the boats."

The alleyway opened up and they were surrounded by light and boats. All around were double enders and wooden boats on their sides. Skiffs that had been sawn in half for wood, cleats and hooks removed, and webbing strewn about. It smelled of damp wood rot. Near the dried creek were grave markers for the Chinamen who died many years ago. There were so many. No wonder her mom said this place was haunted. Now, which boat had the cleat?

"Pick one," he said. He walked around one boat—a large one with a cabin in the bow. Its paint was peeling and the gray wood revealed itself underneath. He pulled at the paint and held a piece between his thumb and forefinger and stared at Ellen with dark eyes.

It happened so quickly that Ellen wasn't sure if she was dreaming things up again, but before she realized it, the man grabbed her. He gripped her arm with one hand and tugged at his zipper with another. Ellen was suddenly aware of all the noises in the cannery—tin rattling the warehouse roof, wind whipping around the corners, and somewhere a flock of seagulls arguing over eyeballs. And the canning engine grinding its gears ever so loud. And then a large seagull with dark gray wings and black spots dived at them. It came so close that Ellen felt the wings beat in her ear drums, and she covered her eyes. The gull screeched.

"Jesus Christ!" The man let go of Ellen and ducked his head under arms.

Free, Ellen ran. Into the alley, she ran from both the man and her mother's squawks. She thought she heard the gull yell at her to get home, but she couldn't be sure over blood beating in her ears.

By the time she made it back to the store, the area was bare, save for a few lazy fishermen inspecting the posted signs on the door. June and Matty were nowhere to be seen, and Ellen felt both relief and immense sadness. Why would they leave? Something shifted and was lost now. She looked down at her feet and saw how the toes were scuffed and encrusted with dust. They were dirty. She was dirty. She pushed the feelings down. She had to get out of this dress and bury it. Or she would feel the vein man always looking at her, pulling at her wrist. She scanned the sky, but not a seagull was in sight. It was then Ellen realized she didn't get a chance to look for the cleat.

Later that night, Ellen sat up and listened to the cannery hammer away. She could practically hear the whine of the conveyor belts as fish were pushed through chutes to be beheaded, gutted, and chopped into pieces. The noise would last all night long, pounding at her. "It's them quiet ones. Don't let them fool you," the elders would say to each other while dipping smoked fish in seal oil. Smoked fish made her think of her mother's smokehouse. And she felt it pull on her. She needed to see it again. Ellen dressed and listened to the deadness of the house to make sure her father was asleep. As she closed the front door, the midnight sun was just beginning to move over the mountains in the west, but it paused at the Killweathers' and peered in the window, casting a long reddish glow.

She walked with her head down, seeing all the things the high tide brought and left along the slope of the beach. Rotten fish, bloated with salt water, were scattered along the path. Long pieces of driftwood and trunks of alder trees lined the shore, and Ellen wondered where they once stood, because it wasn't on this beach. The ground was too frozen to sustain such long limbs. You had to walk across the bay if you wanted to see a Christmas tree.

When she approached her mother's smokehouse, Ellen advanced slowly, almost with fear that it wouldn't be the same building where her mother used to sit and tell stories. Stories came alive in her head as she walked between the grasses, and she didn't notice their cold, wet surfaces scraping against her skin. Ellen almost sighed with relief when she saw that smokehouse. It leaned slightly toward the beach, and its door was completely missing, but the building still had four walls, four rusty walls ready to brave the next cold spell.

"Gee, uh," Ellen said to herself as she crawled into the building. It was cold and damp in the dark room. All the cross poles that had been used for hanging fish were gone, as well as the tin cover for the fire pit. But the room still vaguely smelled of smoked fish, as if the scent were embedded into the skin of the tin walls. Ellen sat next to the fire pit, as she had seen her mother do so many times before. She picked up a piece of damp driftwood lying next to her and began to draw into the ground. She drew a box, a shape for a house, and some figures that would be the family.

"And this family here had a Mama and a Papa and a Nan too," Ellen began. And as she drew, she talked, reciting stories that she had heard and combining them with new ones, ones that she wanted to be true, but knowing that they would always be only drawings in the ground. And as she talked, she heard her voice, its usual thinness grown deep and angry between the four walls. Like a breeze that sweeps over the village, Ellen felt something shift within her, a growing hardness that she had felt only hazily before. She continued to draw into the dirt, but her hand moved quicker, her lines ragged until the area was nothing more than crisscrossed scratches in the ground. And despite the cold, sweat had gathered along her forehead. She didn't feel chilled, but that she had somehow separated from herself and was now watching her hands from outside the smokehouse. Their violent motions seemed to move without her, drawing their own stories into the dirt, and it was making her dizzy.

Twenty-One

The wind picked up. You feel that? From the south, an onshore wind. The tide's changing. It's probably going to be a rough one. I feel you worried. Yeah, we might drown. It's happened before. Like that time out of Kvichak Bay, those poor fishermen got stuck on a sandbar during a storm. They were overloaded with gear and booze from town. Thought they could push their skiff with their oars, but they were dry rot and broke. And then the waves came. Moved them this way and that. Lost all that good equipment too. They found the net tangled in another fishermen's line. Never found the men, though. The tide took them out the bay and into the ocean. It had other plans for them. Can't really fight the waves when they make up their mind.

The tide's changing. But we have time. Time for you to know about the fat one.

John took off for the day as the tide rolled in and fishing boats cruised toward the mouth of the bay. He was flying a fisherman to King Salmon and would be back shortly, hopefully with a bucket of white paint. Now she sat on the front steps and watched as boats were getting ready to set their nets. Some were the unchanged double enders with their massive sails breathing wind, but most boats bobbed without the masts, their nine-horse motors puttering noisily. Their sleek bodies against the backdrop of the mountains across the bay made it seem like they had a long ways to go before they found the curve of the earth. She wondered what it would be like to travel that far, to drift to the place where there was only ocean to be seen. It had to be lonely, and Ellen felt suddenly sorry for the fishermen, that they had to be lonely in order to get fish. She shuddered as the cannery worker's image came to her, and she wondered if she was now dirty like her mama had said. All at once, longing hit her like the pull of the water, and she wanted nothing more than to be rid of it. She looked again to the boats and reminded herself that because they walked on water, they were free, even if lonely.

Ellen leaned on the porch railing and watched Amos's skiff create waves that curled toward the shore. June was probably with him, getting a test ride, and Ellen wondered if Matty was with her. Ellen almost wished the boat would turn over and dump them in the bay. And then she felt bad and could hear Nora's thin voice telling her that the Lord doesn't listen to a mean girl's prayers. It seemed to be a favorite saying of Nora's lately, and Ellen wondered how mean was mean before He decided to quit listening? It seemed to her that he hadn't been listening for a long time, definitely since the day her mom turned blue.

Over the waves, Ellen heard Nora's slow step and swish of her dress as she approached the Nelson home. Nora stopped at the front of the steps, her mouth half-open, as if she were going to say something or recite a prayer.

"Ellen, Kristen was wondering where you were for breakfast this morning."

"I was watching the boats. You been on one, Nora?"

Nora sat down next to Ellen.

"Yes, we came up here on a large boat, a big steamship."

"You mean like those barges that come to the cannery every year?"

"Yeah, something like that. It was quite a cold ride, even in the spring." The ends of Nora's lips rose slightly. "We need some water. You dad said you both need water too. Get Kristen to help you."

"My mama had a boat. A small one," Ellen said. "I even helped her fish in it. She let me sleep in the bow when I got tired, though.

We picked lots of fish, more fish than you ever saw. Silver to the rim, mama always said."

"Yes, your mom was a busy woman." Nora stared at the boats passing by. "Sometimes too busy for everyone around her."

Ellen wondered what Nora meant, but decided it wasn't important. "You ever seen her skiff? I'm gonna fix it up. Papa is going to buy paint today. White paint. I think that will be a good color for a skiff, don't you?"

What Ellen didn't reveal to Nora was how she convinced John to give her the skiff. She giggled just thinking of it. A few days ago, she had woken with her gut twisting and she knew. A betrayal again. It wasn't her body anymore. It came as a flood. In all the stories she heard Anne Girl talk about her period, a flood wasn't part of the language. Neither were the black blood clots. She would end up like Sweet Mary with sweat hidden between rolls of fat. Or worse, she would become Jill now that she was ruined. The thought terrified her, and Ellen wondered what to say to her father, who was piecing together their new wringer-washer. He was so excited when it arrived on the barge, Ellen worried he was going to fall off the platform as he didn't watch where he was going. It took Amos and his son Phil to help John get the washer home. He hadn't stopped whistling since. She didn't want him to stop.

Ellen stuffed her pants with rags until she was sure she was wearing something of a diaper and then she went to the back porch and stood over her father. She tried forming the question in her mouth but couldn't get it out. Ellen wondered if he knew she was draining between the legs and if he could hear it. It was a flood, and she wondered how long she had before she drowned him in her blood.

"Papa," Ellen said and paused.

John looked up, his blue eyes clear like glacier water. "What?"

Just as Ellen was getting the nerve to talk, the opening and slamming of the front door jarred the house. John's expression changed, and Ellen wondered if he too almost thought Anne Girl was walking in.

"I bring your skinny ass *patek* bones." In came Sweet Mary, lumbering from side to side, her stomach forever swollen since the war. She had many lovers during the war, soldiers and all, but only one soldier meant anything to her. Some said that she would have repopulated the entire village if she hadn't stuffed crumbled yarrow and wormwood inside of her until she bled. Despite the rumors about the soldier who never returned for her after the war, Sweet Mary managed to keep busy. She was on the Village Council, constantly trying to find a balance between the cannery and the village and the missionaries. Sweet Mary carried a bowl that was still steaming. She nodded to Ellen. "I think she's shrunk since Anne Girl died. Time you feed her right. No man is going to want a shrunken woman."

"Or a loud one," John said, and wiped his brow. "Finally, we get one of these." He patted the washer. It was glossy, white porcelain with turquoise trim. A heavy gasoline motor was strapped at the feet.

"And all the village will be at your house to wash their clothes," Sweet Mary said. "Look, I promised I would bring you the best dinner if you stayed in one spot long enough. So here I am. You gonna eat it?"

"We wouldn't miss it," John chuckled. "Let me just finish this up real quick. Ellen, you wanted something?"

"I'll stay too. Can't miss my own goodness," Sweet Mary said. "Even Nancy likes my soups." She went to the kitchen, set the bowl, and commenced rummaging through the cabinet for spoons and bowls.

Ellen waited for Sweet Mary to leave the back porch. "Mama's skiff is stored next to the smokehouse. Can we scrape it and paint again?"

John frowned. "I know you want it, pumpkin, but you aren't quite strong enough yet. I was thinking we would give it to Amos. His son is just right for it."

"Phil?" Ellen gasped. She felt her chest tighten at the thought. There was nothing left of her mom in this village but the skiff. "You can't. It's mine."

"You can't go fish by yourself. That's a strong current," John added. "Too many drownings lately."

"But . . . Phil?" Ellen said. The shock of her dad's suggestion was melting to anger. "No!"

John put a finger to his lips. "We can talk about this later."

Ellen shook her head and left the back room. She went to the kitchen where Sweet Mary was humming to herself as she reheated the soup. She probably heard everything that was said, but she made a fuss that Ellen was suddenly standing by her. She pulled on her braid.

"Creepy," Sweet Mary muttered. "No use scaring a woman like that."

"Tell my Papa I'm going over to Nora's real quick."

Sweet Mary frowned and huffed.

"I know. I'll be back. I just gotta ask Nora something."

Ellen ran out the door, feeling the rags adjust themselves with each step. At that moment she felt anger and longing rising from her chest to her throat. It was an anger that scared her, because she would do anything to have it leave her body. She knew that it was the kind of anger that could rest in her hands until it grew to be too big and she would break something or someone. She inhaled the salty air as she watched seagulls and sand hill cranes tiptoeing along the water's edge as if calling for the tide to turn once more. She made it all the way to the Killweather house and realized that she didn't want to tell Nora she was ruined either. No one needed to know yet.

When she returned home, Ellen thought she constructed the image in her head, but she found them in the back porch, next to the shiny new washer. Sweet Mary stood over her father, brushing her thick fingers through his blond hair. His eyes were closed as he leaned his head her in her sturdy hands. It was a private moment between them, but she felt like she was the one naked with bloodied rags in her crotch. She leaned against the door frame.

"Papa," Ellen said loudly. "Nora thinks we should also paint the skiff white. I told her that you will get us some paint up town on your next trip. "

John jerked his head forward and he reddened so deeply Ellen was positive blood clots were spilling from his eyes. Sweet Mary, however, smiled and grunted, not bothered at all. She removed her fingers from his hair without any rush.

"Yes . . . yes," John said. "White paint is good. Mary, Ellen's going to fix up Anne Girl's skiff."

"Ooh, about time this girl learn how to fish good."

John stood up and his knees creaked. "How about that soup, Mary?"

"It's Sweet Mary."

"Yes, it is. Sweet Mary." John said. "*Patek* bones? I don't think I've had that since Anne Girl."

"I know. You skinny bastards need food."

"And a neck rub," Ellen added. She left them and began thinking of ways to get a cleat. She could probably convince her father to buy her one.

Sweet Mary laughed, and her whole frame jiggled with her.

Nora leaned against Ellen gently. "I've come to see if you want to go berry picking with us today. After you get water, of course."

Ellen hesitated. Normally she would jump at the thought, but she was still bleeding and bears smelled blood. They would be hunted for sure. And then they would die. Ellen didn't like how that story sounded. Yet, she thought about the berries. When she was on the tundra with June and Matty, the salmonberries were still hard like beads, and she wondered if they were ripe now and practically falling off the stems. She would show Nora where the good patches were, the secret places where her mom picked. Anne Girl always took long walks, deep into the tundra, passing pond after pond to where the rolling tundra curved and shaped itself into a landscape of forever green. It was there, on the edge of earth, where the berries grew in thick bundles. And her mama said that if you walk that far, you must never waste and you must pick until your fingers hurt.

"Well," Ellen said slowly.

"Well what? It's a perfect day for berries." Nora waved towards the semi-cloudy sky. "Just enough breeze."

"Well, I am gonna need a cup."

Nora frowned. "A cup?"

"For *naivaa*."

"What's that?"

Throwing up her hands, Ellen exclaimed. "You know. Pour. We got to pour the berries into the bucket. I'll run and get a cup from home."

Nora stared at Ellen. "Why do we need to pour them?"

The question threw Ellen off. She didn't know why really, just that she saw her mom pick with a cup and pour them into the bucket while she muttered *naivaa* from time to time. She thought everyone did that when they picked berries. "I don't know. Just that we do."

"Alright," Nora stood up. "Get your cup and come over. I need to see if Kristen is ready."

By the time Ellen made it to the Killweathers', the familiar sing-song voice of Sweet Mary drifted through the door.

"My, my, you're all prepared for winter! I'll run to your house next time we have a flood. I'll wave to all the cold feet on the bluff and say Nora will keep us warm!"

"*Cama-i* Nora, I was looking for Frederik and was wondering if he had any of them medicines left over from up town."

"I think there might be some left. Who's it for?" Nora set down her berry buckets and moved to the counter, her hands scanning the rows of bottles and pill-boxes.

"Ooh, who isn't ill around here?" Sweet Mary's hands went to her stomach as if she was taking in secret pleasure to make Nora search. "Old Paul has a cough that won't go away and he's too stubborn to do anything about it. So I am going to make him tea." Sweet Mary smiled, showing a row of graying and twisted teeth.

"I see," Nora answered. She tapped on the lid of one red bottle. "I think this one mixes well with tea. Give it a try."

"We're going to have a council meeting once the season slows and the cannery clears out a bit. If you could tell Frederik about it." Sweet

Mary took the bottle from Nora and looked around. Her eyes fell onto the berry buckets. "Going berry picking, huh? Lots of people went up there today, so it should be good."

"You hear that, Ellen? There are lots of berries," Nora said.

Sweet Mary smiled and shook the bottle next to her ear. "Thank you for this, and don't forget to tell Frederik." She turned, tucking the bottle under her armpit, and left with her braid swinging behind her.

Nora, Kristen, and Ellen headed out into the breezy afternoon and toward the bluff, each carrying a berry bucket that rattled against their sides. Ellen walked behind Kristen and Nora so that she could pick flowers along the way. Nora didn't walk with the same urgency that Anne Girl used to, with her arms swinging all over the place, so Ellen had plenty of time to pick the late fireweeds and tear off the petals one by one. She grabbed a long fireweed stalk. Its base was bright purple, but stems near the top were still just buds, meaning that there was just a little bit of summer left. Ellen pulled off the purple petals until she had a long, grassy whip. She waved it over her head, and then shot it like an arrow into the grasses.

Before the path curved over to the bluff side, they passed Jill's father, Jerry Wescoat, staggering toward the cannery. His eyes were clouded over in a mist of alcohol, and he gave a cock-eyed grin. "Mrs. Killweather. I hear you . . . I hear you." he paused and swallowed. "Mrs. Killweather! Thank you for telling Jill she needs to go to Mt. Edgecumb."

Nora stepped to the side of the path and signaled for the girls to do the same. "Hello, Jerry."

Jerry approached Nora and lightly gripped her arm, his fingers still stained with scales and dirt. He breathed heavily into her face as he tried to speak. "Thank you for helping that Jill. I told her that she was lucky. I told her . . ."

Without raising her voice, Nora unglued Jerry's grip on her shoulder. "Yes, of course." She tried to step around Jerry and pull free, but the path was uneven and she ended up leaning forward so that his chin touched her forehead. She raised her bucket in the air. "We're going berry picking. If you could just let us get by, we can be on our way."

"Yeah, yeah. Penni went today too." Jerry blinked several times as if that would help him keep upright on his feet. "I'm going for my own berries today." He laughed.

"We'll see you on Sunday then?"

"Always Sunday. Mrs. Killweather, you beautiful soul you." He staggered down the trail, humming off key to "Glory to His Name."

Nora turned to Kristen and Ellen. "And they wonder why Jill does what she does. It doesn't surprise me. Not in the least bit, and thank the Heavens you both know better." Nora fixed her jacket and straightened her skirt by repeatedly smoothing it out. "I wonder if we'll even make it to the berries today."

"He's going to the cannery like that?" Ellen asked.

"Apparently," Kristen answered. "I bet he'll pass out before he gets there, though. I've seen him asleep on the beach before."

Nora began to walk with an uneven but quicker pace. "Now you two stay close. There's too much money in the bay right now."

As the trail exchanged the high grasses for the lichen and moss of the tundra, Ellen's earlier enthusiasm drifted. She soon learned that berry picking to Nora meant berry picking and no running and playing in the gentle mounds. Every time Ellen followed a patch over and down a hill, Nora would call her back and tell her that there were plenty of salmonberries and blueberries where she stood. Nora didn't seem to understand that berry picking meant following berries from one side of the tundra to another, not standing in place like a panicked ptarmigan.

Ellen sat down in the carpet of berries and dropped a couple of salmonberries into her cup. And then she ate a couple, and everything seemed alright, and she could breathe once more. She entered a space where it was only her and the berries, their sweet flavor poking out from the wet ground. She wanted to pick them all, every single one of them, like she had seen her Mama do. She looked around, feeling the cool breeze on her skin, and saw a few women wandering in the distance. Their bodies bent over like elbows, Ellen wondered when it would be her turn. She imagined herself growing up, wearing a *qaspeq* with a large pocket in the front where she could store her cup and pieces of smoked fish. She squinted and stretched her eyesight to the curve of the earth.

"No bears yet, not yet," she muttered.

Kristen came over, her cheeks ruddy, her bucket half-full, and sat down next to Ellen. "How much do you have?" She leaned over and peered into Ellen's bucket. The bottom was barely covered. "You've been eating a lot. I knew you would. You nearly ate all of them."

"A little," Ellen answered. The truth was that she didn't want to fill up her bucket, didn't want it to be heavy with berries.

At that moment, Nora lumbered over the slope and kneeled beside Kristen. Despite the coolness, a thin line of sweat had collected on her forehead. "You girls hungry? We can take a little break."

While Nora pulled out crackers and sandwiches, Ellen leaned over and poked her head into Nora's bucket. Also half-full. The top layer of salmonberries were sprinkled with blueberries that reminded Ellen of salmon eggs. Littered inside the bucket were bits of tundra, small leaves, and twigs that hadn't escaped Nora's careful eye.

Ellen dipped her cup into the bucket until it was full of berries. "Nora, *naivaa*." She poured the berries back into the bucket. They fell in hard, but the breeze took hold of the leaves and twigs and scattered them back into the tundra. "See, that's *naivaa*."

Nora looked up from her preparations and saw how quickly the leaves fell away from the syrupy berries. "*Naivaa*—I see now. That's how you clean them. If I had known that earlier . . ."

"How do *you* clean them then?"

"We spread it out on a pan over the stove, so the ones that aren't yet ripe will separate." Nora handed out crackers to both girls. "See where I grew up, we only picked blueberries. We didn't have these messy salmonberries. And we didn't have to pick all day either." She gazed at the horizon, and took a deep breath as if seeing the treeless land for the first time. "We got lost one time. This was before I was married to your father."

"Who's we?" Kristen asked.

"This young gentlemen who attended the same summer retreat," Nora said, but looked neither at Ellen nor Kristen. "We had made a bet to see who could fill up their bucket first. I won, of course, but we had definitely wandered deep into the woods. Only then did we realize that it was too dark to find our way back to the campsite."

Taking small bites of her crackers, Ellen waited for Nora to continue. She imagined a thinner Nora getting lost in the woods. Maybe her long skirt got snagged on the limbs, like Ellen's clothes always did. Nora still missed her home, wherever that was, Ellen decided.

"How did you get back?" Ellen asked.

Nora picked at some lichen. "We waited out the night and ate blueberries."

"You've never mentioned this one before," Kristen finally said. "Who was this guy, and how old were you?"

Ellen couldn't be sure if it was the snap of wood or the sudden rustle of leaves that caught her attention.

"You hear that?" Ellen asked, and rocked onto her knees. Her skin felt suddenly cold, and she pointed to a clump of alder brushes near the next hill.

"Hear what?" Nora frowned. "That's just the wind."

Ellen strained to hear and thought she could make out a low grumble.

Fear found Kristen, and she stared at Ellen with wide eyes. You would have thought she had never seen a bear before.

"Bear," Ellen whispered.

Nora stretched her neck. "Nonsense. I don't hear anything."

Ellen quickly shook her head, and she thought about the damp rags between her legs. They weren't going to listen to her. She gazed above for circling seagulls, but the sky was empty.

"We have to go."

"Ellen, you are overreacting."

"Please," Ellen pleaded. She blinked to fight the tears. Everyone would know once that bear charged her, straight for her crotch, that she was the reason they were caught in the mess.

All three heard the movement of leaves from the brush, but not before Nora sighed exasperatingly. The alder brushes moved and swayed, and Nora reached for Kristen and Ellen, gripping their shoulders tightly.

"Don't move," Nora whispered.

A long muzzle emerged from the green until two black eyes stared at them as they chewed. Long legs with knobby knees and thick matted fur took a step forward. It chewed slowly and returned to the brushes.

Nora burst out laughing. "A moose, my, my." She patted her chest. "You almost had us scurry from a moose!"

Kristen sighed, and color slowly found its way back to her cheeks. She glanced at Ellen with blue eyes as a smile formed on her lips.

"I don't see what's so funny." Ellen scowled. "That was a bear."

Twenty-Two

Toward the end of summer, Ellen began spending most of her days at the skiff. Her father gave her the bucket of paint he had promised with a brush and didn't mention a word about Sweet Mary. As soon as her father took off or sauntered over to Frederik's for a cup of coffee, she wandered down the beach toward the skiff—her skiff. Often she saw boats bucking the tides and would think, "That's going to be me."

She began with the inside of the hull, scraping the ribs first before moving to the sides. The old flecks of paint came off easily and caught in her face and hair. And then she moved to the side walls of the skiff and carefully watched as the gray wood exposed itself. She was on such a roll that she didn't see her mom until the gull hopped twice on the bow. Ellen jumped back and swore under her breath.

"You think you can get this done before the cannery shuts down?" The seagull tipped its head and peered at Ellen with one eye.

"Mama, where've you been?" Ellen sat down and wiped the dust from her face. Her skin felt gritty. "How come you come now?"

"Down the beach. The cannery has good bits here and there. What you been doing at the cannery? The beach women are cheap with their heads."

Ellen shrugged. "Looking for that cleat."

The seagull flapped her wings and small feathers floated around them. "That cleat," she squawked. "That cleat is still in the boat graveyard. I shat on it."

Ellen wished the bird would leave. "Aren't you hungry or something? *Ampi.*"

Ellen couldn't tell whether the gull was laughing or wailing, but the screeching penetrated her ears. Her mom hopped and flapped her wings. "Good idea. The cannery is dumping some guts right now." And she took off.

On the outside of the skiff, Ellen began with the stern and worked her way forward. She scraped paint, occasionally pausing to feel the wood beneath her fingers. It had been a long time since she felt this close to her mother. This year she didn't make strips with her mom, so she and her Papa would be out. But she had the skiff, and that almost set things right.

Anne Girl visited often. Sometimes she didn't make a sound, just swooped and dived above before allowing the wind off the bluff to push her higher into the sky. Other times, especially when she was painting, she perched too close and Ellen shooed her away, not without getting bird shit dripping off the rails in return, though.

"Have you gotten your red roses?" the seagull squawked. "Never been this stuffed in my life."

Ellen colored. She wasn't going to respond. Her mom didn't need more reasons to tell the entire beach of seagulls about her blood cycle. She could hear them now, announcing it to and from Ekuk.

"Ah, you do then, huh?"

Ellen didn't answer as she dipped the brush in paint and slapped a glob of white at the base. She felt the brush fill in the grains of the wood, as her hand went from right to left. Right to left.

The seagull hopped down the rail and stood over Ellen. Her sharp beak pointed toward Ellen. Sometimes she was so close, the smell of rotten fish hung in the air, and Ellen tried not to gag. "Easy, you don't want to waste paint. Spread it so it dries even too."

As the gull took off, she circled above Ellen and the skiff. The gull's wail was shrill despite her height. "You're ruined now, so use lots of rags and keep them clean in case of bears."

"Who you talking to?" June came out of the shadows of the old smokehouse.

"Ah, just myself," Ellen answered.

June walked around the skiff and surveyed the work, taking on the same posture as her mother. June's eyes were wide. "You did this?"

Ellen nodded and continued to paint. She wished her hair was like June's—straight, instead of frayed rope. Ellen figured Alicia must have shown June how to fix her hair.

"No one helped you?"

"Just scraped and painting now. It needs fixing here and there." Ellen pointed to the stern, yet she felt a surge of warmth flow through her chest. Pride? "It's missing a wooden plug."

June smiled. "Can't wait till we can take it out!"

"Yeah, me, you, and Matty," Ellen said. She dipped her brush in the paint bucket. She wasn't sure she wanted to take Matty out in it first. The first time she wanted it to be with Nora. The seagull came to mind. Hovering. What would she have to do about the seagull? "Oh, no."

"What?"

"Oh, that seagull will want a ride too."

Did she really say that? Ellen was fairly certain the words came out of her mouth by the way June frowned at her with her eyebrows pinched together. So tight. Ellen didn't know eyebrows could squeeze that tightly.

"*Akleng*, you."

Twenty-Three

One afternoon, when Bible school closed for the day, June and Matty snuck through the back door and found Ellen arranging the Bibles on the benches. Both girls had wild grins on their faces as if they were dying to burst out laughing. Their round cheeks were seal gut balloons waiting to be popped.

"Oh my God, you got to come to the cannery," June yelled.

Ellen put her hands to her lips. "Shush, Nora will hear you. Where you been? I thought you were coming to Bible School today."

"At the fucking cannery!"

Matty took one of the Bibles and thumped it against the bench. "Sweet Mary is at the dock—naked!"

"Nah, you're fooling."

June crossed herself like a Russian Orthodox. "Swear to God. She's singing. She's never sung before like that in church." June doubled over.

Nora poked her head around the corner. The worry lines drifted off her face for a brief second. "There you are, young ladies. We missed seeing you this afternoon."

June dropped her hands and stared at Nora. "I had to help out my mom this morning."

Matty smiled. "Me too, Nora."

"Come by tomorrow, if you like." Nora lifted her eyebrows. "I'm not going to interrupt you. I just came in here to get some more paper. Ellen, Kristen, and I will be at Nancy's and then Penni's this afternoon. Watch the stove. We'll have soup tonight when your dad gets home. How does that sound?"

"Good." Ellen stood, leaning on a bench, holding a stack of Bibles against her chest. She smelled the beach in the covers and not the holy smell that Frederik claimed the books had. He claimed that all one had to do was drink in the words of the Lord and his path would straighten out, but her path always seemed to curve right to the cannery or left to the bluff. Hardly a straight path.

Matty punched Ellen on the shoulder. "What you waiting for?"

"For them to go," Ellen hissed. "Help me set these back on the benches."

Five minutes seemed like hours with June and Matty pacing around her. They kept giggling and telling Ellen how she couldn't miss it. Ellen wondered if Sweet Mary had found her old lost G.I. from the war and followed him to the docks.

She heard the front door open and close softly. First Nora's heavy steps swished down the porch steps, then Kristen's lighter ones, and then silence. All three girls exhaled.

"Come on." June grabbed Ellen's hand and pulled her out the door.

Before they had even reached the main section of the cannery, Ellen heard Sweet Mary. Her voice rose above the grinding generators in a high-pitched shrill that lifted and fell like the cry of seagulls. It was circular, her voice, painted around and between the cannery buildings, as if searching for something that was lost years ago. Ellen listened but couldn't recognize the tune.

Sweet Mary sat in a grounded skiff that was still tied to the dock pier. She waved her arms to the men standing above on the dock. Her brown skin seemed unreal against the grayness of wooden piers. Her thick *aamaqs* hung low nearly down to her belly button and swayed in tune with her moving arms. Her underarms were pale as though they had never seen daylight before. Then Sweet Mary stood up, her voice rising with her. All that flesh folded over on itself, rolled itself into pockets of dough. Her black patch of hair was hardly visible because her stomach sagged low to her thighs.

The men on the dock stood in hip boots pulled down to their knees, gloves in their back pockets. They chewed snuff and spit it over the side, and they laughed. Even the seagulls found piers and roof ridges to perch on, and stared at her with open beaks, ignoring the leftover fish being pumped out of the gutting room.

The girls found a sawed-off pier and scooted close together. The cannery men had gathered around them. Some were murmuring about how it seemed that all the villagers were drunk now that fishing was nearing an end for the summer. "They can't hold their liquor, these Eskimos," some said. "No wonder, they're lazy," others said.

Ellen realized that it wasn't a song coming from Sweet Mary, but cries that seemed to grow deeper and louder. And to think Sweet Mary was just at her house a few weeks ago with marrow soup.

June and Matty laughed and Ellen shuddered. She wondered why no one was doing anything. Where was the superintendent now? The men on the dock just stood there, shifting from one foot to another, licking their lips.

"And she's on the council!" June exclaimed.

"Why doesn't she get out of the skiff and go to the bathhouse?" Ellen asked.

Matty shrugged and stared. "Came back from town and must have just woken up. Too bad your mom's not there to sing too." Matty elbowed Ellen.

"What would you know, Matty? Your mama only comes to church because it's on the way to the cannery," Ellen said, and clenched her fists. "We all know it. As soon as the service is done, she runs out the door!"

"You guys are mean," June said.

"Everyone knows that your mom liked to sing with all the men at the cannery. She had many." Matty counted on her fingers.

"Your mom sang louder than Sweet Mary down there," Ellen said, and she motioned to Sweet Mary. "You'll be like that too soon. I'll come watch. Maybe clap too."

"If only," Matty said. "I will need more booze than Sweet Mary guzzled to sit like that with my *aamaqs* down to my knees. She probably steps on them."

Matty giggled. Ellen felt the sides of her lips curl, and she saw June doing the same despite herself.

"No, she rolls them up first. You know, like if she was making bread," Ellen said, and motioned with her hands.

Matty punched Ellen on the shoulder, laughing. And then they saw Sweet Mary again, this time doubled over, her chin touching her knees as she retched. The curve of her backside reminded Ellen of a seal, large and fleshy. Her long braid swayed in front of her, catching bits of juice as it waved back and forth.

"Why doesn't she put on her clothes?" Ellen asked.

"Maybe she doesn't want to. She's hollering for one of the men to come for her. I wonder which one," June said.

"Maybe there's more than one," Ellen said.

A cannery worker exited the store and walked by the girls. Ellen held her breath. She recognized him by the length of the vein that traced down his forehead. His expression was shaded with grease and dirt. As he walked by them, he grinned, and the vein bulged like a worm in the morning. Bits of snuff were caught between his teeth. "You girls going to be like that when you grow up?" He laughed.

He was beginning to walk on, carrying his can of snuff, when his eyes caught Ellen's, and she looked away. "I remember you. Where'd you go last time?" He spat. "You girls want to see how the cannery works? Want to see how fish are steamed shut into the cans?"

Matty leaned against the wooden stump. She matched his stare and bit her lower lip as if contemplating a response that didn't seem too childish. "What you think? We never found your mom's cleat anyway." She looked at June and Ellen.

June's eyes grew large and her cheeks reddened into apples. "*Caa una!* What are you thinking? With him?"

"Nah, we can go another time," Ellen said. "I'll find another one."

The cannery man stood heavily on one leg and spat a string of brown juice as he waited. He seemed to have all the time in the world as he stood.

"Come on! We've never seen the insides of the cannery before," Matty said. "There's the net loft, mechanic's shop, carpenter's shop . . . all kinds of places to see, not just the fish."

Ellen kept her eyes locked on the man, although she was thinking about how it would be a perfect time to get the cleat. "You go ahead, Matty, and we'll meet you later."

"I don't need your permission." Matty huffed. "Geez, both of you bums! Fine, I'll go but I'm not telling you about it. You'll have to see for yourselves. He'll probably let me go inside the old boats too! I'll write my name on them." She stood up and dusted her knees off.

Matty shot Ellen and June a look and followed the man. Ellen watched Matty walk away with her head high, her arms swinging at her sides. She seemed to have grown over the short distance between them and the docks. It was then Ellen noticed that Sweet Mary's low wail had become silent in the thick hum of the cannery generators.

When the cannery man and Matty rounded the corner into a narrow alley between the Filipino bunkhouse and the machine shop, Ellen and June caught each other's eyes and broke into a run toward the alley. They rounded the corner, panting but determined not to let Matty have all the fun.

The machine shop window was broken in the top corner and a glass piece in the shape of a red salmon fin was missing, so they could hear the sounds of metal cutting over the man's raspy voice. You'll like it, just don't know it yet, he told her. He warned her of biting, telling her that the cannery was big with many rooms that no one *ever* goes into.

Ellen and June stood on the lip of the wall to peer over the window ledge. The machine shop was dark inside with metal glistening from grease and sharpened edges. It was difficult to see past the outside light, but the worker stood with his legs apart—his head bent down, looking down toward his catch. His hands held Matty's head, her black hair messy between his greasy fingers, pulling her head toward his pelvis. Matty was gagging, clutching his jeans. He pulled up her shirt, showing her brown, smooth skin. "Isn't this nice," he said. "Isn't this nice." He moaned.

Ellen dropped down to the ground. Her stomach felt funny, and sweat tickled her neck and crotch. Isn't this nice, she heard again.

June pulled herself away from the ledge, her face white like October snow. "Let's go to the store. I'm hungry."

"No," Ellen pulled on June's arm. "No, let's go to the boat graveyard. I know a quick way."

The noise continued to radiate from the window. June pulled Ellen up. "Okay." She breathed. "Okay."

Memory was a funny thing. The alleys and corridors of the cannery came together against all the noise, and Ellen found the Chinamen graveyard and then the shape of boats, rising from the grasses likes a flood of the past came into view. It was just like how Ellen remembered, and she mentioned that.

"When were you here last?"

"Oh, never mind that. Com'on!"

It was an area of the cannery where the boardwalk ended and the edge of the sandy and grass continued. Driftwood was scattered between each boat as the fall tides had no problems reaching this side of the village.

The girls separated and peered into the boats of the old-timers. Most of the boats had nothing left in them, except old coffee mugs, tools, and other fishing items, like a bucket of corks and some web from old nets. Ellen picked up a rusty blade curved in a shape similar to a banana that ended into a sharp point. The handle was smooth and worn, with the end carved into a fish tail. Lines were cut into the tail, making the texture of the fin seem real.

Ellen heaved herself over the side of the NN42. Inside the boat, she was shocked to find that most of the hull had rotted out. The ribs that had once maintained the body's shape were twisted and splintered. Blue flecks of paint had peeled off and scattered along bottom surface.

"What you see in there?" June hollered.

Careful not to step on a nail, she catwalked along the boards to the cabin in the bow. Unlike the body, the cabin seemed untouched. The weather had not yet made her mark on the wood.

"Nothing really," Ellen muttered, as she catwalked along the hull. "Look for a good cleat. One with bird shit on it."

"Ew."

"That's what I said," Ellen hopped over a row of broken boards with their nails still pointing upwards. Her stomach continued to do flip-flops, and she took a deep breath to steady herself.

"We should go back, huh?" June asked. She had crawled over the side of another wooden boat, an old double ender with its mast entrenched into the ground. Sweat glistened on her brow from the effort, although she stared at Ellen, expecting an answer.

Ellen felt her throat tighten on its own. She didn't want to return to the machine shop or run into the man again. Matty was okay, or else why did she run off with him anyway?

"Let me see this one boat, and then Matty," Ellen said. She jumped off the boat and climbed into another where the entire bottom had dry rotted. Only the sides and bow remained, which gave the feeling that the ground was swallowing it whole.

"I found it!" June hollered. She stood and kicked at it. "You want a cleat, yeah?"

Ellen ran to the vessel that June stood on. She stood on her toes and peered over the side. There, fused into the wood, was the cleat—galvanized steel with little rust and bird poop on it.

"Holy shit! That's it."

They tugged at it, but the bolts were sealed in place from the marriage between salt and rust. In fact, there was no evidence that they were getting anywhere.

June groaned. "It's not coming off. It didn't come off for your mom, you know."

"Yeah," Ellen said quietly. She rested her forehead on the wood, suddenly aware of how her arms ached. "It's stuck like mud. Com'on."

Twenty-Four

I thought this skiff was going to save me. This is the second time I'm wrong. And so here we sit. You know, I don't want you in my life. And again, here we sit.

When the village learned about Sweet Mary being anchored to the dock piling with nothing but a pair of rubber boots on, it responded with its usual rumors that crawled up and down the bluff side. Some laughed, saying that Sweet Mary was holding onto her ways like it was still war time. They wondered if she still practiced the blackouts, closing her blinds every night and waiting for her soldier to return to her bed. Others clicked their tongues and said they'd be glad when fishing was over and the village would become quiet again. Caribou season was just around the corner, and once the men brought home some meat, people wouldn't have to worry about making runs to Dillingham to spend all their money.

"You're a godsend!" Penni exclaimed when she opened the door to Ellen and Kristen. Age never hid itself on Penni's face, even when her eyes were glassy and her skin smooth from the booze. With the purple marks under her eyes and creases around her lips where her teeth once were, she always appeared as if she were one step from falling on herself. The circles under her eyes seemed only to have deepened since Jill's belly stretched like a seal gut balloon. Although in public the villagers asked about the coming baby, they avoided the Wescoats since Penni announced she was going to be a Nan during a *maqi* at Alicia's. And that was the reason why Jill didn't make it to the boarding school that fall. They spoke in the *maqis* about Jill and how she needed to sew her legs up now. Or they wondered out loud, over the splash of water, how large Jill's *aamaqs* were getting. Tell her to walk through the doors fast now, they said to one another, or maybe she'll get pregnant again as soon as this one pops out. And although they laughed between steams, the villagers avoided the Wescoats even during the rare times Jerry and Penni managed to make it to the church. Even Ellen avoided the path that went by the Wescoats, because it reminded her of Matty and the man with the vein. But Kristen was the only one who didn't care, and she made weekly trips to check in with Jill.

Jill never complained, but it was clear that she was drained. Once Ellen mistook her for Penni and asked her if Jill felt like seeing Kristen. Jill didn't even crack a smile, but through tight lips responded that *she* would like that very much.

"Hi, girls," Penni said, and she eyed Ellen carefully. "You not going to Bethel, Ellen? I couldn't hack the place either. I got cousins that way, real dark ones. Different kind over there in Bethel and in the flatlands. They run out of food in the spring, before seals come and go crazy."

Her tongue lingered on Bethel, and Ellen could smell the alcohol wrapped around the *th* and *l*. It was too bitter for the beer from up town, and Ellen wondered if Penni made it herself. Or maybe she got some from Sweet Mary, who was probably still on a binge.

"Is it okay if we come in?" Kristen said carefully. And she reached out and touched Penni's arm.

Ellen looked on and noticed how Kristen had emerged from a façade she wore around Nora. She had a natural touch with people, and Ellen wondered what she was supposed to do. Penni was drunk. One more drink and she would be on the floor.

"Jill here?" Kristen asked, and nudged Ellen.

"That little whore," Penni hissed. "She sleeps and sleeps. Go wake her up. Tell her that she has company." Penni pointed to the doorway that was covered with a blanket.

Despite what her mother had said, Jill was not sleeping. She was sitting on the edge of her bed with her shirt off with her teeth pulling at her left nipple. She looked up when Kristen and Ellen entered and left a round wet mark over the purple skin. Ellen couldn't help but stare at the size. Like a beluga's belly, her breasts were swollen and stretched to the limit. Ellen wondered if Jill was crazy.

"You need to get out more," Kristen said when Jill's eyes met hers.

Just then Penni pulled on Ellen's arm. "Go get water from the beach, will you? It will be good and salty right now. *Aamaqs* need fresh air. They are going to be worse when your pup comes."

"Mom might know what to do," Kristen said.

Penni waved the response way. "Nah, we don't need everyone to know. We'll just cook up some saltwater. It will help the pain."

"You're going to boil her *amaaq*? How much you drink already?" Ellen asked.

Penni winked unsteadily and pushed Ellen out the door. "Just maybe yet we might boil them; now get out of here and get me some water."

Outside, Ellen ran toward the beach, soaking in cold air that smelled of a coming storm. The moisture hung in crystals, and Ellen breathed deeply. She detoured toward her mama's old smokehouse, where the white skiff lay in the grasses. The smokehouse leaned toward the bay even more so than before, as if the current was pulling on it. She approached the building, smelling both the mixture of smoke and wet earth. How comfortable it felt to be here again, she thought. And that's when she noticed the skiff.

Ellen blinked. The little people were playing tricks. The cleat she and June left at the boat graveyard was securely fastened at the bow as if it had always been there. And then at once her eyes cleared. Along the length of the skiff gashes were chipped into the wood. *Whore* was carved near the bow, perfectly straight as if it was the name of the vessel. Ellen traced the letters with her fingers, and splinters stabbed at her where the letters went against the grain of the wood.

"I saw you coming down this way," Matty said, as she walked around the corner of the smokehouse, waving a cigarette in the air as if it were a wand. Matty frowned and sat on the edge of the skiff, letting her legs swing. She jutted out her chin in the direction of the village. "They got an early start tonight. I have to wait until Mom quits being funny, and then I can go back home."

An early start meant someone brought alcohol back from Dillingham, and they were shoving it down their throats like berries. Everyone knew that Matty's mom only got nicer the more she drank. But there was always the time in between, when she lashed out against anyone who was within an arm's distance. Matty called it the funny time.

Ellen had hardly seen Matty since the ground froze up. She didn't come to the chapel or the Girl's Club any longer, and even though Nora urged her to come to school, Matty rarely left her house. Ellen saw her once up on the tundra, picking cranberries. Her long, black hair was loose that day and reminded Ellen of the old sailboats' sails whipping in the wind. Today, Matty's hair was short, sheared unevenly around her face, making her eyes seem big like they were hungry for light or food.

She was dressed in a thin shirt and shoes not made for the winter. She threw the cigarette in the grasses and looked at Ellen, blowing smoke in her direction.

"The skiff's name was from me. Phil and June," Matty nodded toward the bow, "did the cleat."

Ellen dropped the bucket and fell to her knees. The rush of earth hit her nostrils and she tried not to cry. "At the same time?"

Matty's laugh was high pitched. "No, I finished up after they left. You like? I think it's good for you."

"Why you do that?"

"How did he know you?" Matty's eyes narrowed.

A rush of noise entered Ellen's ears. Matty knew something about the secret she tried to pretend didn't happen.

"He said you . . ." Matty paused. She scratched her face, creating two red lines down her cheeks like stained cranberry juice.

"What?" Ellen sucked in air and felt it rush coldly into her chest. She twisted her knuckles until they burned. "What he say?"

Matty dipped into her shirt pocket and pulled out a matchbook. She lit one match and traced its flame in air. Her wrist moved, making a fan of her hand. Ellen saw then an older Matty, with age lines circling her mouth, and her eyes sunken in from too much drink. The tips of her fingers were rough and dry from putting up fish and berries. Ellen blinked.

"Nothing. Maybe it should have been you in the machine shop."

Ellen saw Matty walking down the alleys of the cannery, smelling like the mixture of fish slime and oil, as she looked for June and Ellen. Smells stick with you, and Ellen wondered if it followed Matty around—over the tundra and in the *maqi*. Did the smell of the cannery worker's crotch still linger in her nostrils? Heat swept through Ellen, and she felt her skin burn as she realized she felt simultaneously relieved for herself and sad for Matty. She pulled a thick stalk of grass and chewed on its root.

Matty extinguished the flame. "Yeah, it should have been you." She tapped the wood with the heel of her foot. "You can't take this out anyway without a motor. You think you were going to row?" She tossed the match into the grasses and walked away.

Twenty-Five

Our kicker is shot. I said that already, I know. I know. Shit. No, no, I'm not surprised, but I was hoping. You laugh. How about laughing when you learn that it's keeping our stern anchored tight. I'm short on ideas, minus that oar. And that damn cleat. Yeah, I kept the cleat. So when the time comes to jump ship, I'm taking the cleat.

The water is rising, and quickly too. Now it's coming to take us. Until now it has been easy not to think of you, easier than I thought. But the tundra air can wipe away memories or any aches in your head. I went to look for berries. I don't think they are going to be much this year. All day here. I wouldn't have said anything if Matty didn't guess. She guessed right, though, which is odd because it was a lucky guess. And that's the truth. She just wanted everyone to see my shame. My mama would have said I have no shame. Maybe Nora would agree. But does it matter now? They didn't see the changes in this village that make you want to tread circles. Mama just saw fish and Nora just saw pages of the Bible, specifically Luke. That was her favorite. They didn't see. See what? How we are stuck here, even when money flows through our fingertips in the summer. You'll see soon, with all of your eyes. Or . . . my head hurts.

The year Alaska made its bid for statehood, Ellen found herself boat-hopping at the docks with June and Matty. Ellen was seventeen and hungry—hungry for money, for fishermen, and a ticket out of the village. She could no longer stand to see her father, lying on the couch, waiting for Sweet Mary to make him feel better. Ever since he rolled his plane and Sweet Mary nursed him back to the world, he rarely left her side.

Ellen was with the women when John's plane did a cartwheel down the snowy beach in January. Some said that they saw the propeller dive then flash into the air with the rudder and tail following it. Others, who only admitted this during the few moments before chapel, claimed that the plane, with its silver-winged tips, twisted like a top on its wings before falling belly up. But Ellen didn't listen to their stories that they intertwined in the air. She heard the rivets rupture at the seams and then a thunderous crash fall around her. She would remember that day as being a cold one, where the winter sun was far in the horizon and the sky was blue. And she would remember Nancy's hand instantly coming down over her eyes, so that she could only see black and breathe in the caribou marrow from their lunch.

"John's home," Ellen announced. "He missed the runway again. He missed it again, dammit." The words just seemed to come out on their own.

"Shame on you," Nancy said. Yet she didn't move her hand, even after the scream of metal changed to the sound of wood snapping. Bones cracking.

"Jesus Christ, it's still moving down the beach!" Sweet Mary yelled. She grabbed her parka and ran out the door, her thighs moving from side to side.

What Ellen would remember was how chaos traveled slowly toward the bluff side of the village. How everyone in the kitchen dropped their pots or food and ran to the door, leaving the caribou burning on the stove and water boiling over. How her legs acted as if they were asleep no matter how hard she tried to get them to move. What she would remember of her father's first and only crash was the stories she pieced together from those who found him in the wreckage. And she would come to know those stories as if she herself made it to the plane to see where it laid on its side in a crunched up ball.

Despite Sweet Mary's heftiness, she was the first one to the plane, which hissed and steamed in the snow. It was difficult to tell which part of the plane was the cockpit and which was the tail. Sweet Mary yelled John's name, but when there wasn't any answer, she kicked at the metal pieces, moving them away from the chunk of metal. By that time, the entire village was on the beach, yelling and prying at the twisted pieces. A trail of letters was scattered around the plane as if dumped from the sky, and they found a coffee cup still intact with a coffee stain line along the rim. But they didn't find John, and someone wondered aloud if he jumped.

"Jump? That man couldn't even find the ground if he jumped," Sweet Mary yelled. "He was better off in the plane. We'll find his stick legs just yet."

Nervous laughter rippled through the site, and everyone commented that they knew this was coming sometime, that thank God or hell fishing is over. No one would care when the run was hitting the bay.

It was then that both Sweet Mary and Amos simultaneously spotted the blond, thinning hair of John's. Splashes of blood cut through the ice and snow, forming puddles around his head. He groaned under the weight of his cockpit chair, as they pulled off the broken glass and instruments.

"Look what you did to yourself," Sweet Mary said. "Jesus Christ, we been telling you about landing on the beach." She bent down and pulled off airplane metal with the strength of half the men in the village. The only sign that she was straining was the steam of sweat radiating off of her neck.

"Holy hell," Frederik said, and froze when he saw John's battered face. Pieces of glass stuck in John's cheeks and a streak of blood ran from his ear to his chin. "Holy hell," he said again.

"My legs," John whispered. He groaned again.

Amos nodded but didn't say anything. They worked to cover John and his legs that bent in four places like a polyline. Phil brought his sled dogs, and they lifted John, who screamed louder than a fallen moose. They positioned him as flatly as they could onto the sled although he continued to scream, which one day Sweet Mary would compare to a young girl's voice—a "girl child," she would say.

All this Ellen pieced from the stories that Nancy and Alicia told her over tea. She had no other choice but to listen, because if she hadn't slyly saddled herself next to them, she wouldn't have remembered anything about that day.

Since the plane crash and Sweet Mary's tedious work to put John together, Ellen couldn't separate herself far enough from them both. It wasn't his laziness that drove her crazy, but his patience for Sweet Mary's flesh. He was persistent, carefully limping around the house, messing it here and there, and planning for the woman's arrival. It was like a routine between them, a bizarre dance that she didn't get. During the day, he would sprinkle sugar on his oatmeal and take bite after bite, and then leave the bowl at the edge of the table. His clothes—he left them by the door, stained in a crumpled pile. And then to Ellen's embarrassment, he hobbled on his good leg to the couch and waited. Worse than a magpie begging for leftovers, he was. He watched the door, and when Sweet Mary entered, bringing the salt of Nushagak Bay with her, he acted surprised. But Ellen couldn't blame him entirely; Sweet Mary played her part just as well, if not better. She always lumbered in loudly, exclaiming how her feet were sore. She scolded John, and told him that he should know better by now. But when she approached the couch, she always leaned over and kissed him while her hand ran down his thigh. It made Ellen want to gag.

Despite John's discouragement, Ellen worked part-time in the cannery store. She was curious about boats as much as she was curious about men. She wondered how long it took for the wood to become swollen to keep a boat afloat. All kinds of boats, she loved. She felt their wooden spines beneath her feet when she walked on them and could feel how they took on the waves, whether gliding through swells or if they allowed water to fly over the bow. Boats, skiffs, and dinghies not only unlocked the secrets of the bay, they were home for Ellen. People can leave their troubles on the water. Boats. She had one.

A skiff. Her chest tightened when she thought about taking it out. She could still feel the wood biting her skin at the tip of the W. She and Matty never spoke of that afternoon again, but it seemed that it was always between them. Matty was waiting for the right time, Ellen figured.

When most of the fishing vessels were lined up on the dock, she counted all of them to Phil's boat—the old bow picker that rocked twice as much as the other boats. After the nine o'clock coffee break bell sounded, Ellen closed the store and walked to the dock. She scanned the boats tied to the wooden piers. A seagull perched on one and cocked its head to the side so Ellen could see the profile of its sharp curve. Dammit. What was *she* doing here?

"Sweet Mary would be jealous of you getting all the eyeballs," Ellen muttered. Who was docked up today, she wondered.

"Sweet Mary's fat," the bird chirped.

"You're not too skinny either."

The seagull flapped its wings and jumped to flight. Ellen watched her for a moment as she circled the edge of the dock in smooth glides until she landed next to the screeching gulls fighting for the processed fish waste.

Her attention returned to the docked boats. There were good days—days where the boats were lined around the dock, jostling against each other for space. The sound of buoys rubbing against each other and the clanking of the flag pole at the dock was a good day. Fishermen lingering in the carpenter's shop and the net loft was a good day. She had her pick. Fishing days were a little bitterer, and although Ellen was busy stocking the shelves with food and gloves and canned goods, there was less for her outside the store when everyone was fishing.

Today, though, was a good day. The fishermen were rearing to go, waiting for the sign from Fish and Game that they could pull up their anchors and cruise to the mouth of the bay. Anticipation and impatience lurked in the air, making Ellen's skin tingle. Phil's boat was three boats out, right next to the *APA 41*—a wooden log that made everyone wonder how it managed to float. Phil and Amos's boat was called the *APA 39.* Most of the boats were owned by the cannery, the Alaska Packer's Association, but the fishermen called the wooden vessels their own anyway.

Ellen climbed down the ladder and stepped onto the first boat, feeling it shift under her weight. A fisherman with scales stuck to his face emerged from the cabin and waved at Ellen. She nodded and jumped over the bins to the next boat. When she reached the *APA 41*, Cooper Harland's head jerked up.

"Ellen, Ellen. It's been a long time," he said, looking her over. He was leaning against the boat rail with a knife in one hand and a net in the other. His eyes stayed on her as he slid the knife against the cork line, separating it from the web. "Where've you been?"

There wasn't much that Ellen regretted. But she did regret Cooper, a lazy fisherman who didn't know a woman's body from a fish's, although he thought he was the greatest contribution for all the women in the village.

"Apparently not far enough," Ellen said. How did she let him get to her that night, she wondered as she stepped onto the railing to straddle between the *APA 41* and Phil's boat. The waves were sympathetic and the boats gently bobbed against each other.

"Oh, Ellen—be nice to a poor dirty fisherman," he said, and laughed. "Come, give me a kiss. I'll take it with me down the bay."

"Dirty is right. You won't get another night with a girl if you don't wash up at the showers once in a while."

"It worked for you, yeah?"

He grinned at her, and Ellen could feel his dirt rubbing into her skin, staining her. She rolled her eyes and jumped in the *APA 39* where she found Phil steadily working. He was on his knees, scrubbing the floorboards with a bucket of water next to him. How she liked the look of his hands. Even in the cold, they were strong and veiny, always ready to take charge.

"*Waqaa*," he said. His voice was rough, but not angry. Working always made him focused. He looked up at her. Scales were scattered in his thick, black hair, and a streak of salmon shit was smeared on his forehead. When she reached over and pressed it away with her thumb, his half-grin reminded her that they weren't together, except in secret. The thought made her sad.

There was a time when they were together. It was brief, though, and it reminded Ellen of spring break-up. One week the bay was littered with ice chunks. The next week the chunks allowed the silty tides to take them around the peninsula to the ocean. Ellen broke it off, because it was clear to everyone up and down the beach that Matty loved Phil, and Ellen couldn't compete with that kind of attention. She didn't have it in her to give Phil her time day after day. Maybe a minute here and a night there, but that was all she craved, all she needed. Matty, on the other hand, had grown into "women's work." She boiled heads, put up fish, and skinned rabbits like all the other women on the beach. She offered to watch his dogs while he fished and enjoyed being with him on the quiet days. That's how Ellen explained it to Phil, that Matty was better suited for him. She didn't tell him that she owed it to Matty, that she wished she could erase that afternoon on the docks. Ellen had half-expected Phil to fight for her, but she hadn't anticipated him to agree so vigorously. But Phil wasn't picky. He liked salmon in the summer, *pateq* bones in the winter, even long-faced Matty. So when he nodded with his lips shut tightly, Ellen regretted not taking him up to the net loft for one more night.

"Where's Matty?" she asked.

"You tell me," he said, and stood up. "I haven't seen her yet. I thought you two would be together."

"I haven't seen her or June all day," Ellen answered. "The store's been busy—last-minute food stuff people want."

She hated lying to him. She had in fact seen Matty walking toward the bluff side carrying a king salmon by the gills. Matty was making head soup for everyone, even brought some beer down from Dillingham. She told Ellen to come by, if she wanted. They could have *maqi* together, drink a little.

Nodding, Phil looked out toward the water where the changing tide brought waves that rocked the boat. "Yeah, I think Matty was making us all dinner before we head out. You know, got to get your last meal in before setting the net. Who knows when we will be back?"

"So fishing's been good then?"

"Ah," Phil said, piercing her with his black eyes. "I dunno. Could be a pink year. We got a few good reds. What you up to just now?"

"Just seeing if Matty and June are bugging you."

Phil picked up a length of coiled rope and threw it to the bow. He liked his lines to be free of the net. Like his father, Phil was a meticulous fisherman. Everything had its place on the boat—from the can of coffee to the nets and buoys; everything was lined up so that when the word was given, all they needed to do was untie the boat from the docks.

She could see that he was being a perfectionist, and as much as she wanted to amuse herself by throwing things out of place, she picked up the cork line of the net and began to coil. They stacked the net in silence, listening to the water lap against the sides of the boat.

"I miss you sometimes," Phil said at last.

"Well, you know, sometimes I have other rounds before I could settle on this boat."

Phil let go of the net and stepped toward her until they were face to face. She could feel his heat, despite his layer of gear. "And who else would you need to visit?" He leaned against her while his hand traced her hips.

She jutted her chin toward the *APA 41* and laughed. "Cooper."

"You're on the wrong boat, then," he whispered in her ear. "You took too many hops to get to this one."

"Well, maybe I changed my mind today." She pressed her lips to his cheek, feeling the salt of the Nushagak between her lips. Sometimes she tasted scales—today it was just the salt. "I got booze in the store. You want to have a drink?"

"I'm not thirsty yet anyways. Let me get warmed up," he growled, and slid his hand beneath her shirt. His fingers were cold like the ocean.

They backed into the cabin and fell into a bunk, where the water could be heard lapping against the wooden sides. She pulled off his shirt and let her lips touch his chest, tasting salt again. He always brought the bay with him, and she felt it every time. His hands found pockets of exposed skin, touching her stomach and thighs. She felt Phil's breathing deepen, his chest expanding against hers as if he were sprinting down the beach.

"Phil?"

"Hmm—"

"We can't meet like this anymore."

Phil pulled back slightly and let his lips linger over her skin. He sighed. "I know. We shouldn't, but we never said . . ."

She didn't let him finish, and she pulled him to her. She felt his hands, his lips, his heat against her body and thought that maybe she would feel something more than the growing urgency between her legs. She thought she would feel something more with his touch. Each time she thought it would be different, and when she found herself in this place, she was surprised that there was nothing more than just sweat and low groans. How many times had she found herself here? This boat—that boat. It was too many to count. And she couldn't even try to count when her skin ached for more pressure.

Later, with her head resting on Phil's chest, Ellen listened to water against the boat and pictured the shape of each wave. No matter what happened in her day, the tide would rise and fall in its own perfect rhythm. It was like breathing, and the bay would never stop. She was about to tell this to Phil when she heard Matty's voice on the dock. Ellen sat up quickly and hit her head on the top bunk.

"God damn and shit," Ellen said and rubbed her brow. That was going to leave a knot.

"Shit," Phil cried. "You gotta go." He reached for his pants and fishing gear.

"It's too late. She's coming down the ladder. Can't you hear her?" Ellen got dressed quickly. "Like I'm going to jump in the ocean now."

"Well, hide then," Phil said. "I don't care what you do."

Ellen combed her hair with her fingers. "Who cares? I am just down here visiting you, helping you sort shit out. I am off work now."

Phil groaned. He reached for the cabin door and looked at Ellen with dark eyes that appeared black in the shade. "Yeah, I guess so."

And then he went outside to greet Matty who just crawled over the railing.

Ellen listened to Matty and Phil greet one another. Matty's voice was loud and seemed to reverberate into the cabin. Ellen's feet felt like stone, as if they wanted Matty to find them, with only one shoe on. She looked around the room to see what she could use to make herself useful. A handful of tools—crescent wrench, screwdrivers, and a used oil can were set on the table. Crewmembers' fishing gear hung on the wall and empty coffee cups were scattered about. She heard their muffled voices and then silence. How could he kiss her now, she wondered. Standing there in the shade, Ellen became aware of the distance between her and the dock ladder. She took the oil can and smeared whatever oil she could squeeze out of it onto her wrist, cheek, and shirt. She grabbed the tools and went outside.

Ellen waved the tools. "Thanks, I'll bring these back when I am done." She met Matty's eyes. They reflected the light in the bay yet were unreadable.

"Shit, Matty. What you doing today? I'm getting a used Evinrude for my skiff. Got a good deal on it. Going to hook it up."

"Oh." Matty frowned. "No wonder I couldn't find you." When she wasn't smirking or being boastful, Matty was probably one of the prettiest girls in the village. Her skin was brown and matched her dark, slanted eyes. And even though it was rumored that they never had enough for dinner, she always managed to order the same things from the catalog as June did—blouses, saddle shoes, skirts, and slacks—things that Ellen was too embarrassed to order for fear her father would open the packages.

Phil sighed and adjusted his shirt. "Yeah, take your time. We aren't going anywhere until the tide changes."

As Ellen climbed the ladder back up the dock, she saw June hop from boat to boat with her shoes in hand as she raced to get back to the dock. She too had a little visit that needed to be attended to. From which boat, Ellen couldn't be sure. But it was alright, because June would tell her in her own time, perhaps over tea at the mess hall. Their boat visits were secrets that only the two of them understood, even as all the village women shook their heads and pointed at them, saying they should know better than to let people talk about them. Even Sweet Mary, who shared her *aamaqs* with her dad, had something to say. A couple of times, Sweet Mary entered the store to get sugar, and when she saw Ellen she would shake her head and say, "I must've rubbed off on you, hanging around this joint." And then she would plop the sugar or canned goods on the counter for Ellen to ring her up. Sweet Mary's words often lingered in Ellen's head far after the woman lumbered from the building, and Ellen would feel a wave of heat pass through her as she tried to come up with a response. Yet, Ellen couldn't tell Sweet Mary what she thought was true, that if she didn't find a boat to leave the village, she was going to become her mother, roaming the beach until the snow hit. Hell, she would probably freeze to death as well.

Twenty-Six

Although it was after ten in the evening, the length of light shimmering across the green bluff made it feel as if it were noon. Summer had a way of erasing the grayness of winter. Ellen walked toward the bluff side, feeling the wind touch her cheeks. This summer would be different, Ellen was positive. And it had nothing to do with the lack of fireweeds. All winter long, she saved the Sears and Montgomery Ward catalogs, pinching the corners for the dresses and blouses that she wanted. No one said anything, especially her dad, but Ellen knew that she was the mirror of Anne Girl. The small, bony hands and short, thin legs were hallmarks of her mother's blood, though her dark brown hair was shoulder length with slight curls at the end, making her feel like John's daughter after all.

She crossed the runway, which was busy this time of year. There was a bag of mail sitting at the edge of the runway. Letters for the Filipinos and Chinese workers, love letters from home, Ellen wondered. It made her sad to think that some didn't know that their lovers died here and were buried behind the spit. The Chinese graveyard was the largest in the village. Some mounds were marked only with a piece of wood off a boat—others had nothing. It was said to not walk alone over there, because those dead cannery workers still wanted to go home. It was said they still walked around the men's *maqi* and waited for their turn to clean themselves. They were still waiting to board the barge to return home.

"What you doing this way?" June asked, panting. She emerged from the path, carrying her shoes. It was difficult to tell which boat she came from this time, but Ellen guessed it was the Greek's vessel. June's hair was wild, tucked behind her ears and her shirt was unevenly buttoned. But she didn't seem to notice or even mind. She extended an arm toward Ellen.

They stood near the new BIA school building. It was only a couple of years old, but it leaned left as if that was the best the BIA could bring. Last fall, the green teachers arrived with thin, cotton coats, and Nora was finally relieved of her school teaching duties.

The Killweathers moved to Igushik shortly after the opening of the new school. It was time for them to leave, Frederik had announced during one sermon. His eyes were so bad that he had ordered new glasses from Seattle twice in the past year and was embarrassed when Amos asked if they were fogging up. He announced that they were going to Igushik to help with the Youth Ambassador program, but Nora qualified their "assistance" after services, saying they would be there until they weren't needed anymore.

The women in the village had elbowed each other when Frederik made the announcement, saying that they were surprised Nora lasted this long in the bay. Everyone knew that Nora was itching to be closer to her daughter. The women thought Nora was a saint as they muttered they wouldn't have put up with Frederik's wanderings like she did.

Now all children in the village went to the BIA school. Teenagers had the option of going to Mt. Edgecumb in Sitka for high school, but most of the teenagers in Nushagak, including Ellen and June, thought that Mt. Edgecumb was too far—half a world away.

"Too far to just go to school. How will we *maqi?*" June had said when Alicia suggested it. She had stood in the front of the mirror, tying her ponytail with a bright fuchsia scarf.

The grasses—wild and just beginning to grow their seedy tips—beat each other with the wind. Ellen hadn't realized that she had walked this far, but somehow her legs had taken her here, to where the bluff meets the beach. Where she stood, she could faintly hear the rumble of the cannery generators, but the wind muffled the clanking of the gears.

"You seen my brother?" June asked. "That bugger leaves me a big mess at home, and Mom is on my case." The wind teased her hair, flipping it into her eyes. She pulled it back irritably. "You think I should go on Fred the Greek's boat anymore?"

It was hard to say. Fred the Greek had a nice boat, but Ellen knew that nights with him were less than pleasant. When he drank, he liked to *uyug*, and it was rough like the current. He had no rhythm, moving every which way, and it was hard to tell whether he was in or out. It made Ellen believe that he just brought women on board so that the other fishermen would see them over their bows.

"*Ayii*, you like that kind?" Ellen asked. "There's lots of boats this summer. Don't get stuck on only one kind."

June agreed and said that the Greek's boat wasn't as nice as it used to be anyway. "He don't clean it good like we know how, you know scrub the scales off the bins and walls. He's too dirty for me."

"Hell, like Cooper." Ellen laughed and fell into step with June. "After this opener and when all the fishermen get back, come to the docks, and I'll show you which men are good." Ellen paused. "And they aren't from this village."

June stopped and slipped on her shoes. Her voice dropped and fell with the sounds of the grasses. "That's all we got, huh? Just the boats that dock here?"

Ellen pulled the stems of the grass. The wind was dying as the tide shifted. For a brief second, Ellen heard all the voices of the women in the village mutter under their breaths about how quickly the tide changed. And then you are old, they said.

"Nah," Ellen answered. "You can go to Mt. Edgecumb. Or be like Nancy when you are old, which means going to chapel every time it rains." And then Ellen giggled. "She had them all in her day. At least that's what Sweet Mary said."

June wiped the hair from her eyes and nodded. "Yeah, her and Sweet Mary. My Mom said they had all the good stories. I don't think we will get any from Nancy. She clammed up once she got to church."

The wind swirled between them. Ellen took June's hand. "I need some tea. The store was busy today."

A couple days later, Ellen was waiting for June at the dock, swinging her legs and counting all the boats anchored to the pilings. There were boats that she recognized, like Cooper's boat with the flaking paint. She thought that someone should tell him to paint it or it would sink. But then there were new boats in the village—ones that had pretty women names. Only boats from out of state were foolish enough to name a fishing work boat *Mrs. Beautiful Jean* or *Heather Hopeful Miller.*

When she peered toward the direction of the village to see if June was on her way, she spotted a tall, blond-headed fisherman carrying two sacks from her store. At this point in the summer, it was *her* store. She knew every can and box on the shelves. From the way he walked, Ellen assumed he was all business. His steps were short and his upper body was stiff, like his spine was nailed together. She waited for him to walk the dock to the ladder before asking, "Where you from?"

Ellen scratched her neck. He didn't hear her, or he was really good at ignoring women on the dock. "Hey, you in the orange jacket, where you from?"

She followed him down the ladder. He didn't ask her to come, but she felt like it. And, hell, it wasn't like he was going to pull anchor soon. She needed to see his hands. Hands are money, and she needed to see if they were worth anything. She followed him down the ladder, trying not to get her feet caught in the rungs.

Like a tightrope walker, he moved from one boat to another, balancing himself on the rails with ease. Ellen wondered what boat he lived on and if it was the last one tied up.

"What you get from the store? I work there," she said. She felt heavy and uncoordinated, as if her shoes were put on backwards, as she climbed over one railing to another.

"I know," the fisherman answered without looking back.

When he stopped at one, a newly painted gray boat, a sleek twenty-two-footer called *Mrs. Chanel* with the real name *APA 29* beneath it, Ellen laughed. "Ah, you are on this one. Where are your partners?"

His name was Sigurd Kristiansen, and he was fishing for the first time with his brother. For all of his aloofness, he didn't seem to mind when Ellen settled herself on a stack of brailers and started chatting. She watched him carefully unload the sack of goods—a pair of gloves, potatoes, and cigarettes. He rolled up his sleeves and began to work, starting with the net. Veins crisscrossed his hands like cables to his elbows, and the scales dotted on his skin shimmered in the afternoon light.

Ellen took in the details of the boat, its curved shape that moved smoothly with each swell, the wooden planks worn down to the grains, and the light smell of flounders. She imagined that Sigurd's scent was that of a flounder—a little sweet like a bit of honey. Perhaps there was salt there too.

"Here, if you want to talk so much, coil these lines." He handed her some rope. His soft expression didn't match his tone, and Ellen took it as a sign to continue to talk. She hadn't fished since sitting on the bow of her mom's skiff, but Ellen still knew how to coil lines. They slipped easily through her fingers as she coiled a figure eight in no time. "How do you like that?" she said when she was finished. "I'm a master coiler. You should have me on your boat."

"Not my boat," Sigurd said. "But it could use a woman. Maybe for food. Neither my brother nor I can cook on that little stove. What's that? The Swede stove?"

They fell into an easy conversation. Ellen learned that he was from Bellingham, that he got seasick often, and he enjoyed reading books like *Moby Dick*, Thoreau, and other obscure names she hadn't heard of. Sigurd wanted to know if she helped herself to everyone's boat or if this was a special trip. She reminded him that the Village of Nushagak was hers right down to the last fish, and he smiled crookedly as if deciding whether to believe her. His blue eyes flashed at her, and he looked more like a boy than a muscled fisherman.

Abruptly, she felt like telling him all the secrets she held in her pockets, and she didn't know why. It wasn't the typical urge that clutched her when she was boat hopping. Occasionally, Sigurd looked up and his blue eyes flashed a smile. This one was different, she thought.

Ellen would have stayed on board all day if she didn't catch sight of June's slow walk toward the end of the dock.

"Oh, hell, I forgot about June," Ellen interrupted herself and jumped to her feet. "We need to get her fixed up good."

Sigurd looked at Ellen gratefully. "Thank you for keeping me company. It was awfully nice to talk to you."

It wasn't a compliment she heard often, and Ellen felt suddenly silly. "I probably just filled your ears with a bunch of village talk. I'm surprised you didn't call your brother to rush him back to the boat."

"No, it's nice. My brother speaks about four words a day—'Pick faster. Hurry up.'" Sigurd looked down at his hands, which moved so swiftly knotting webbing that they didn't seem connected to his body. "I feel like I know you," he said.

He said this so quietly that Ellen wasn't sure she heard him over the waves. The tide had shifted, and suddenly it was as if the dock were filled with ants, preparing to work the long hours. "I hope you stay longer next time." And then Ellen heard herself saying, "*Kitak cali taikina*," just so she could watch Sigurd's head turn sideways as he stared at her, straining to make sense of what she said. For a brief second, she wondered if he had heard those words before, and she thought she saw his lips curl in response. She turned toward the dock ladder, before he could respond. Ellen imagined his eyebrows raise and maybe his lips would bend into a slight smile. He would probably tell his brother that the village girls were pushy.

Twenty-Seven

As the season wore on, Ellen relied less on the changing tides and more on the bells sounding out lunch, breaks, and dinner. Occasionally she wandered to the docks and scanned the boats for the blue *APA 29*. It may have only been weeks since she was sipping tea with Sigurd, but it felt like months. A whole fishing season seemed to have passed by and returned. Her skin craved touch, and she hungered for a taste of salt lingering on his neck. She imagined that lying against him would be like sinking into a warm *maqi*.

More and more Ellen found herself spending hours on the dock to fill time and the empty space in her chest. Goldman's boat was the talk of the cannery. The rumor was that his boat could hold twice as much poundage as the APA boats. The cannery workers in the machine shop made the boat sound as if it fell from the sky in one large wave, and Ellen finally had to see for herself. After work, Ellen invited herself to his boat. Deep in her pockets, she carried a pair of leather gloves and a bottle of beer. She thought about sharing but noticed that Goldman had his own flavor of alcohol that he was sipping on. It was true. Goldman's boat was crafted for speed. Its narrow bow was long and sleek for slicing the waves and keeping the swells in check. But she didn't find a fathom of net—small or large web. What kind of fish was he planning on harvesting without a net, she had wondered aloud.

Goldman's fingers, which were long and bony, produced a pack of cigarettes and bottle of whiskey out of thin air. He laid them delicately on the counter next to his small pot of coffee, which he had secured with braided rope. "Nets?" he asked. "I need one, I know. You would know where I can get the best one, yes? I only want the best." He popped the lid on the whiskey and offered her a swig. "I only want the best. And you know this bay, yes? Eskimos know the bay better than any cannery man."

His fingers, which didn't have an ounce of work in them, made her think of Sweet Mary's hands—large, plump, and scabbed from the years of fish that this man probably only read about in an article on the steamship to Anchorage. He was white with a freckle on his nose, and it was the first time that someone so pale made her want to drink and lie.

"Yeah, I know good nets," Ellen answered, and she took the bottle before he could change his mind. "I know good nets for every kind of fish. You want a net, I want two suitcases."

Ellen felt the boat's ribs shift against the swells. She told him how she was going to order two blue suitcases with red stripes. And then she explained that she was going to travel to Europe, that although she appeared that she had never left, she had in fact already been to Norway. She went on a boat with her father, who was from there. She told him that her two suitcases would be the finest with pockets in the interior.

Goldman nodded and murmured that he lived off the coast of Cyprus for years before he decided to head north. By this time his smile was becoming blurry. He offered her more of the bottle. And she took it, because a free drink was good.

What Ellen thought would be only a survey of the character of his boat turned out to be a tide's worth of drinking. Leaning against him, Ellen promised him a net—one with square webbing made for reds and kings. She told him of the net loft and how many fishermen wasted webbing that was still good, still strong for fishing. She promised him that she would make him learn to fish with his fast boat, and that in the end he would wish that she was his captain.

It hadn't been her plan to sleep with Goldman, but it was difficult to make plans that the tides didn't interfere with. On the shore, the tides were king, bringing fish and people to the village. One didn't go against the moving shore but followed its rhythm. Plus, his touch was new, softer than Phil's and most of the other men at the dock. She had moments where she believed she was with Sigurd, and then Goldman's fingers told her otherwise. Yet, the effort to leave was too great, so Ellen spent high tide on his deck and waited for the offshore wind to shift.

Twenty-Eight

Late July, Ellen knew that she was pregnant, not when her cramps failed to arrive, but when she instead felt the rush of a cold fever at the smell of grilled eggs. At first she suspected the fever was because she was standing over the stove, but when the urge to vomit spread to the smell of *pateq* bones and smoked fish, Ellen knew. Not even a *maqi* could warm her muscles, and she kept taking long steam baths and hoped that the humid heat would quiet the nausea. She began taking one during every break she had—lunch breaks, coffee breaks—and when the cannery workers closed up shop near midnight.

After the last bell sounded, Ellen walked toward the back of the cannery to the men's *maqi*. Located next to the wooden water tower, it was the bathhouse for the native fishermen who preferred to steam rather than take showers in the dorms. It had been here since her childhood, and she remembered hiding in the grasses with June and Matty to watch the men come out with steam rising from their brown skin as they retrieved more driftwood. They giggled at the men's bodies, their hairless chests and purple penises. The fishermen probably knew the girls were there, but joked loudly anyway.

Most of the fishermen were out fishing right now, and Ellen only wanted some heat. The steam room was damp and cold as if it had rained inside. The smell of urine filled the room and coated her nostrils, and Ellen imagined that the drunk ones were too lazy to pee around the corner. Light came through the gap between the stovepipe and the roof, but she saw that there was enough wood to start a fire. There was water in the basin, so she gathered wood and stuffed it into the stove. There was a can of kerosene near the door, and she poured what was left in it on the wood. She dug into her apron and pulled out some matches, striking them on the drum. The fire started like the wind, and Ellen felt her skin burn from the shock of it. But it felt good.

As the flames fed on the kerosene and the wood began to pop, Ellen shut the opening in the drum with a metal sheet and felt the heat fill the room. She started sweating and her clothes stuck to her skin. She undressed and stood naked in front of the heat, thinking of what she had to do. The heat stuck to her and she breathed deeply, closing her eyes. She wondered which boat made her this way.

What would Kristen think? Nora? Ellen giggled when she thought of Nora finding out. Her hand would cover her mouth and guard her tongue from unleashing a string of disappointments and shames. Thank goodness she wouldn't have to witness Nora's reaction. Ellen laughed and then felt the weight of the heat get to her. Tired all of a sudden, she sat next to the stove with her head between her knees, smelling the ammonia radiating off the stove. She had to leave the village.

She heard footsteps moving the gravel outside, and she opened her eyes. How much time had passed by? The room was hot and she couldn't breathe. But she didn't move, for fear the door would open and a half-naked fishermen with beer and wood in arms would be ready for a steam. The sound of wood being dragged across the gravel continued. Scratching and more scratching. The sound of grasses rubbing against each other, and Ellen imagined someone walking knee deep in them to pee. She hoped she didn't know him. The wood crackled and there was a bump against the wall. The door rattled slightly.

"That's it. They can fuckin' wait a minute," Ellen muttered. She grabbed the Folgers can handle—a long piece of wood nailed to the can—and raised it above her head as she opened the door.

And there in the light an ermine jerked his head up and looked at her with piercing eyes like black berries looking through her. He was digging for mice, but upon seeing Ellen, he sniffed the air and took two steps forward.

"Oh, it's you," Ellen said, relieved that it wasn't one of the fishermen ready to hop in the *maqi*. It was bizarre to see an ermine in broad daylight, but Ellen stood naked and felt his eyes on her as his whiskers twitched and scanned the air. He continued to advance forward, even after Ellen rattled the can as if it were a ptarmigan wing. The ermine didn't flinch, but boldly crawled toward her, his vanilla white belly painting the ground. She didn't have to think about it. She hit him on the head with the Folgers can, feeling the impact shake her elbows. The ermine backed up and stared at her, stunned.

"Get, you filthy rat," she yelled, and shook the can at him. With each swing of the arm, the ermine jumped back.

"What you going to do now?" the ermine asked, his whiskers trembling. His voice wavered. "Beat me over the head? That fucking stung."

The heat blasted from the steam room. Ellen gripped the wooden handle until the splinters dug into the palms of her hands. She gaped at him, both aware that sweat was trickling down her back and that she was talking to an ermine.

"There's no mice here," she finally said.

The ermine scraped the gravel with his front paw, dipping his nose here and there. "You don't know any better. I saw a fat one sneaking around here. I'm hungry." He moved away, following the scent.

Standing naked in the *maqi* doorway, she felt all the eyes in the cannery tracing the triangular shapes of her *aamaqs*, the creases in her skin, and the indentations between her ribs. She felt the stares, even though the alley was bare, and between the buildings she could see the rising swells of the current coming at her.

That summer the fireweeds didn't show up on time. It was a sign—a reminder of that summer storm when all the double enders turned upside down. The village women whispered to each other about why the fuchsia-colored stalks refused to break the earth's skin. Each had their own theory, their own speculations that they traded while splitting fish and pulling in the nets off the beach. Their ideas ranged from the warm winter to the lack of rain early in the spring. Some even believed that death was hanging around, and they told the young children to watch out for birds hitting the windows. The children shook their heads as they rushed through the grasses, laughing that no one believed in *those* kinds of stories anymore.

The tide was out, and it seemed as if one could walk across the gleaming mud to the ships anchored in the bay. Ellen was tempted but knew that the black mud was deceiving, that it was a suction cup around the calves. She was tempted, because farther down the beach, the younger village kids—naked black bodies running under the sun—were mud slicking near the shore. She was tempted to strip one last time, but Nancy asked her to help with the net.

"Mend a little, yeah," Nancy said. "I need to put up more fish, and no one taught you nothing about fishing, so it's time you get busy. There was no time between your mom and nana. Gee, you are almost old now, and you know nothing. When I was your age, I put up fish for everyone, including Old Paul. I fed this whole village!"

Nancy pulled the holey net down from her fish shack and dropped to her knees. For an old woman, her strength seemed to come from the ground, and she could still work a net faster than most. "You know how to mend nets? Your mom teach you? We need to hang this over an oil drum so that the web is square. It needs to hang right or you won't catch nothing." Nancy pointed to the lead line. "You're strong, but don't hurt your eggs. You will want them someday."

Ellen took the lead end of the net and heaved it over the drum, so that a portion of the net hung to the ground and the worn holes could be seen. She pinched the webbing with her finger, thinking that she should know already how to mend a net. What did Anne Girl teach? Ellen couldn't remember right then. Scraping guts over the cutting board came to mind, but Ellen could barely feel the image, which made her wonder if it was real or not. Memories of Anne Girl came and went in blurry waves.

"Like this. You gotta do it like this," Nancy said. She pulled the web straight, so that the hole was completely visible. With the needle and string, she looped, weaved, and double-knotted a new square. It matched the original. "You try."

Ellen mimicked Nancy's hands and wondered if this was how her mother mended nets, on her knees as if praying, as her hands caressed the webbing into knots that could withstand the changing current. Anne Girl's hands—scabbed and callused. Ellen could see them in her mind, their knuckles scraped and red from the salt.

She dropped the sewing needle and stretched her hand out. Smooth skin, like that of the women in the catalog. It was obvious that she had spent her summers between the four walls of the cannery store, stacking cans and piling high the barrels of gloves. Anne Girl would only shake her head and tell her that she'd turned out like John after all.

"You spend too much time at the docks," Nancy said. She pulled on one end of the net. "No good. People talk, you know?"

"What they say?"

Nancy gave Ellen a sideways glance, her black eyes glassy from the years of judging and staring at others. "You know, uh. They say you like to close the cannery store early so you can roam like a seagull on the beach. Are you hungry for leftovers and guts? We got good salmon in this village, you know?"

Groaning, Ellen pulled on the string and weaved the needle until her knots formed tighter and tighter. Squares were starting to replace the holes, and it was easy to imagine this net dropping in the water again. "Salmon? Aren't we talking about men and *uyuging*?"

Nancy's eyes widened, and Ellen couldn't tell if it was from shock or shame.

"*Ayii*, now you're talking funny. Gees. Don't be too proud now. You'll be like Jill there, bloated again. I took *maqi* with her, and her *aamaqs* hang low from all that milk. Hiding her button on her stomach. They should send her away again, instead of letting her show her belly for all people down to Ekuk to see." Nancy hissed as she cut the twine short. "Now what about that Phil? He's not lazy or too proud."

Ellen looked away, hoping her expression didn't reveal how she felt. Pride was bad and not something a woman wanted in man. But she had to agree—Phil was not full of too much pride. He never boasted his catch or his furs. Yet, Phil was Phil. He didn't want anything more than dinner at night and a net full of salmon. Ellen didn't understand him not wanting. All she did was want—a mother, men, and to flee away on her skiff.

"Phil loves Matty," she answered.

"You'll need to feed him then, huh?" Nancy poked at Ellen with a finger. "And look at your father. He would die if it wasn't for Sweet Mary. No man wants a too skinny woman."

The waves crashed on the rocks and the tide sucked them back out again. The grasses pulled with the wind, and Ellen could see the snipes falling off the cliffs. Falling or running and jumping, it was hard to tell. Nancy—no wonder everyone called her nosey. Gil must have gotten tired of her, so now she had to talk to everyone in the village, snag whatever ear she could find.

"Your Nan's smokehouse still stands," Nancy said, pointing with the needle.

Yes, it still stood—patched with corrugated tin sheets and dry, rotted strips of wood. It hadn't gone untouched from the bay, though. Yearly floods that brought in trunks of pine trees from Dillingham lifted the base of the smokehouse so that if one really wanted to, he could crawl inside like a squirrel. The fire pit was chockfull of alder brushes, ash, and tin cans from the boats. It hadn't burned in years, and it struck Ellen that Anne Girl was the last to push smoke through the seams of the walls.

"Uh-huh," Ellen grunted. The work seemed harder than usual today. Her shoulders ached and her fingers continued to slip, yet she couldn't let Nancy outwork her.

"My smokehouse is no good, and Gil is too slow to fix it. He missed the barge order for wood this year. I'll use your smokehouse, huh." Nancy said. "I'll keep it good so that when you are ready, it will be here for you."

"Yeah, good. That's just good," Ellen said, rubbing her temples. It was hard to think about smokehouses and ever being ready to put up fish. It was hard to think about anything but the growing being in her belly and the urge to run away.

"Here, pull." Nancy motioned with her needle. Her brown fingers were bent around the handle like dried twig. "You get me wood, though. We'll smoke good strips now."

Twenty-Nine

The keys jingled in her hand as Ellen slipped them into the door and turned the lock to close the store. The six o'clock coffee bell rang, and all the cannery men were moving toward the mess hall, forming a line that circled around the building. Dressed in overalls and boots, the Filipinos, Chinese, and Japanese all looked the same to her against the blue buildings. Each one came out of their shops whenever the bell sounded. It was a rhythm structured so opposite of the wind and tides and it had taken Ellen weeks to realize she was supposed to lock up the store whenever the bell rang. And now the key didn't want to fit in the lock.

"*Usuuq!*" Matty said as she approached. She licked her lips. Her tongue was fire-red, and it was easy to imagine where it had been. "Aw, the store is closed? I was trying to hurry from the boat." Matty's dark eyes rose and fell with her words.

"Yep, six o'clock. Coffee time, you know that," Ellen said, and she jammed the key.

"Just one minute?" Matty raised her forefinger. "I need some soap and Phil wants some Spam or something. One minute? Phil said hi to you. How's the Evinrude coming along? Got it all hooked up to your skiff."

Ellen stared hard at Matty, who didn't seem to notice. The skiff, her only choice to leave now. She wasn't going to admit anything related to the skiff to Matty. And there was no way she was going to say that she recently ran into another fisherman at the store, who said he had the fastest boat in the bay. Goldman, who paid for his grub by letting his long fingers rest on the counter, didn't look like he had ever been on a boat, let alone own a boat. His fingers were made for the organ in the chapel, not for nets and salmon. A boat is a boat, and Ellen had to see it for herself. Now she wished she was standing anyplace else but next to Matty at that moment.

"So you can carve up the other side of the boat?"

"I didn't come to start another fight," Matty said. She stepped closer with her palms facing upwards, which reminded Ellen of Frederik pacing in the old chapel.

"The store is closed," Ellen answered. She was tired, and her legs ached from standing all day. "What you want then?"

Matty always wanted something, yet Ellen didn't know what. She asked Matty if she wanted an apology for that summer years ago.

"Ellen, you still think that?" Matty asked incredulously. A smirk played on her lips. "Shit! Yeah, I was mad at you back then. Really pissed. I can't feel mad anymore. Just don't feel it," Matty said. She dug into her pocket and fished out a match. "You were all over the chapel shit and it bugged me."

Relief spread like hot water over Ellen's limbs. The heaviness she carried all this time was suddenly removed, and she had to hold onto the door handle to keep from being picked up by the breeze. She momentarily forgot what she was doing.

"You going home? I'll walk with you," Matty offered.

Ellen chuckled. "Actually, I need a new bushing on the lower end unit of the kicker and was going to see if I could rob one off a broken one down by the boat graveyard."

Matty smiled, curling her lips until her eyes twinkled. She looked hard at Ellen. "*Usuuq.* No wonder you've been quiet all summer. Who's the papa?"

Matty playfully hit Ellen on the shoulders, wearing a look of all smiles.

"How the hell you know?"

"It's all over your face." Matty pinched Ellen's cheeks. "Your cheeks are fat."

"Shit," Ellen muttered and reddened. The heaviness returned, and she wanted to sink into the ground.

Matty leaned against Ellen so that their foreheads touched. The onshore breeze whipped their hair around them. "No time for skiffs now. You need to learn to make clothes and shit, like Sweet Mary and my mom. It's so good for you!"

Thirty

The end of July slowly rolled into August. Some of the villagers had made their way up the tundra and reported that the salmonberries were scarce, which Sweet Mary took as a chance to rumble, "Death comes in small ways, I'm telling you. We need to pack our sheds with whatever we can . . . if we can't make *akutaq.*" At the same time, Sweet Mary wasn't bothered by the lack of berries. She walked along the bluff side of the village to the cannery side, making runs between the village, picking up booze for herself and others under the bluff.

"I was waiting for you to get here," John said excitedly when Ellen came home from the cannery one evening. She tossed the store apron onto the table and went to the stove and moved the kettle over the heat. The August wind rattled the stovepipe, and the heat felt good on her skin. Her eyes scanned the kitchen shelves—three cans of tomatoes, nails, matches, a moldy lump of dough, and a block of hardened salt. In the middle shelf were Sweet Mary's stacks of bottles with long and short necks—unashamed. John never said anything about the drinks Sweet Mary brought home. He never looked the other way, just nodded and made more room for her concoctions.

She picked up a bottle and twisted it open.

John's bad leg was propped up on the chair, and he leaned back, surveying her with a toothpick in his mouth. All day long he chewed on toothpicks. Never a cigarette. It embarrassed Ellen when Sweet Mary came and lit up. He could have at least tried to smoke, just for the sake of looking like he belonged.

"How's the new kicker working?" he asked. "Did you hook it up?"

Ellen's hand went to her mouth as a whiff of salmon hit her nostrils. "What you cooking—Jesus, that stinks."

"You're not feeling well?" John asked. He looked concerned as his eyebrows folded together. "Mary's making fish head soup. Nancy gave them to her. Thought you would like them."

Ellen's glance jerked in his direction, and she saw her father's curved figure molding to the chair as if he never had left. His blue eyes flickered like the stove, and he looked with his mouth open, waiting for her to respond.

"You wanna take the skiff out now? Go ahead, I'm tired. The kicker needs oil."

With both hands, John pulled his leg off the chair and set it easily on the floor. He did this in one swift motion, such that Ellen bet he could fool anybody about the leg's tenderness if he wanted. He had Sweet Mary wrapped around his finger. Only the scar above his ear, where the hair refused to keep its roots, made people stare. Even during services, people looked up from their hymnals and took peeks at him. He grumbled about it first but now carried the scars as if they made him belong.

"Yeah, I thought me and Sweet Mary would take a ride to up town," John said. "She would handle the tiller, of course."

Ellen laughed. "Of course. After what Mom said, you aren't going anywhere near steering that thing."

How did he get on without his plane? The parts were buried now at different places in the village. The wings went to the cannery, to the boat graveyard to be piled high with those double enders that the village women didn't chew up with their fires. The tail and the engine were stolen for parts. Sweet Mary did manage to obtain the prop. And she polished it before giving it to John. When she did give it to him, she told him that if he forgot who she was, she would hit him on his soft spot and make him remember. John had nodded meekly while Ellen giggled in the back kitchen.

Sweet Mary tumbled through the door, smelling of tundra and *piivaq*. She carried a small bottle under her armpit. "*Usuuq*! Home brew, drink up, child." Sweet Mary nudged the bottle toward Ellen. "I come to get your father. We're going hunting, and he's going to work for a change. No more lazy-ing around. If I can quarter up a moose, so can he."

Ellen raised her eyebrows, feeling laughter boiling inside. Her father worked? Anne Girl was going to pull herself from the dirt for this one, no doubt. She thought she had seen a seagull flapping her wings on the ridge of the roof earlier. "Oh, good. My skiff is safe for another day. He's all ready for you. Work him hard."

John stood up hesitantly, although it was obvious that he was holding himself back. He was thrilled to see Mary, Ellen knew. Now they would begin their ritual dance, where in the end, Sweet Mary would have John either dressed in a parka or down to his long underwear.

A whiff of fish hit Ellen's nostrils. She breathed in, and salmon went straight to her stomach. Her stomach lurched. Ellen brushed by Sweet Mary and dived for the pot of heads and strode out the porch, holding her breath.

"What you doing with them," Sweet Mary demanded. She marched after Ellen, holding tightly to her bottle and swinging her hips like she was entering a private dance. "Those are fresh, still good yet! Jesus, you're being wasteful. Don't you dare dump them out!"

Hollering over her shoulder, Ellen swung the pot with the force of a gale. "Something's wrong with them. They smell like rot." The heads flung from the pot and scattered on the beach, and immediately the seagulls lunged for the eyeballs.

Sweet Mary pushed Ellen aside, shoving the bottle into Ellen's hands. She rushed down the beach, swaying her arms from side to side. "Damn you, wasting. We can't waste—we don't waste here. You never know when we might need them, when the Japs might buzz us again."

No matter how many times Sweet Mary came over, slept on the couch or tucked inside John's bed, Ellen couldn't get used to the larger woman's movements. They were heavy, like a low ice fog that could suck air from the lungs. Ellen wondered how John could handle it, but then maybe he was used to having a woman sit on him. Sweet Mary had sworn that she didn't want to be next to the noise of the cannery and that new BIA school building. She wrinkled up her nose and said that she liked the bluff side better—more things to eat that way.

Ellen took the bottle and drank greedily. She surveyed Sweet Mary's *qaspeq*, and how it only partially hid the skin and made her seem wider and taller than she really was. A part of Ellen, the part that she didn't want to admit existed, wanted Sweet Mary to set up camp in their house and become a Nelson. Anne Girl wouldn't mind sharing for just a little bit.

"No worries, Mary. We know you'll be ready if them buggers want back in the country," Ellen said. She breathed deeply now that the fish were out of her sight.

Huffing and grumbling, Sweet Mary shooed the seagulls and picked up the fish heads one by one. The rumble of the ocean and the wind didn't conceal Sweet Mary's protests and glowering. "Wasteful—worse than sleeping up at the docks."

Mocking her, Ellen waved the bottle at them both and edged toward the door. "I'll be *maqi-ing* with June. We want a good rack, Dad. Let Sweet Mary skin it."

From the dock, Ellen could feel the shift in the current pull at the piers. She wondered how long they would last before they rotted into the beach. It was nearing September, and most of the boats had pulled up and tucked into the sheds for the winter. The cannery men had mostly deserted the small city on the spit. The Chinese and Filipinos were the first to escape, jumping in planes and boats with the cash in their pockets and never looking back. The cannery windows were barely boarded over with leftover planks from torn sailboats. Sigurd and his brother stayed for a couple of days while they overhauled their gear for the winter. Seeing him was like seeing Phil, except he existed mostly in her imagination.

Only the Native fishermen, including Amos and his son, lingered on the water, waiting for the run of silver salmon to hit the shore. They would fish until the moon didn't set.

Amos climbed the ladder, which shivered under his weight. Ellen, along with June and Matty, watched him from above. His hat hung to the side, but she could see bits of gray crawling out from under the wool. If Phil held his years just as well as his father, Matty had nothing to worry about.

"Hello little ladies," Amos said. "He's on his way up. We come back for a *maqi* before we go out again. Maybe a little *pateq* bones if we can. Tell him I'm at the house."

"There's no fish," Matty said, giggling. She peered over the side of docks, seemingly unbothered by its sway. "Hurry up, Phil, we don't got all night." She pulled out a cigarette from her pocket and dropped it into the boat for Phil, before passing the pack to June and Ellen.

June sucked on the cigarette and stared out to the bay, which was naked without most of the fishing boats. She looked sad, sucking on the cigarette, like it was her last love. Fred the Greek had left the bay last week, sailing back to Seattle. Although June didn't say anything, Ellen suspected that June had wanted to go with him, because now she followed Matty around listlessly, groaning about how she was tired of picking berries. She didn't even like them, she insisted.

"*Akleng*, you're too sad." Ellen said, putting her arm around June.

By then Phil had climbed onto the docks, bringing a two-week-old fish odor with him. He wore his rain gear and overalls with slime smeared into his clothes. "Shucks, we're not that bad. You make us sound like the Wescoats." He sat down next to Matty, swinging his legs over the edge. His lips were chapped, and there were scales permanently suctioned to his skin. His hair had grown long in the past few weeks, and Ellen was tempted to part it down the middle.

He glanced over to Ellen with a thoughtful expression before looking away. It made Ellen feel as if her ears were burning under the pressure between them.

For all the weeks apart, the group was silent. The swells rocked the boat below, and they listened to wood rubbing against wood, creating new scars and scrapes.

"Jerry Wescoat spotted a bear toward Ekuk. Thought he was going to shoot it, but tripped up and shot his foot instead," Phil said.

"Oh yeah. He's up in Dillingham? I never seen Penni yet," June answered.

"You don't see much of anything right now," Ellen said. "Fred the Greek this and that."

"Yeah, like you too. Where you go all the time?" June asked. "What you going to do now all the boats are gone?"

Shrugging, Ellen tried to loosen her shoulders. They were so tight with her lies. "I dunno. Sweet Mary always has something cooking."

"So where's Penni now?" Matty interrupted them. Her hand was inside Phil's rain gear, creeping up his thigh, moving like a tundra mouse under the surface. It was difficult not to notice, and Ellen thought she better give them the key to the cannery store if they were in such a hurry.

"*Ik'atak*, Matty." June punched Matty on the shoulder. "No loving right now."

Phil gently guided Matty's hand to her own lap, and straightened his posture, as if freeing himself from Matty's strange possessiveness. Ellen gave them the winter until Matty would become pregnant too.

"Penni's been laid out drunk for the past week. Jill's up in Dillingham with Jr.," Ellen said, to change the subject again. "Nancy's been bringing her all the leftover heads, maybe to make herself feel better, I don't know."

"They should just let Jerry's foot rot off," Phil said finally. "It's going to fall off anyway."

"Yeah, one less part of him anyway." June lit a cigarette again.

"Don't be that way when you become a mama, Ellen," Matty said.

June turned to Ellen, her eyes were wide. Phil's expression was one to remember—a mixture of fear and nausea.

"Ellen!" June exclaimed. "Really?"

"Yeah, it's true," Matty said. "Can't you tell?"

Ellen shot Matty a look.

"I didn't know it was a secret," Matty shrugged.

"Because I've been announcing it all over the bluff, huh?" Ellen snapped. "Give me another cigarette."

"What you going to do?"

Sand hill cranes passed overhead, their wide wings beating at the sky. They were leaving the frozen land, heading south for the coming winter. Ellen wondered if they were leaving too early as the grasses on the bluff side were still tinged with green and had not yet seeded. Winter and the coming darkness made her limbs feel heavy and her eyes slow.

"I don't know," Ellen stood up. "But I'll make sure to announce it this time when I figure it out. You will be the first to know."

She left them sitting on the dock as she walked toward the bluff, toward the one thing that had been her safety all these years. Taking the beach route, the mixture of the salt and rotten fish had never seemed so strong, and Ellen wondered if the earth's scents were rising with the tide. As she neared the smokehouse, Ellen's heart thumped. How sweet her skiff looked with the fifteen horse kicker hooked up on the end. It was easy to look past the gashes when she had a motor.

Ellen used her shoulders and hips to push the skiff on the beach. It took all of her effort and held breath to get it to move. The tide was moving quickly out, and she pushed the skiff until it caught water and began to float. She hopped in, and with two pushes of the oar, the skiff caught the current and she was drifting toward the mouth of the bay. She took a deep breath and felt sudden relief. She dropped the kicker and pulled to start until it was rumbling smooth. She didn't have anywhere to go, only a need to be away. A need to hear her own thoughts.

As the bay widened and the silty green waters stretched as far as the curve of the earth, Ellen settled herself in the stern and pulled the motor to life. Once in gear, all Ellen could do was put distance between herself and the village. The bay was calm, and the skiff bow cut through the waves effortlessly, and finally she could breathe.

In her effort to get as far away from the village as possible, Ellen didn't read the waves telling her the tide was going out. It only occurred to her when a strange grinding noise came from the engine and the skiff halted in mid-flight. She flew forward, watched one and then two wooden benches go by as she tumbled in the bow, hitting her head on something cold and metallic. The shape of the cleat flashed through her mind.

"Son of a bitch!"

Ellen lifted her head and pain shot through her right temple. Laying back down, she closed her eyes and chuckled. "Well, you're not going anywhere now are you, Ellen?"

She patted her abdomen. "What kind of fisherman can't read the waves? Looks like we are going to be here a while, my girl. The tide is going out."

For a second, Ellen thought she was two inches from crazy, but she blinked, and her mother was perched at the bow. And she was still sitting on the sandbar. There was light clicking of her mother's toes as she waddled up and down the skiff and stretched out her wings repeatedly. It was difficult to determine at first, but the gull was clearly her mother. The short shape and the dark gray wings with black spots gave her away. Her mom flapped her wings and shuddered. She seemed grayer than when Ellen had last seen her.

"*Usuuq*, he still can't fly yet," Anne Girl said and nipped at her under-feathers.

Ellen shook her head stiffly. Her hand came to her temple and she felt a knot the size of cork. "Not even if you paid him. Maybe you had it right all this time."

Anne Girl grunted. "And what about you? What shape is this?" Her beak snapped. "Good thing I wasn't there. I would have sent you to Sitka long time ago. You need to sew your legs up."

"You got fat since I last saw you," Ellen answered. "Must be eating lots."

"The southeast is better. I'm moving down that way. Maybe you should come. Winters are easier, almost not even like Alaska. I sat on top of a boat near Shelikof Bay and let the wind flatten my feathers, thinking that you should come down that way. It feels like Nushagak and lots of fish. Lots of fish," Anne Girl said. "I'm never hungry."

Twisting her head around, Anne Girl looked at Ellen with one eye. It was more beady than Ellen remembered, and Ellen averted her own gaze. "I wish I didn't crumble up that bread for you," she said quietly. "It was hot bread. Just baked."

The seagull cawed and laughed, snapping her beak. "That bread? I wouldn't have eaten it if you gave it straight to me. I wasn't hungry that night, Ellen. But if I knew you were creeping at the door, I would have made you get some dry wood."

"You had wood in the porch," Ellen answered. She leaned against the window sill, and stared at her mother, a shape she hoped she wouldn't have to return to anytime soon. "I saw wood leaning against the water bucket."

"Dry wood, dear, dry wood," Anne Girl answered impatiently. "Enough about that. If you get off this sandbar, ask that fat Sweet Mary for help. Nancy's good too, sometimes."

"Who said I'm having any kind of baby?"

The seagull walked to the peak of the skiff. "I like the name Sara," Anne Girl said. And then she fluttered her wings, spraying snow over the windshield, and took off. The tips of the wings were bent slightly downward as she gained lift. She was following the tree line south toward the inlet. From there, Ellen figured her mom would go either east to the Inside Passage or down to the Aleutians. Wherever her mother decided to visit, Ellen knew that she would be back, with a beak full of new instructions and demands. She would return, and Ellen hoped that it would be soon.

Thirty-One

The cannery churned loudly at the edge of the spit as Nancy, Sweet Mary, and Ellen began to put up fish for the winter. The cannery was at the peak of the season, turning its generators to a low rumble as they took in slabs of salmon into their chutes.

This year the cannery also packaged roe for the large Japanese ships waiting in the bay. It was rumored in the village that the cannery didn't even want the salmon anymore, that they squeezed the females for the eggs and gave the rest to the seagulls who pecked out the eyes in single gulps. It was also rumored that the cannery was going to quit taking in the salmon all together. The old women in the village twisted their tongues when they heard this and said that it was a shame to waste all those good heads. But most in the village agreed that it didn't matter what the cannery did with the fish, because at least there was a store that sold cigarettes and onions for the summer.

From the cutting table, with her *uluaq* poised in her hand, Ellen searched the shore's edge for a sign. She glanced toward the village sitting in the grasses. A long row of one-story homes, including the community hall, sat perched on stilts alongside the gravel beach until they reached the water tanks nestled on the sloping bluff. The other side of town, at one time, used to be the center, where families attended the chapel and gossiped. Ellen thought of how these buildings appeared dead with gray-weathered sidings and boarded windows. There was the missionary's house and the chapel. She imagined that the Bibles were still sitting on the wooden pews, gathering dust. Yet, on clear days, their tin roofs reflected in the sunlight, still boasting how they shaped the people in Nushagak.

Ellen slid the *uluaq* across the rounded stone and sharpened the half-moon blade. With the flick of her wrist, she turned it over and ran the *uluaq* again. It screeched against the roughness of the stone. Ellen wiped the hair from her eyes, smearing blood and slime across her brow. Beads of sweat trickled around her ears in small rivers that followed her neck line. From her waist down, Ellen was covered in blood and slime. It soaked through the small holes in her rain gear, and she felt it crawl down her legs, past her ankles, before settling between her toes. On the table, in puddles of slime and thick blood clots, lay a king salmon, stiff yet still slimy. He's a fat one, she thought, probably a she. Only the females were fat with extended bellies. Ellen glided her finger along the belly, feeling for eggs. A thin string of light pink pellets flowed from the anus area as her fingers reached the tail fin. She had two more to split after this one. Every time she picked up an *uluaq*, Ellen felt her forearms twitch with the desire to mimic Nancy's clean cuts. But no one ever said how hard it was to chop a head off and that the spine didn't want to be split into two. She worried that Nancy and many of the old women in the village talked about her sloppy fish when they walked the beach looking for agates.

The tide was out, and she could barely make out the curl of the waves on the horizon. It was mud, black mud as far as the eye could see. She wondered how far one could go before the mud would decide to hold on forever. She remembered the time two boys walked out on low tide like they were going to walk across the bay. They went too far and the mud held on to their legs. And then the tide changed. By the time the people on the beach saw the waving arms, it was too late. The tide rose and the boys disappeared under the curl of the waves.

Over the sound of the cannery and the wind, Ellen heard Nancy and Sweet Mary trade news of Jill's youngest child, the flat-faced one, that hadn't learned to walk yet.

"Spirit got his legs tied up," Sweet Mary said.

Nancy sharpened her *uluaq* on the round stone and waved Sweet Mary off. "She's knocked up with another one. My God, what are these kids coming to! Not enough Bible school is what I say."

Sweet Mary chuckled. "Or too much."

Ellen ran the *uluaq* blade over the stone again in quick strokes, grinding the metal. She had looked forward to putting up fish with Nancy and Sweet Mary all summer. She had looked forward to doing more than feeding and washing Sara. But now that she was out here sharpening her blades, she realized that she had forgotten about the incessant chatter between Sweet Mary and Nancy.

Ellen looked over to Sweet Mary and Nancy, both bent over the bloody table, cutting and slicing, and then she glanced down to her native white daughter. Next to the cutting table, Sara slept in a wooden crate taken from the cannery. She was wrapped in two blankets made by Nancy and Sweet Mary, who both insisted that their blanket softened the wood's hardness. It surprised Ellen that Sara could sleep with the flies trekking over her forehead, but many things surprised Ellen nowadays. How the tide kept coming in and going out, how the bay and slough shifted directions each day, and how easy it was to forget.

The sound of footsteps in the gravel coming startled her. She looked up from the cutting table and almost believed her mother was walking toward her. And then the wind rustled, and she heard the seagulls chatter as June solidified on the beach.

"Ellen, you been splitting all day, uh," June said, as she approached. She walked slowly, leaning from side to side with each step, her blouse moving with the wind. She was always up to date with the fashion and wore bright colors with patterns that weren't Alaskan. Ellen wondered if June was showing off the fact that her father made good fishing money.

"Oh, it's you." Ellen smiled, relieved that she wasn't seeing spirits. She wiped her hands on her rain gear. "Yeah, we got good kings here."

June leaned on the cutting table, careful not to get her shirt dirty. Her fingers traced the blood clots on the wood. She looked into the crate and sucked her breath. "Don't look much like you today. Some days she does look like you." She stood up and faced Ellen. "Haven't seen you much this summer. Even Matty wonders where you been."

"Because she's not playing down at the cannery no more," Nancy butted in. "You should take a couple of tips from her. Get out of that shirt and help us put up fish. We need lots of help this time of year."

June wrinkled her nose and rolled her eyes in Ellen's direction. It was true, though, that the cannery visits had not lost their appeal to June. She knew every boat and fisherman from the Filipino bunkhouse to the Native bunkhouse. At times Ellen envied June's freedom. Being able to crawl onto any boat and pretend she was made from the current while she tried on different men. She smiled at Ellen. "When you're done, bring Sara over and we go up the tundra and then *maqi*."

"Nah, Sara's coming to see her papa. Ellen, you go *maqi* with the girls. Bring me back some booze, though. I know they got lots," Sweet Mary said. She motioned with a bloody finger at the crate Sara slept in.

The mention of booze made Nancy grumble, and she took her *uluaq* blade and chopped a head clean so that it appeared as if it didn't belong to a fish at all. The motion made Sweet Mary giggle. Getting a reaction out of Nancy was all Sweet Mary wanted.

"We're almost finished here anyways," Ellen said. With one swoop of her hand, she pushed the remaining intestines, livers, and tails with fins spread out like fans into the gut bucket. She wiped her hands on her pants. The blood, though, would linger in the fabric long after the sun set for the winter. "Here, take some heads for soup later. Sweet Mary has enough already."

June took the heads gladly and made her way back to the bluff side. Ellen watched June leave, feeling suddenly left out. But the noises of the beach, the engines, and the williwaws gusting by brought Ellen back. She heard the drone of the cannery's generators, the fishermen hidden in shiny rain gear, selling salmon at the edge of the village. The hum was loud and insistent, promising another good season.

Sara opened up her eyes and blinked. They were blue, like John's, which brought Ellen some comfort. The girl was at least related to one part of her. Sara kicked at the blankets and began to cry.

Ellen picked up Sara, smelling the fresh soap and milk in Sara's skin mix with the stink of fish blood. Bouncing her, Ellen whispered in Sara's ear. She didn't know where to start, but supposed that now was just as good of a time as any. Sooner or later, Sara would know about *carayaks* and the little people. "You want to know how your Nan became a seagull when she wanted to be a raven? You haven't heard that one yet."

Glossary

Translations courtesy of the *Yup'ik Eskimo Dictionary,* compiled by Steven Jacobson, published by the University of Alaska (1984), and distributed for Alaska Native Language Center.

aamaqs ▸ female breasts
akeka, or akaa ▸ 'ouch!'
akleng ▸ 'pitiful,' 'poor thing,' or 'so sorry'; used when one feels sympathy
akutaq ▸ an edible mixture of berries, sugar, shortening, and fish; commonly referred to as 'Eskimo ice cream' in English
alingnaqvaa ▸ how frightening!
ampi ▸ hurry up!, let's go!
assiipaa ▸ 'how bad'
atem ▸ look
ayii ▸ go away; leave
caa una ▸ what are you doing?
cama-i ▸ hello; greetings; nice to meet you
carayak ▸ bear
ik'atak ▸ ugh!; yuck!; so disgusting
iqmik ▸ tobacco
kass'aq(s) ▸ white person; Caucasian
kita ▸ here, take it; there it is
kitak cali taikina ▸ please come again
maqi(s) ▸ steam bath
naanguartuq ▸ 'he is playing with toys'

naivaa ▸ 'he poured it,' or to transfer from one container to another by pouring

pateq ▸ marrow

piivaq ▸ beer, homebrew

potlatch ▸ potluck

qasgi(q) ▸ men's community house for sweat baths, dances, and feasts, no longer used in modern era

qaspeq ▸ thin hooded garment worn as a parka cover or dress, also spelled kuspuk

qayaq(s) ▸ kayak

quyana ▸ thank you

uluaq ▸ traditional woman's knife shaped in a broad arc, also called ulu

usuuq ▸ hey you!; you there!

uyug(ing) ▸ to have sexual intercourse

waqaa ▸ hello

Acknowledgments

I love my solitary life, but sometimes even I need people. So unfortunate. Thank you so much to Wyn Kelley and Dale Peterson for your immense support and kindness and opening up your home for my writing vacations. I don't have the words to describe what this has meant for me.

Thank you to Heather Miller and Carey Carpenter. I love you both.

Thank you to Stephanie G'Schwind and Rhonda Gardner, because I just need to.

Thank you to my teachers Leslee Becker, Steven Schwartz, Judy Doenges, and David Milofsky who read various versions or sections of this book.

Katherine Ellin. Thank you. Always.

Thank you to Peggy Shumaker for championing this book from so long ago. Thank you to John Gosslee for keeping the pressure on.

Thank you to my family, the real storytellers: Nina, Theron, Rob, Heather, and Joe.

Of course, thank you to the Red Hen Press team. You probably know it already, but you are awesome.

About the author

Born in Illinois and raised in Alaska, Mia C. Heavener is of Norwegian, Polish, and Yup'ik heritage. Her experience in rural Alaska is both personal and professional. After graduating from MIT with a degree in civil engineering, Mia returned home to design water and wastewater systems for Alaskan Native villages. Her childhood summers consisted of commercial fishing in Bristol Bay where she would catch glimpses of stories traded between her mom and friends over tea, in the *maqi* (steam bath), or between tides.

Mia is a licensed professional engineer with over ten years of experience designing water and wastewater systems throughout Alaska. She believes water is a basic need that everyone in the twenty-first century should have access to, and she hopes to close the gap on those communities still without running water.

Despite being an engineer, the desire to create stories and separate worlds remained. She obtained an MFA from Colorado State University. Her fiction has appeared in *Cortland Review* and *Willow Springs*. Mia currently lives, works, and pays rent to her cat in Anchorage, Alaska.